Mercedee Meehan, Acadian Free Spirit

The true story of loss, growth, and perseverance in 1890s Nova Scotia

Sue Ryter and Derek Ryter

DEDICATION

This book is dedicated to the enduring and adventuresome
spirit of Aimee Beatrice Mercedee Meehan Ryter

CONTENTS

ACKNOWLEDGMENTS

The authors would like to thank our great friend and family member, Don Potier of Tusket, Nova Scotia for helping with the history of the Eel Lake area, providing pictures and miscellaneous historical knowledge. We also thank Judy Frotten of the Argyle Township Court House and Archive for providing images of St. Anne's Church as it was in 1892. And we would like to thank Mary Flynn, Congregational Archivist, Sisters of Charity - Halifax for providing valuable information on Sister Rosalia and both the Mount Saint Vincent Academy in Halifax, and St. Anne's Convent in Eel Brook as they were during the 1890s. Thanks to Shaila van Sickle for help with the manuscript. And thanks to Nikki Haverstock for valuable insights as we developed this story for publication.

PREFACE

Forty years before this book was written, Ruth Mercedee Ryter MacDonald said, "Sue Ryter, will you type these old letters for me? They are letters that my mother Aimee Beatrice Mercedee Meehan wrote to her parents William and Agnes Potier Meehan starting in 1893, and later her future husband. No one will type them for me!"

I grimaced looking through boxes full of hand-written letters and diaries in ornate script but agreed to take on the task. I didn't know that the letters spanned forty years of correspondence. As I deciphered the beautiful handwriting, I came to know and fall in love with the child, girl, and adult Mercedee Meehan. "What happens next?" I asked after practically every letter. After two summers, the task was complete, compiling around 600 pages on an old mechanical typewriter.

Over the years I explored the genealogy of Mercedee's family and revisited the letters often until I realized that this compelling life of Mercedee Meehan would probably never be shared by more than a few in our family with the patience to go through the letters and pictures. The story needed to be told.

I enlisted the help of my son Derek Ryter, Mercedee Meehan's great grandson, to turn the true story into a readable novel. He was also drawn into the amazing story of his great grandmother's life. Derek and I travelled to Nova Scotia, Boston, New York, and Colorado and met relatives along the way who showed us where Mercedee and her ancestors had lived, helping the story come alive.

The story begins with Mercedee living in a convent near Eel Lake, Nova Scotia, in 1893, and follows her childhood trials and adventures through her teenage years in New York to her marriage to John William Ryter and life in Colorado. She rose from an impoverished Acadian girl to a strong woman in Colorado. This book encompasses Mercedee's time in Nova Scotia where she matures quickly and develops traits that will guide her through her life. We hope Mercedee Meehan's life journey is as interesting and entertaining for you to read as it was for us to write.

1 AN UNWELCOME LETTER

May 15, 1892, was breezy and cool on Eel Lake, Nova Scotia. The placid lake pulled the sun's rays into its deep-blue depth under the northern sky dotted with a few small cotton-ball clouds. Deciduous trees were replacing their leaves, and day by day, the temperature warmed. Everything seemed fresh and new, as announced by the birds that darted from branch to branch in shoreline trees. The birds chattered from perches high in conifers stretching their branches skyward to compete with the deciduous trees for sunlight.

In a weathered rowboat on Eel Lake, fourteen-year-old Aimee Beatrice Mercedee (pronounced Mer-se-day) Meehan sat tall on the stern bench beside her friend Kitty Hughes, a smaller girl of twelve. Mercedee, who had an oval face and a strong jaw, sent a measuring look to two boys, George and Sylvain, as they sat on another bench where they held oars and faced her. Mercedee could be forceful with the boys, and although they all had gotten on well that day, she watched them carefully as she adjusted her dark, wavy hair pinned in a bun on the back of her head. Her eyes could appear mischievous, suspicious, or vulnerable, but at that moment, they were at the mischievous end of that spectrum.

Mercedee nudged Kitty and smirked at the two fourteen-year-old boys. The nudge tilted Kitty's dark flat-brimmed hat with two feathers adorning one side as it perched on her light-brown hair. As Kitty righted her hat, Mercedee told her softly, "I'm sure George had to spend all day at home after missing the coach yesterday"

"I did not spend all day there, Mercedee," answered George. Through a shock of blond hair, he squinted at her. "You shouldn't start teasing if you want to get back to the shore dry." He feigned splashing Mercedee with the oar but sent a drop of water into the air. It landed on Mercedee's ankle-length dark skirt that was belted at the waist.

Mercedee smirked and rolled her eyes. She brushed a fly from her white blouse, its long sleeves fitted at the wrist and loose in the shoulders. The collar was snug around her neck. "You get one more drop of lake water on me, and you won't make it to shore at all!" Mercedee growled, and George recoiled.

"You were stuck there long enough to make your mother plenty mad, though." Sylvain, who spoke with a French accent, grinned. He sported a newsboy cap over his straight dark hair. He used his oar to take a short stroke that turned the boat slightly.

"That's enough, Sylvain." George clenched his teeth as he dug his elbow into Sylvain's thigh.

"Ouch!" Sylvain yelled.

"You had it coming," George said.

Sylvain rubbed his leg. "Well, it hurt nonetheless."

"Will you two please settle down? You know this boat isn't the steadiest craft." Kitty held her hat on and steadied herself against the gunnel. The dark-blue water appeared very deep, which she found disconcerting in the rocking rowboat, particularly when the gunnel neared the water's surface as the boat tipped.

"I agree," Mercedee said. "We have only one week left in school, and if we end up in the lake, God only knows

2

what Sister Carmel will do to us."

George scowled. "There's no need for carrying on. aren't going in the lake with me and Sylvain at the helm this fine boat." He smirked.

"I was worried about coming out on Eel Lake with y two." Mercedee sighed. "Perhaps I should take over t rowing duties."

Sylvain and George glanced at each other.

"Not just yet," George said. "First, we'll give you lesson in rowing!"

They pulled on their oars in unison, lurching the boat toward the center of the lake.

"Hey, George!" Mercedee called out. "I know what you're going to be when you grow up—a sploosh maker."

"And just what is a sploosh maker?" George sounded suspicious.

Mercedee picked up a small rock from the bottom of the boat and tossed it high, and it landed with a *sploosh*. Her eyes sparkled, and she laughed loudly.

The others joined in, and George said, "You're a terrible tease!"

George and Sylvain resumed rowing. They pulled on the oars, but George called out, "Ouch!" and stopped. He wrapped one arm around the oar to keep it above the water and clasped his other hand. "I got a splinter. These old oars are terrible." He bent down and examined his hand as Sylvain looked on.

"Is it bad?" Kitty asked.

"No. I've had worse," George said. "But I suppose you can row for a while, Mercedee, while I dig this out. Sylvain and I could have kept going right on across the lake, though, just so you know."

Mercedee rolled her eyes. With utmost care, she and he friend executed a tense exchange of places so that Kitty sa between Sylvain and George, all three facing Mercedee, wh held the oars with extended arms. Mercedee leaned bac pulling hard on the oars of the roughly built rowboat. T

oar locks complained with muffled squeaks, and the hull creaked under the load as the boat and four occupants moved across Eel Lake. She pushed the handles down, raising the oars above the water, and paused as the boat drifted and slowed to a stop. Mercedee's exertion felt good, both to work her arms and fill her lungs with the cool, clean air. She looked past her companions at the houses on the far shore only a couple hundred yards away.

On the east side of the lake, a man led a large cow toward a barn and the scattered houses of an area known as Belleville. Mercedee had relatives there, and her late grandfather Ambroise's farm wasn't far to the north. She wished she knew her Potier relatives in Belleville better and thought again of Mamma Agnes in Concession. Rowing always helped her release her loneliness, uncertainty, and sometimes anger.

"Are you going to row or stare at Mr. d'Entremont and his cow?" Sylvain laughed.

Mercedee pursed her lips and took another strong pull on the oars as George called out, "I got it!" and held up a small splinter between his fingernails. He dropped his hand over the side of the boat and washed a small amount of blood off in the chilly water.

Mercedee worked the oars until the boat had nearly reached the eastern shore of Eel Lake. They looked at the low hills as the *clip-clop* of a horse and the rattle of a wagon on the bumpy road through Belleville echoed across the lake. Mercedee rested the oars and looked at her companions. Kitty sat clutching her long, bulky gown in her lap. Sylvain and George leaned against their respective gunnels, in part to make room for Kitty's hat. A diminutive girl, Kitty had brown hair hanging in a long braid down her back. She and Mercedee had met when Mercedee arrived at the convent the previous autumn, and they'd immediately struck up a friendship. Sylvain and George were sons of lobstermen who harbored boats in Tusket, a few miles northwest toward Yarmouth. Local boys liked to meet the

girls attending the convent boarding school, and Mercedee was a shameless flirt, though she always kept the boys at arm's length.

Mercedee grinned as she lifted an oar then smacked it on the water, sending a spray into the air and raining down on her friends, who cried out at the chilly drops. The boat rocked precariously as Mercedee pulled on the oars again, jostling the boat forward.

"That was cold!" George said as Sylvain shuddered and smiled.

"You're going to drown us!" Kitty squealed, grabbing George's shirt and steadying herself in the rocking boat as Mercedee guffawed.

"Don't be a sissy," Mercedee mocked. "I'm not going to tip the boat over." She lowered the oars into the water and leaned forward. "And if it does tip, we can all swim to shore unless you're afraid of the sea monsters. My uncle Lezin lives on the shore over in Belleville"—she gestured at the wooded northeastern shoreline then pulled on the oars— "and he says the lake is infested with eels that will devour anyone who falls in." She chuckled, knowing Lezin had told her that in jest when she was much younger. However, the name given to the lake by the indigenous Mi'kmaq people did translate as "place of eels." She took another big pull on the oars, causing the others to lean back.

"Do be careful! You'll never live to see your fifteenth birthday if you keep being so wild and reckless," Kitty cried. "And it won't be those fantastical eels. It'll be the icy cold water. You'd never swim to shore in a skirt anyhow."

A gust of wind pushed Kitty's hat off her head, and it rolled across George's lap. Kitty nearly fell onto George as she lunged to rescue her bonnet before it could go over the gunnel and into the lake. George clasped his hands in his lap as Kitty pulled her hat back. Their eyes met briefly, and Kitty blushed and turned away.

Sylvain adjusted his own hat and addressed Mercedee. "I went swimming here last summer and didn't see one eel.

You're a fibber."

"They probably just didn't want to find out how you tasted." Kitty laughed.

"Oh, stop it, Kitty." Sylvain nudged her with his elbow. "They'll go after George anyway since he put blood in the water."

"Hey, Mercedee, row us across to the shore before it gets too late," Kitty said. "We have to get back to the convent before beads."

"We have to get back to Eel Brook too," George said.

Mercedee raised the oar, threatening to spray them again, and they ducked and cringed. "I could row over there twice before Sister Mary Anne gets her rosary in a knot. And we're not nuns." Mercedee felt a tinge of panic, wondering what time it was and how the sisters would react if she and Kitty were late. Sister Mary Anne was stern but understanding. Sister Carmel was not. She was very strict and had no qualms about physical punishment. Mercedee's favorite sister was Sister Lucilla, who was young and helpful. Sister Lucilla didn't let the girls do as they pleased, but she certainly wasn't the enforcer that Sister Carmel was.

"Oh, sure, Mercedee. Always showing off on Eel Lake, eh?" Sylvain said.

"She's the best rower in Eel Brook," George interrupted. "I'll bet you none of the other girls could beat her in a race." He appeared to admire Mercedee's strength as she pulled on the oars and pushed them forward. He leaned forward, looked past Kitty, and faced Sylvain, who was lounging against the gunnel. "Do you think you could beat her?"

"She might beat me if she gets both oars in the water." Sylvain chuckled.

"Ha ha. Very amusing," Mercedee said.

"I doubt I could beat you now." Sylvain grinned. "But I'm getting stronger. You just wait."

"Nonsense!" Mercedee said. "I would be even faster if my papa would have let me row in Boston. He was always worried I might get hurt."

"Well, where *did* you learn to row?" George asked.

"My older brother, Ferdinand, taught me how to row a boat faster than anyone when Mamma and I were in Digby last year," Mercedee said.

"I thought you were an only child. Isn't your mother too sick to have any more children? Isn't being a consumptive bad for having babies?" George asked.

"That's right." Mercedee looked somber. "Ferdinand is actually my half-brother by my father's first wife, who died when Ferdinand was young. My grandmother Meehan raised him in Digby. He's clever and extraordinarily talented." Mercedee's powerful oar stroke sent the boat in a tight circle, and the crew giggled and grabbed the sides of the boat.

"Ferdinand now lives with Tante Monique in New Jersey," Mercedee continued, using *tante*, the French word for aunt.

"That's enough about Mercedee's mother, George." Kitty looked at him from under the brim of her hat.

"It's all right." Mercedee studied her hands gripping the oars and the frilly cuffs on her sleeves. "Mamma will be fine," she said, mostly to herself. "She's always been sick, but she'll be fine with Tante Mathilde in Concession."

Mercedee continued to row, suddenly reminded of "Mamma" Agnes. Mercedee looked forward to the end of the school year and returning to Concession to care for Mamma. Everything about being away from Mamma at St. Anne's was new, and the loneliness and worry at times battled with Mercedee's wry, clever, and mischievous nature. Mamma wasn't well. When Mercedee had seen her during Christmas break, she was weaker and more frail than ever. Mercedee would be able to help Mamma as she had in the past if she could get to Concession. She kept telling herself the school year would be over soon, and for the moment, rowing in Eel Lake with her friends was a welcome reprieve.

Kitty interrupted Mercedee's shenanigans and the

playful banter with a warning. "Seriously, Mercedee. We had best get back to St. Anne's. If we're late, Sister Mary Anne will be furious with us. It's almost time for beads. And furthermore, you're out in the sun without a hat. The sisters will be upset if you go back burned by the sun."

Mercedee looked around, and the boat was drifting eastward in the breeze. They would have some distance to row, as well as the walk to the convent. "All right, we must go. But Sylvain, you need to help me row. Let's see how strong you are."

"Yes, we'll see." Sylvain rose from his seat, remaining bent and steadying himself with one hand on the gunnel. "Move over. I'll take an oar, and you try to keep up so we don't make a circle." Sylvain smiled as he turned and dropped down beside her, just missing Mercedee's hip as she moved quickly aside. Sylvain teasingly pressed against Mercedee's side, looking up into her pretty face. But her grin faded as she wrinkled her nose and looked ahead at Kitty as she prepared to row. Mercedee and Sylvain dipped their oars into the water and tugged.

The small boat lurched and glided across the smooth water, picking up speed as Mercedee and Sylvain found a rhythm and matched each other's power. The boat moved away from the wooded shoreline and toward the sun that pierced strips of clouds in the western sky. A cool, brisk sea breeze ruffled their hair and teased the girls' full skirts and ribbons.

Sylvain and Mercedee rowed in tandem past a small island, glancing at each other and matching the other's effort. George and Kitty looked past them at the west shore, and the boat put in at a naturally open spot.

"Watch out!" George cried.

A small sailboat with five or six men sitting on the gunnel and standing on the deck appeared around the end of the island at a good fetch from the north. Mercedee and Sylvain stopped rowing, staring over their shoulders as the sailboat passed no more than fifty feet from them. The men waved and called out as the boat turned away from the rowboat and quickly sailed on to the south.

"Phew!" Mercedee said.

"I thought we were done for." Kitty sighed.

George looked across the water at the boat sailing away. "It wasn't really all that close but shocking nonetheless."

"Close enough for me." Sylvain glanced at Mercedee and pulled on his oar.

Mercedee took the cue, matching Sylvain's pull. "All clear?"

"Yes. Clear sailing to the shore." George looked to his right along the axis of the lake.

The water sparkled as the two made short work of the last hundred yards, guiding the boat onto the rough shore. As the boat's bow scraped the rocky ground, Sylvain released his oar and hopped over the bow gunnel onto dry land. The boat rose in response, and Sylvain grabbed a rope tied to a rusted iron hasp on the bow as Mercedee followed him out, holding her skirt up and taking a long step to avoid getting her boots wet. Sylvain pulled the boat as far as he could onto the shore and held out his hand to Kitty, who took it tepidly. She used her other hand to raise her long dress so she could step over the side of the boat.

George hopped out on the opposite side, stretching to reach across the water. He followed Mercedee to a primitive road that skirted Eel Lake.

"Thank you, Sylvain." Kitty looked around nervously as if one of the sisters from the convent might see her touching a boy's hand. Exiting the boat, she quickly pulled her hand away and walked up the shore.

"No problem at all," Sylvain replied, perhaps knowing that he was getting under Kitty's skin. He tied the rope to a worn branch of a maple tree on the bank.

The foursome walked south on the primitive road to a main road, Chemin des Bourque, which connected the villages of Eel Brook and North Belleville. Fifteen minutes later, the foursome reached the hamlet of Eel Brook, where

Chemin des Bourque teed into Main Post Road. They turned right on Main Post and passed the Eel Brook Post Office.

"I thought you two had to go to Argyle. Shouldn't you go that way?" Mercedee pointed east.

"We have to pick up a package from my uncle first," Sylvain replied. "He lives just right up there." He pointed past the post office.

"Oh," Mercedee said, relieved. She was concerned because looking west on the Main Post Road, she could see the steeple of St. Anne's Church less than a quarter mile ahead. The nuns strictly forbade them from making any contact with local boys.

George and Sylvain stopped after reaching the junction. They clearly wanted to say goodbye. "See you tomorrow, eh?" Sylvain asked.

Mercedee squinted at the boys. Kitty looked at her shoes.

"Maybe…" Mercedee muttered, not wanting to give the boys the idea that she enjoyed their company. She was also worried about being seen with them and knew that she and Kitty were already pushing their luck.

"Maybe it is, then," George replied.

The two boys walked away on the dirt road as Kitty and Mercedee headed toward the convent. The girls heard the boys talking in the distance.

George was needling Sylvain. "And maybe tomorrow, you'll finally impress Mercedee with your rowing, and she'll give you a kiss."

"Shut up! I don't even like her. And maybe tomorrow, you'll get more than Kitty's hat on your lap!"

George responded with a punch on Sylvain's shoulder. "Shut up, or I'll tell your mom you're in love with a nun." George ran down the road with Sylvain sprinting to keep up.

Mercedee and Kitty walked on toward the convent as the boys' voices faded. They walked over a small rise then into a swale.

"Well, that went rather well," Kitty said.

"I suppose. Why do you say so?"

Kitty looked ahead. "George used to be such a nincompoop. He's more respectful now."

"Oh. Yes. In that respect, it did go rather well," Mercedee said. "Last fall, he wasn't on my good side at all."

"Nor mine," Kitty said. "No one would have been blamed for giving him a good slap on the cheek."

"True. And I still don't trust him. However, if he keeps this up, he can row with us."

Mercedee's mood turned dark, and she gazed solemnly up the road. "I'm getting the feeling I will soon be all alone," she said softly to herself.

Her comment wasn't lost on Kitty, who obviously suspected the source of Mercedee's sudden melancholy was because of her sick mother in Concession. Kitty asked, "How's your mother faring? I hope her health is improving. The warming spring air must be helping."

"I got a postal from her two days ago. I can't stop thinking about it." Mercedee sighed. "I feel that I've abandoned her. She says she's been feeling weak." Mercedee looked at her scuffed leather boots, appearing then disappearing under her worn skirt hem as she walked. Her mother had been sick with tuberculosis for as long as Mercedee could remember. Agnes had returned home to Nova Scotia to be cared for by her sisters. She wondered if the move would be a healing time for her mother, or the last act in the tragedy of illness.

"Mamma wrote that she was fine and said not to worry, but she always says I shouldn't worry," Mercedee said, feeling overwhelmed. "Tante Mathilde is taking care of Mamma. I don't think she's going to die or anything. She's just always so sick. It's really tiresome."

"I can only imagine." Kitty sighed.

"We can never have a house or stay with Papa in Boston," Mercedee said, "and now I have to stay here at St.

Anne's Convent while she is... is..." Mercedee put her face in her hands.

Kitty seemed at a loss for what to say. "Don't you like St. Anne?" Her voice conveyed that she valued Mercedee's friendship and hoped Mercedee knew that.

Mercedee stopped, and she and Kitty faced each other on the narrow, dusty road. "I'm sorry. You know that's not what I meant." She looked across the fence at the forested, rolling landscape and distant water.

"It's my fault. That came out wrong," Kitty said. "Whatever happens, we're still friends. I want you to know that."

"You're one of my best friends in the world." Mercedee turned back to Kitty. "It's me, not you or the school. It would be nice to have a home like other people. Mamma and I have lived in many different places. Just when I get settled and happy, I must pack up my trunks and move again. Sometimes, I pack them five or six times only to unpack again if Mamma gets worse. I never expect to stay anywhere."

"I'm sorry you've had such a hard time, but think of how hard it is for your poor mamma. She can't be with you or your papa and must live with her sister and feel so bad."

"I know very well that Mamma is the one suffering. I may sound spoiled and selfish, but I really don't mean to. It rips my heart into pieces not being able to be with her." Mercedee cried.

"I'm sorry—"

"Mamma told me that we would stay together, that we would all die together because she knew I was so afraid for her. But that was a long time ago. Now I wonder how much longer she can go on. I despair it won't be another fortnight." Mercedee wiped her eyes as she gazed at wispy clouds. "My papa hasn't been to see us since last year. I do miss him, and if she passes... I already feel so alone."

Kitty gave Mercedee a quick hug, and they walked on toward the church, which was situated on a rise just east of a large tidal lagoon. In the distance, Mercedee could see men working in a salt marsh as they dug narrow drainage trenches in the soft silt and marsh grass that would be harvested for hay in a couple of months. She wondered if those men had families and homes.

"Come on," Kitty prodded.

"Of course," Mercedee replied, and they turned toward the convent schoolhouse and the majestic church beyond, its bright-white walls contrasting with the tall, dark trees.

The girls walked quietly past the church to a path that took them to the three-story, square Victorian convent trimmed by dark concave roofing that wrapped around the top. They stepped up onto the small front porch and toward a large wooden door.

Pushing the door open, Kitty exclaimed, "I smell sugar candy! Mercedee, Sister Mary Anne is making sugar candy! Hurry, hurry. I must see if she's going to put peanuts in it. I can't wait!"

"But Kitty, your hat," Mercedee reminded her as Kitty darted down the hallway to the kitchen in the rear of the building.

Kitty stopped abruptly and turned. "Thank you," she said, clearly remembering the strict rule about not wearing hats indoors. She took off her hat and looked around, impatiently searching for a place to hang it.

"Over here." Mercedee pointed at a hat-and-coat rack in the corner.

The hat hooks were beyond Kitty's reach. "Would you help a short girl out?"

"Of course." Mercedee accepted the hat. "You know, I'm so tall because I was born in the shadow of Bunker Hill in Boston. At least, that was what Papa said. That makes me a real Yankee, I suppose. But sometimes, I wish I wasn't quite so tall." As she reached up to hang the hat, her dress lifted above her ankles, and she quickly lowered her arms. "Now let's see about the candy."

The girls hurried down the poorly lit hall into the warm

kitchen, still breathless, fresh cheeked, and excited from their excursion. In the soft warm light of several oil lamps hanging on the walls, Sister Mary Anne was busy dipping a sweet concoction from a pan. The sister allowed the girls one piece of sugar candy each. To their joy, Sister Mary Anne had indeed included peanuts.

"Mercedee, there's a letter for you in the office. We picked it up earlier. From your father, I think." The sister motioned to the office door, and Mercedee hurried to pick up the thick packet.

"Thank you, Sister." Mercedee smiled as she followed Kitty down the hallway and up the stairs. At the upstairs hallway, Kitty turned left and Mercedee right. At the third door on the right, Mercedee gripped the round, brass, patina-covered handle. She turned it and gently knocked on the door. "Clara?" She opened the door and stepped through.

"Hello," said a girl lying on one of two beds.

The room was just big enough for two beds extending from one wall, separated by a nightstand. Light from a window opposite the door illuminated the room. A mirror hung over a table holding a small washbasin and pitcher. Mercedee moved past the first bed where Clara lay and sat on the second.

"How was the lake? I hope you're not in trouble again." Clara placed a bookmark in the book she had been reading, closed it, rolled over, and faced Mercedee.

Mercedee rolled her eyes. "It was quite fun. And as far as you or Sister Mary Anne know, it was just Kitty and me paddling the rowboat calmly on the lake."

Clara frowned into Mercedee's eyes, then they both broke into laughter.

"Of course, of course!" Clara sat up and put her feet on the floor, facing Mercedee. Clara was substantially shorter than Mercedee and her hair a light brown. She wore a white blouse with billowy upper sleeves and a buttoned collar with a narrow black ribbon tied in the front. Her dress, like

Mercedee's, was ankle-length and belted at the top. Her clothes were noticeably newer than Mercedee's and with fewer repairs.

"And that's all I'm going to say about it." Mercedee chuckled.

"We had better get down to the abbey for beads," Clara said.

"Yes." Mercedee tucked her letter into her desk drawer. She brushed her dress to remove dirt and plant debris. Then she went to the mirror to fix several strands of hair that had escaped her bun. She finally resigned herself to pulling the pins out, brushing her hair, and rebuilding the bun.

"All right. Shall we go?" Mercedee asked, but before Clara could answer, there was a knock at the door.

"Sister Carmel says we must go now," Kitty called from outside.

Mercedee opened the door. "You have perfect timing. We were just about to leave."

"I want to go to the conservatory after beads for a few minutes to find a book for tomorrow," Clara said. "Do you want to come?"

"No, thank you. I'll see you when you get back to the room. I feel like lying down for a bit." Mercedee thought of her waiting letter, still unopened.

After beads, Mercedee hurried to the convent. She walked up the stairs to her room as quickly as possible without raising the ire of Sister Carmel and placed the letter on the small desk. She slipped her finger under the envelope flap and slid the letter out. As the letter unfolded, Mercedee smiled at her father's ornate cursive writing in a purplish ink and the familiar warm greeting.

My very dear Daughter Mercedee,

I send you a thousand kisses and a fond embrace for your charming and well-composed little letter and sweet little flower, so appropriate for your loving Papa's birthday—Sweet William. That is the common name for the flower. Now can you find out the scientific or botanical name? I think Mr. Cullen will be able to tell you. You see, dear, Geography is the science of the earth or world; so Botany is the science of Knowledge of flowers & etc. And every flower has a Latin name, because Latin is the language used in the sciences throughout the world so that the Frenchman or Englishman, or the German or the Russian, etc., could all have the same name of the flower, in only one language, the Latin, and understand it everywhere. That is why Doctors write their prescriptions in Latin, and that is why the Catholic Church prescribes Latin for its principal service, so that if a Dutch priest went to Eel Brook and could not speak a word of English, he could still say mass to the satisfaction of the English and French who might attend. When you go to Wellesley College, you will have to study Botany. Oh! It is so interesting.

Mamma tells me in her letter what a nice time you have bathing! It is splendid exercise for you, darling, but you must never go in if you are in perspiration nor stay in after you get chilled. The moment you begin to chill, come right out & dry yourself well and quick & then run about or exercise until you get warm. If you are in perspiration, wait awhile before going in, & get cooled off. Then there will be no danger.

I have your photograph right before me on my desk as I write. It is there always, looking right at me. It is the one that was on the mantel in Melrose Highlands & is in the frame that the Bricknells gave you. Do you remember it? Well, I have put that little bunch of "Sweet William" in the frame, right under your nose, just as if you were smelling it. And when I put it in the frame, I kissed you a dozen times. I wonder if you love me as much as that? No! I don't wonder at all, any such thing, for I am sure my darling little daughter loves her dear Papa and Mamma with all her heart, and we love you the same! Kiss me!

Mamma writes that you are a very good girl and helped her to sew for two hours every day you were in Concession with her.

Now be careful what you eat. If you keep your digestion right by using proper food, your skin and complexion will be beautiful always.
Your loving Papa, Wm. Meehan

Mercedee read the letter slowly and then a second time

to digest all the information. Papa was always passing on lessons about math or science. She thought about what he had written and reflected on her last few days. She didn't swim often, but the advice was good to remember.

She folded the letter, slipped it back into the envelope, and took out a small composition book that her father had sent her some time ago. On the inside front cover, he'd written, "This book could serve as a sketchbook. Perhaps you could sketch a boat at the harbor or your little rowboat."

Mercedee chuckled at the picture she could draw of Kitty and the boys ducking as she splashed them with the oars. He would surely not approve! She drew a small bouquet of Sweet William flowers and placed a heart at the bottom. She tucked the book into the nightstand and snuggled into her blanket with a smile.

The next morning, Mercedee and Kitty were joined by their friend Mamie Gardner. Shorter than Mercedee, Mamie was a year her junior. Mamie usually wore a white bonnet on her curly blond hair. The trio set out on the ten-minute walk to the post office to see if a postal had arrived from their parents. The girls skipped along and enjoyed the fresh, damp morning air, and the warm sun made Mercedee optimistic.

"I hope we see Sylvain and George today." Kitty laughed. "They were sure surprised at how well Mercedee can row."

"You didn't do anything silly, did you, Mercedee?" Mamie asked. "We know all too well how you are when you get a chance to show off and tease those boys."

"I did no silly things. I simply asked them if they wanted to go rowing. It's not my fault I'm better than they are."

Kitty giggled and stumbled over a root protruding from a small tree whose branches hung over the fence. Several brown and black cows grazed lazily in the field beyond. The girls paused in the shade.

"You did, too, Mercedee," Kitty said. "Mamie, you

would have laughed. Mercedee splashed water on their heads."

"I wouldn't call it silly," Mercedee said. "Those boys just want to have fun. Someday, I'm going to be done with the sisters and rules. I'm going to see the world." She stepped over to the wooden fence and looked across the field. "I'll be traveling while you're with your new beau, George." Mercedee rested her forearms on top of the fence.

"Oh, stop that." Kitty's hands were firmly on her hips. "Don't believe her, Mamie. My hat blew off and landed in George's lap. And that was that."

"I believe you," Mamie said, "but you *are* blushing."

Kitty looked toward Eel Lake and asked. "And just how are you going to travel the world, Mercedee? You'll need a rich husband and fancy dresses. I've seen how adults travel on the steamships and trains."

"My father says I must finish the convent school and become a presentable woman," Mamie said. "I'm not sure what that means exactly, but it doesn't include running off to see the world."

"Yes, my father has the same house I was born in, and we'll never leave," Kitty chimed in. "I don't suppose I'll ever get on a steam train to places in the West." Mercedee moved restlessly, and Kitty added, "But it's scary anyway."

"And Mercedee, you said you weren't sure that your father could even afford the tuition at St. Anne's," Mamie said.

"Stop it. Stop all this negative talk. I will do it. You'll see." Mercedee faced them and repeated, "You'll see." But Mercedee knew the odds of Papa William making a deal and funding her for another year were not good.

A breeze picked up, and Mamie gathered her brown wool shawl around her. "It's so chilly in the morning. I can't wait for summer so it'll get warmer. I wish it were warm enough to go bathing."

"I wish the weather would make up its mind," Kitty said. "I wish it were either cold enough to ice-skate or warm enough to bathe because it's tedious having to do beads all the time."

"According to the calendar, summer starts in three weeks, but it's still chilly here. When Mamma and I lived in Georgia, it was already too hot," Mercedee said.

Mamie turned toward Mercedee, who was still looking at the field. "Georgia? You've been to so many places. I wouldn't know what to do."

"I wish I'd never been to Georgia"—Mercedee turned back to the girls—"because that would mean that Mamma wasn't sick."

"Because of her consumption?" Mamie asked.

"Yes. She and Father were sure the Boston winters would be too harsh. The cold air made her cough so much I despaired that she would survive." Mercedee looked at her hands. "And Father would write letters saying she could get better by staying warm and eating the right food. He still tells me that, but I'm not sick at all."

"I'm sorry," Kitty said. "That must have—"

"My papa says that we should never go bathing if we're in perspiration or stay in the water if we get chilled." Mercedee wanted to change the subject. "If we get chilled, we should run around until we're warm again." She looked thoughtfully into the distance. "We would surely be chilled if we went in today. It's the middle of May, and it feels like there's still ice on the wind." Mercedee pulled her scarf tighter over her ears and put her hands into her fur muff.

"But your father always tells you such stuffy things. If you actually did all of them, you'd never leave the convent," Mamie teased.

"I know. He does go on dreadfully, doesn't he? I'm glad I wrote him a letter today because he gets so cross when I forget to answer his letters. I haven't seen him for a year, anyway, since we came to Nova Scotia. He's so busy with his business."

"The choir concert was delightful, don't you think? Do you think we'll get to sing again?" Kitty asked, changing the subject.

The girls heard voices and turned as five boys appeared on the road. Sylvain and George and three other boys were walking in the opposite direction, having crossed Eel Lake.

"Greetings, Mercedee," George called. "Sylvain says he likes you because you can row so much better than him!"

Sylvain punched George's shoulder, and he and the others ran past the girls. "Did not!" Sylvain blushed as he and Mercedee's eyes met in passing. The boys stopped a short distance down the road, looked back at the girls, and whispered and chuckled before walking on. Sylvain said something to the other boys then took off running as George chased him.

Mercedee set her lips in a thin line. "Now they're laughing at us! We aren't here for their amusement." She folded her arms and pursed her lips. "Who needs them anyway?"

"Mercedee!" Mamie exclaimed. "Your garter has fallen down. That's what they're laughing at."

Mercedee pulled her skirt up. Her garter had fallen to her ankle and was visible just below the hem of her dress, which was a bit too short when she walked. She was growing faster than she could alter her skirt or get a new one. Her face flushed, and her lips tightened. Looking down the road to be certain the boys were out of sight, she lifted her skirt, tugged the garter up, and hid it. She dropped her skirt. "Come. We must get to Eel Brook. I've had my fill of this." She fumed with embarrassment.

The three girls looked at each other for a tense moment, then Mercedee glanced down the road. She turned to Mamie and Kitty, and they exploded with spasms of laughter.

"This is a terrible day," Kitty said sarcastically, giggling. "But the boys always like you best, Mercedee. I can't believe you're upset."

The tension fading, they hugged, laughter turning into tears. Mercedee, Mamie, and Kitty walked on to Eel Brook. They checked for mail at the small post office and headed to the convent empty-handed. The sisters had probably picked up the mail and taken it to the convent for distribution.

At Rocco Point Road just past the schoolhouse, the girls hurried to the convent and hung up their wraps. They walked down a dim hallway, where afternoon sun brightly lit a window at the far end. A dark figure walking out of the light caused the girls to slow, squinting. Sister Mary Anne, Mother Superior for the convent, approached slowly and appraised the group. She wore a black habit with a black headpiece trimmed in white. A broad white scapular covered her upper chest to her shoulders.

"Oh. Hello, Sister Mary Anne," Mercedee stammered upon seeing the sister's measuring look. "We were just at the lake, Eel Lake, looking at birds."

"And rowing the boat," Kitty added.

"Yes, the boat was good exercise," Mercedee agreed.

"Right," Sister Mary Anne replied tersely. "I sincerely hope you're not engaging in untoward behavior. The school year is nearly over, and you haven't been reprimanded for some time." The sister looked at Mercedee. "You want to end the year in a positive fashion."

Sister Mary Anne was a stern Mother Superior but also compassionate. Mercedee cringed at the strict rules but also knew Sister Mary Anne was capable of being understanding. Along with the six other nuns in the convent, she was a member of the Sisters of Charity visiting from Halifax, Nova Scotia.

"Of course," the girls replied reverently.

"Now, go freshen up before beads and dinner," Sister Mary Anne said, but Mercedee knew they all probably looked like deer in the headlights. "You had better be on your way," Sister Mary Anne said, breaking the tension. The three girls walked quickly to the stairs.

At the top, Kitty said, "See you soon, Mercedee, when we go to beads?"

"Of course," Mercedee said as she reached her room.

"Knock on my door if I don't knock on yours first." Then Mercedee knocked on her own door and entered.

The room was empty. Mercedee sat on her bed, adjusted her pillow, and leaned against the headboard. The room was terribly quiet. She looked out of the window at the bay. The tide was in, and what at low tide was a tidal flat at that hour reflected deep blue in the afternoon light. High clouds and coastal haze created diffused light that gave the landscape a surreal look. Birds hung in the wind then darted away. Mercedee relaxed. That part of Nova Scotia was beautiful in a way she hadn't seen before.

She stared at a painting of St. Mary on the wall and thought about Mamma in Concession. Her parents had sent her to Eel Brook in part because it was close to her mother, and Mercedee hoped she could stay there. She had stayed with Tante Matilde and her husband, Avite, on their small farm in Concession the previous summer and looked forward to going back. Their son, Peter, was about a year older than Mercedee, and they had exciting adventures. The farm brought in meager money, but it provided subsistence.

Tante Adelaide was helping Tante Mathilde care for Mamma. But Adelaide wasn't terribly friendly. Mercedee didn't enjoy her company, as she was always critical and dissatisfied.

Mercedee heard footsteps in the hallway outside her door and choked back her tears. She pulled a handkerchief out of her pocket and wiped her face. She quickly rose and walked to the window. She looked out at the bay as a knock echoed through the room. "Come in," she called over her shoulder as Clara turned the handle and peeked through.

"There you are. I've been in the recreation room reading. I expected you would stop by there on your way back." She closed the door and dropped onto her bed, clearly happy to see her friend.

"Oh, I would have, but I just got back." Mercedee dabbed her nose with the handkerchief while looking out the window so as not to alarm Clara. "And Sister Mary Anne said I should freshen up before beads."

"Of course."

The room became silent, and Mercedee took a deep breath, still not looking at Clara.

As the moment grew uncomfortable, Clara spoke up. "Are you all right?"

"Yes, yes of course." Mercedee faced Clara.

Clara looked into Mercedee's swollen red eyes and noted her flushed cheeks. "Mercedee!" She gasped and leapt up from the bed. Clara quickly crossed the small room and embraced her friend.

"I said that I'm all right." Mercedee paused. "I suppose you can tell I'm not?"

"It's going to be all right," Clara said into Mercedee's shoulder.

After another long moment, Mercedee said, "Even if it's not, I have to go on. I won't cry anymore."

"Well, that's always all right. Sometimes you must." Clara sighed and stepped back, bumping into the steel tubing of Mercedee's footboard and nearly falling backward. Reaching for the footboard behind her, Clara found only air, but Mercedee had grasped her other hand, and Clara regained her balance.

The two looked at each other and burst into laughter.

"These rooms are insufferably small, aren't they?" Clara asked.

"I would say so," Mercedee said. "Now let's get ourselves ready for beads before one of us gets hurt!"

They laughed again, and Mercedee looked in the mirror. She wiped her eyes with her handkerchief and fixed her hair in a bun. Just as Clara and Mercedee decided they were presentable, a knock sounded on the thin wooden door, causing it to bump against the metal latch.

"Mercedee, are you in there?" Kitty called.

"I'm here with Clara, Kitty," Mercedee replied, pulling the door open.

"Very good." Kitty panted. "I was just downstairs, and

Sister Mary Anne is taking everyone to the chapel."

"Thank you so much for alerting us." Mercedee and Clara followed Kitty down the hall then descended the stairs. They crossed the grassy area between trees and followed a stone walk to the church building, quickly reaching the other students already walking to the chapel. Fortunately, the youngest girls, who were from five to ten years old, were walking slowly and gave them time to catch up.

Under the watchful eye of Sister Mary Anne and a scowling Sister Carmel, the girls said their prayers, rose, and went out of the church and back to the convent in single file. The nuns led the students to the back of the building, to the kitchen and communal dining area. Sister Mary Anne looked at a sheet of paper pinned to the wall behind a counter in the food preparation area and read aloud five names, directing them to help with the meal. Then she read five more names, including Mercedee and Clara. "You're to help with dishes after our repast."

After Sister Mary Anne's announcement, some of the girls not involved with food preparation sat at one of two long tables in the dining room. Other girls, including Mercedee and Clara, moved to a table in the recreation room next door. The room was quiet except for the patter of feet and the creaking of the floor outside.

The door opened, and Kitty and Mamie joined Mercedee and Clara. Clara got out of her chair and looked at books on two shelves set into one wall. Cupboards below a thin counter contained activities and supplies for the students. She picked out a book and pulled it from the lower shelf.

Grinning, Clara returned to her chair and softly asked Kitty and Mercedee, "What did you two really do at Eel Lake?"

"I told you, we just rowed the boat around." Mercedee stifled a smirk.

"I think George is sweet on Mercedee," Kitty said, and

Mercedee looked at her, wide-eyed.

"Oh? Well, who was holding hands with Sylvain LeFave?" Mercedee shot back.

"That was an accident," Kitty said.

"Hush you two, or Sister Carmel will hear you." Clara glanced at the door as if trying not to laugh. Then all three covered their mouths and suppressed guffaws.

Clara's eyes widened. "You *were* with George and Sylvain, then. I thought you didn't like them. Didn't George grab your arm last month, nearly getting slapped by you?" she asked Mercedee.

"I didn't need to slap him," Mercedee said. "George tried to take my arm while walking next to me, but I used my elbow to nudge him aside. That's all that happened."

"That nudge almost sent him sprawling onto the road." Kitty grinned.

"Yes," Mercedee whispered, "and I informed him that he must use his manners around me."

"When we were going to the post office with Jean Ekens," Mamie told Mercedee, "George was so rude that I almost slapped him."

"I was certain that you were going to," Mercedee whispered.

"George will learn soon enough that this isn't how to get attention from girls," Mamie said.

Clara put her elbows on the tabletop and rested her chin on her hands. "I think he learned his lesson because he's been much more respectful since that day."

***

A week later, on Sunday, May 23, 1892, the weather turned cold. Dark, low clouds rode a strong wind from the Atlantic to the southeast. Waves lapped the shore near the convent, and its walls were battered by cold rain. After mass, the girls and nuns hurried from the chapel to the convent.

"It's too cold to go for a walk today," Mercedee told her friends. "Let's make scapulars and write messages to send with them. We can practice our calligraphy."

Clara and Mamie agreed and rummaged in the craft cupboard. Clara pulled out some heavy paper and a bottle of ink. "I'm going to be a professional calligrapher." She chortled.

Mamie rolled her eyes. "That'll be a sight to see! If you keep practicing, you'll be able to write your name!"

The group spread out their supplies and spent the afternoon creating.

As Mercedee made her way to the recreation room with a book, she saw eleven-year-old Jean looking out the window of the dining room. She looked profoundly sad. Jean and her younger sister, Kirsten, were from Yarmouth and kept to themselves.

Mercedee walked softly to the window beside Jean and looked out. "Do you miss your home?"

Jean sniffed, buried her head in her hands, and ran from the window and through the door. Mercedee looked after Jean as her footsteps echoed in the hall, then she heard heavy steps on the stairs. "Oh my," Mercedee whispered to herself.

Jean was a quiet girl. Mercedee wasn't sure what she was thinking most of the time. She remembered when Jean's parents had dropped her off at the convent. When Mercedee had arrived, she had kissed her mother and cried, but Jean and Kirsten seemed distant when they got out of the stagecoach and their parents led them up to the door of the convent building. It was an odd scene.

The end of the school year is coming up. Maybe she doesn't want to go home? Or does Jean miss her parents? Mercedee shrugged and walked to the recreation room, where Mamie was reading.

"Hello, Mercedee." Mamie didn't look up from her book.

"Hello, Mamie." Mercedee took a chair across the table from Mamie. "I'm concerned about Jean."

"I think we all are." Mamie folded her book on her finger, saving her place. "If you have any ideas, I'd like to hear them."

"I saw her looking out the window, and I asked her if she were homesick."

"Oh?"

Mercedee exhaled. "She ran off to her room."

"Perhaps she *is* homesick. But I don't know," Mamie said.

"I read stories to her when she was sick. She listened and seemed to enjoy the stories but never said anything."

"Oh well." Mamie sighed. "She's never spoken to me, so I can't say."

"I agree," Mercedee whispered, opening her book.

They read in silence for some time until there was a knock on the door, and Nellie Rolston poked her head in. "It's almost time for biscuits."

"Thank you," Mercedee said.

She and Mamie closed their books and headed for the dining room. Sisters Carmel and Mary Anne were organizing the girls for their ten o'clock biscuits. The older girls—including Clara, Kitty, and a friend, Evangeline—were seated at the main table. The younger girls— including Jean and her sister, Kirsten Ekens, Nellie, Lennie Smith, May Babin, and Mary Ida Sheehan—were seated at a smaller table with smaller chairs.

Sister Lucilla came to the older girls' table and asked Kitty to help get water. Kitty nodded, and they went to the kitchen, which had a hand pump on the counter. Kitty worked a lever up and down, filling a pair of porcelain pitchers that Lucilla held beneath a spout. They took the pitchers and porcelain mugs to the tables.

As Mercedee and Mamie walked into the dining room, Sister Carmel said sarcastically, "Oh, mercy. Thank you for gracing us with your presence, Miss Meehan and Miss Gardner."

Mercedee and Mamie looked down and took their seats.

"Yes, sister," Mamie said.

"Attention, students," Sister Mary Anne said. "I've

added an extra seat at the older girls' table. Because she's almost ten, I'm asking Miss Jean Ekens to sit with the older girls."

Jean looked at Sister Mary Anne as if shocked. She slowly got up and walked with her head bowed to the empty chair.

"Let's welcome Jean to the table," Sister Mary Anne said.

"Welcome, Jean," Mercedee said, and the other girls followed her lead.

As Jean fidgeted with a shock of her straight black hair, Sister Lucilla carried a plate of sweet, light-brown biscuits over to the young girls, and Sister Carmel set a plate in the middle of the older girls' table. Both tables had white saucers in a stack. Each girl took a saucer and a biscuit.

It was apparent that Sister Mary Anne had noticed Jean's malaise and was trying to help her. Jean looked down at her plate and nibbled on her biscuit.

After they ate and returned to their room, Mercedee and Clara were talking when they heard a commotion downstairs. Investigating, they found Jean out of sorts and crying behind a door in a small, dark study. She was calling for her sister to let her out.

"You must calm yourself, Miss Ekens," Sister Carmel said through the door. "As soon as you're finished crying, then you may come out."

A half hour later, Jean finally quieted, and Sister Carmel allowed her to come out and join the younger girls listening to Sister Lucilla read fairy tales. Older girls read books or played games until it was time to go to beads at the chapel before dinner.

Mercedee whispered to Clara, "Sister Carmel wasn't very nice to Jean, shutting her up in that dark closet! I would've been crying, too, if she'd done that to me. I feel so sorry for Jean."

"It was harsh punishment for poor Jean. She's so unhappy, and the nuns just try to punish her. I hope she'll feel better after beads." Clara looked around, probably to see if Sister Carmel was listening.

The storm had let up as the rain stopped, but it was still windy and cold. So the girls gathered up their jackets. Things seemed back to normal when Kitty called out, "Where's Jean?"

Sisters Mary Anne and Carmel came quickly from Sister Mary Anne's office down the hall.

"Does anyone know where Jean Ekens is?" Sister Mary Anne asked. "Is she not in her room?"

"No. She's not, Sister Mary Anne," Kitty said. "I looked on my way down, and I didn't see her in the recreation room either."

"Her coat and hat are gone too." Mercedee pointed at the coat rack.

"Where could she have gone?" Sister Carmel asked.

"I do not have—" Sister Mary Anne was cut off by sobs from the back of the group.

Jean's sister, Kirsten, stood with her head bowed, crying. Sister Mary Anne moved through the girls, and they spread around Kirsten.

"What is it?" Sister Mary Anne asked.

"I'm so sorry." Kirsten sobbed.

"Why?" Sister Mary Anne asked.

"Please forgive me." Kirsten wiped her nose on her sleeve. "Jean told me not to tell."

Sister Carmel frowned. "Did she say where she was going?"

"No." Kirsten sighed.

Sister Mary Anne appeared to think for a moment. "I have an idea. Sister Carmel, you and Sister Lucilla take the students over to the chapel for beads. I'm going to look for little Jean. I have an idea where she may be headed."

"Yes, Mother Superior," Sister Carmel said.

Sister Mary Anne knelt in front of Kirsten and took out a handkerchief. She wiped the little girl's eyes and nose and gave her a hug. "You stay here with Sister Lucilla and Sister Carmel. Everything will be fine."

"All right, everyone. Line up and absolutely no speaking," Sister Carmel said as Sister Mary Anne walked to her room and got her cloak.

After beads, the students walked to the convent from the church, led by Sister Carmel. Feeling the cold wind in the fading twilight, Mercedee, at the rear of the line and behind the younger girls, whispered to Clara, "Do you think Jean's trying to walk to Yarmouth?"

"She might be," Clara whispered back.

"Jean would have to know she would never make it before dark," Mercedee said.

"Yes, but where else would she go?" Clara asked. "Unless she knows someone or has family near Tusket, she'll be out in the cold all night."

"I'm worried—" Mercedee halted as Sister Carmel reached the convent door, turned around, and looked directly at Mercedee, who stood without making a sound.

Sister Carmel opened the door and led the girls to the kitchen.

Later, midway through dinner, as darkness fell on the convent, Sister Mary Anne returned with Jean and led her to a chair at the young girls' table. Jean silently nibbled on her food. Mercedee never heard Jean say another word for the next few days. One morning, Jean's parents arrived in a wagon and took her and Kirsten back to Yarmouth.

***

The first of June was warm. In the small school building, Mercedee fidgeted. Thoughts of her mamma Agnes consumed her. She hadn't received a postal in more than a week, and her mind started playing games with her. Mercedee daydreamed that Mamma had passed or that she was asking for Mercedee to come but Mercedee had no way of knowing. *Maybe the postal has been lost in transit from Concession?*

"Mercedee? Mercedee?" Sister Carmel, who was teaching grammar, suddenly came into focus.

"I'm sorry? What was the question?" Mercedee asked as

the other girls chuckled.

Sister Carmel pointed at a sentence written on a slate blackboard. "Can you tell me which word is the adverb?"

"Oh, right. Yes. I believe the adverb is 'quickly.' The fox ran quickly from the hunter, so 'quickly' modifies 'ran,' which is the verb." Mercedee's father hadn't been present much of her life, but he'd placed a high value on grammar and writing coherent letters, which were their only form of communication.

"Very good, Miss Meehan. Well done." Sister Carmel began dissecting the sentence into phrases and subject and verb.

Classroom time ended in the early afternoon, but Mercedee felt like she had been in the little schoolhouse for a week because her thoughts kept drifting to Mamma. Only two weeks of school remained, then she could go to Concession to help care for her mother. But right then, she was going to the Eel Brook Post Office to see if she had a postal that the sisters had missed. In the best case, there would be a letter from Mathilde telling her that Mamma had improved and would be fine until she got there. Mercedee shuddered to think about the worst case.

As the students rose from their tables and headed for the classroom exit, Clara spoke up. "Mercedee, Kitty and I are going to go to the activity room to play games with some of the other girls. Would you like to join us?"

"I may later, but first, I must walk down to the post office and see if there is a postal," Mercedee said solemnly.

Clara seemed to notice Mercedee's mood. "Um, Kitty, I'll meet you in the convent a little later," she said over her shoulder as she skipped and caught up with Mercedee. They walked quickly toward Main Post Road.

Soon, Mercedee and Clara were walking east. The afternoon sun was hot on their backs, and after the recent letter from her father, Mercedee hoped she wasn't perspiring.

"You're worried, aren't you?" Clara asked.

"Yes. You could tell?" Mercedee sighed sarcastically.

Clara rolled her eyes. "Don't you suppose that Sister Mary Anne would have told you if there was a postal?"

"Yes, she would have. But I have to check. It may not be likely, but I need to be sure. What if it fell behind something at the post office? At least I'll know if I go and check."

"Yes. If this will help, then certainly."

"It will help." Mercedee glanced at Clara as if to say thank you then said, "You're such a good friend."

The gravel road wandered over two rolling hills. The white post office sat alongside the road near Eel Lake. A sign showed the way to a door on the side of the building.

Mercedee pulled the door open and walked inside. Behind a counter, boxes labeled with names lined the wall. Seeing no one in the room, Mercedee quickly rang a bell on the wooden counter with a mottled patina. A man emerged from a doorway that led into the rest of the house.

"Ah, hello, Miss Meehan. You're looking for mail, eh? Perhaps from your mother, Agnes, no doubt?" He rested his palms on the counter. "It was so delightful to see her last fall when she came here with you. I hope she's recovering."

"Yes, Mr. LeBlanc. I just wanted to check to see if any postal had come…" Her voice trailed off as Alphonso turned toward the back wall, where he had placed bags and letters on another counter.

Alphonso looked in a canvas bag with a bundle of letters beside it. He picked up the bundle and cut the string with a pair of scissors before thumbing through envelopes of various shapes and colors.

"Ah yes," Alphonso said. "This is for you."

"Really?" Clara asked.

"Yes." He held the letter in the air. "Here you are." He handed Mercedee the letter, and she accepted it with trembling hands.

"Well, thank you," she said softly and headed for the door.

Alphonso rubbed his chin. "She will get better, and you will see her soon, yes? I hope the letter has good news."

"I hope so too. Thank you so much," Mercedee said over her shoulder as the door closed behind them.

"It's no problem at all for you. Good luck!" Alphonso called out.

Mercedee and Clara walked in silence. Clara was unsure what to say, and Mercedee was afraid to read the letter. Finally, they reached the top of a rise and could see the steeple of St. Anne's Church above the trees up ahead. Mercedee stopped and slid her finger under the envelope flap. She peeled it back and slid out a small, folded piece of paper.

My Dear Mercedee,

I have been so weak. That is the reason I have not written, and I am sorry to say that I am not as well as I was. I have a terrible cough and raise blood dreadfully, and it is lasting so long that I am weary. I am sending for the doctor today. Ask Mr. Surette how long coughs are to last. This is eight weeks now that I cough and raise like that. I have moved downstairs where I can get fresh air. I will try to write soon. Everything is alright.

—Your Mamma

"Oh my." Mercedee looked at the stationery.

"What is it?" Clara asked.

"Mamma isn't doing well."

"Oh, I'm sorry."

"But she's still alive and trying." Mercedee reread the cursive handwriting. "She says that she's raising blood but has called for a doctor. She says she'll be all right, but she seems worse than I have heard or seen in the past." Mercedee thought for a moment. "This letter is different."

Clara put her arm around Mercedee's shoulders. "It'll only be a week or so, and you can go back to Concession. Then you can help her get better."

"Yes," Mercedee agreed. "If she can rest, and the doctor

can help, I'll be there soon."

Clara and Mercedee walked quickly toward the intersection with the road to Belleville, just wanting to get back to their room. After a short distance, Mercedee noticed George Blauvelt up ahead, leaning against a picket fence in front of a house. "Not now," Mercedee said softly.

"Ignore him," Clara replied.

"Hello," he said as they approached. "I was just walking to the lake and saw you go into the post office."

"Yes." Mercedee walked past him.

"Are you two in a hurry?" George trotted after them. "It's a great afternoon for a paddle around the lake, don't you think?"

"I'm sorry," Mercedee said. "We have to get back to St. Anne's."

"Yes," Clara added, "we don't have time today."

"Could I walk with you for a piece?" George was walking alongside Mercedee. "I enjoyed rowing with you and wanted to say I'm sorry for how I acted before. I need to go to Sylvain's house over toward Tusket. It's the same direction you—"

"George," Clara interrupted, "you should know better than that."

"What?" he asked.

"If the sisters see us walking with a boy, we'll be in more trouble than you can imagine." Mercedee's hands went to her hips. "You should know that by now."

George's eyes grew larger. He raised his hands and backed up a step. "Oh," he said softly. "I didn't mean to get you two into trouble."

"Well, you haven't gotten us in trouble. Yet," Mercedee said. "Please do us a favor and wait until we've gone and then start walking so that no one at the church sees us close to each other. The convent is behind the church, but one of the sisters could be out near the road."

"Sure. Sure, Mercedee. Maybe some other time, then?"

"Maybe." But she wasn't in any mood for making plans

to paddle around Eel Lake. "Goodbye, George."

"Goodbye," he answered.

"Bye," Clara said.

As the girls walked away, they saw George as he stood on the edge of Main Post Road and looked west toward the church as if looking for a sign of one of the nuns.

The sun was bright and hot, but a cool breeze was a small relief. Mercedee looked forward to getting to the shade of the large trees around the convent.

Back at their room, Mercedee took out her mother's letter and read it again. She was both optimistic and pessimistic. *Why would she write the letter? She's been raising blood for weeks.* The only explanation was that her mother felt she was near the end. *Or did she want me not to worry during the last few weeks of the school term?* Either could be true. However, Mamma didn't say goodbye. And she didn't say to return to Concession at once.

Mercedee returned the letter to the envelope and slid it into her bound diary.

The next day, June 3, Mercedee, Kitty, Clara, Evangeline, and Mamie attended classes, and Mercedee read a story to Lennie, one of the younger girls. After lunch, Mercedee and Clara walked to the post office again.

"Hello, girls." Alphonso greeted Mercedee and Clara as they entered the post office. "Would you like a couple apples?"

"I don't think we should," Mercedee said.

"Please. I have many." He pushed a large basket across the counter.

The sight of the fresh apples with green and red skins was too much, and Mercedee and Clara picked two each.

"You will like them," Alphonso said.

"You're very kind," Mercedee said. "But you know why we're here, yes?"

"Of course, of course. But I'm sorry," Alphonso said. "The sister… what is her name? She must be new because I can't remember."

"Lucilla?" Mercedee offered.

"A-yes! Lucilla. She was here earlier and picked up several postals for the convent. I made certain that was everything for today. She's very friendly. I like Sister Lu—" His words were cut short as the girls thanked him and raced out of the office.

Mercedee and Clara ate the sweet and sour apples as they walked along the road, and tossed the cores into the fields and forest. Mercedee tossed her last core over the fence just as Sister Carmel appeared over a rise in the road, followed by the younger girls out for a walk. Sister Carmel frowned.

"Hello, Sister," Clara said.

"Beautiful day for a walk, isn't it?" Mercedee said cheerfully.

"Yes," Sister Carmel replied, then she turned to the girls behind her. "Keep up now, students."

The girls waved at them and walked on past.

When Clara and Mercedee reached the convent door, they let themselves in. They walked toward Sister Mary Anne's office, but before they were halfway there, she emerged and called to them.

"Mercedee, please come in. I need to speak with you."

"Do you think Sister Mary Anne found out we got apples?" Clara whispered.

Sister Mary Anne stood in a ray of light filtering from her office and casting her shadow onto the hardwood floor of the hall.

"How could she?" Mercedee whispered back. "We were far down the road, out of sight." Mercedee turned to shield Clara from Sister Mary Anne's view. "Don't worry about a thing. I'll be right back." Mercedee walked confidently down the hall.

"Please come in," Sister Mary Anne said as Mercedee approached.

Walking past her and into the office, Mercedee noticed Sister Mary Anne's solemn expression. She held a postal.

In the narrow office, Mercedee paused between a heavy wooden desk and two chairs facing it near the door. The musty scent of books filled her nostrils as she moved between the chairs and waited. The pause was too long, and Mercedee started to worry. She was often reprimanded for one thing or another, but it seemed as if the sister was a bearer of bad news.

Sister Mary Anne walked behind her desk. "I received a postal from your aunt Mathilde today. She says you're to come to Concession as soon as possible. Your mother isn't well. Mathilde enclosed two dollars for train fare." Sister Mary Anne handed Mercedee the envelope.

Mercedee's heart sank as she accepted the postal with a trembling hand and pulled out the letter and bills. She read the note as tears welled in her eyes.

My Dear Mercedee,
Your mother, Agnes, is not quite so well. Please find the enclosed two dollars and return here at once.
—Your Loving Tante Mathilde

Dread clutched at Mercedee's throat as the meaning of the message became clear. She bit her lip to keep from crying, and her face turned pale. She looked at the envelope. "This letter was written yesterday, and today is June 5." Mercedee sighed. "She's been in this dire condition for one day already."

"I'm afraid so, child," Sister Mary Anne said softly.

"How shall I get there, Sister Mary Anne? I must go at once. I must go quickly!" *Mamma cannot be dying!* Mercedee held back tears and looked wide-eyed at the sister.

Sister Mary Anne said, straightening the letters on her desk, "Perhaps it would be best for you to go to Belleville and hire a horse to take you to Yarmouth to the rails. If you find someone to take you, you could be in Concession by evening. You have family in the area. That, I know."

"Yes," Mercedee whispered. "There must be a way."

"The Lord will protect your mother, I'm sure." Sister Mary Anne took Mercedee's hand. "She's suffered so terribly. Go now, and Clara can go with you if she's willing. You could use the boat. Rowing across Eel Lake will be quicker. Perhaps the two of you will make easier work of the rowing." She hugged Mercedee and pressed a kiss to her forehead before sending her back to the dormitory.

Mercedee left the office and hurried towards the front door. A door to one of the dorm rooms opened, and Clara looked up. "Is something wrong?"

Mercedee paused in front of Clara, looking at the letter. "Well." She sighed, then her voice cracked as she said, "I need to get to Yarmouth as soon as possible. My mother is ailing in Concession, near Church Point, and I don't have much time."

"How can you get there?" Clara looked concerned.

"I'm going to row across the lake to Belleville to find a horse." Mercedee glanced up from the letter. "My uncle Lezin Potier lives there, and he'll be able to help me sort this out."

"Would you like me to go with you? I can help," Clara said.

"Would you? Thank you so much. Let's go quickly." Mercedee pocketed the letter.

They hurried to the end of the hall, down the steps, and out the door. Maintaining a steady pace, they soon reached the Belleville Road, where they headed to the boat landing and saw the rowboat moored. They pushed the boat into the water, and Clara hopped in. Mercedee lifted her skirt and stepped in as she pushed the rowboat from the shore.

Clara took the stern bench, and Mercedee took the oars. Mercedee pulled on the right oar to turn the boat to the northeast and pulled hard, pushing them into deep water. "Tell me if we're not headed right up the middle of the lake. My uncle Lezin lives in a house across the lake and north of here. It'll be a white house, but we won't see it until we're almost there," Mercedee said in gasps between strokes.

"I will," Clara replied.

Mercedee rowed desperately across the lake. Sobs punctuated her labored breathing. She powered the boat on, and the shore on either side moved slowly past. Mercedee breathed harder, not letting up.

Clara tried to calm her. "Don't try so hard. You're going to be exhausted. Let me row for a few minutes."

Mercedee ignored Clara for a few paddle strokes then blurted, "But my mother is very ill! I must see her! And I can row the boat faster than you. I'll be fine." Mercedee calmed her sobs and pulled hard on the oars. She was right, but she was also pushing too hard. She rowed for several minutes, heading the boat toward a landing with a small rowboat on the shore above it. Then Mercedee reached her limit. She dropped her head and lowered the oars, emotionally and physically exhausted.

"Let me take over," Clara said. "It's not too much farther. Don't worry. We'll find a horse. There's nothing more we can do."

"All right." Clara and Mercedee exchanged places, and Clara oared the boat on northward past a small peninsula on the east shore.

"We're almost there." Mercedee looked past Clara. "I think I see the landing."

Clara took another pull on the oars and gasped, "I'm quite relieved I won't be paddling too much longer. How far do you guess?"

"We're almost there." Mercedee searched the landing for any sign of people but saw no one. "Do you want me to finish rowing?"

"I think I can make it." Clara panted and continued.

"All right, turn a bit that way." Mercedee pointed to her right.

Clara rowed on, and they were soon at the small, weathered wood dock where they tied off the boat. They climbed onto the dock and walked to a trail that led through some large maple trees, then they climbed onto the low upland. They continued across a large field toward a small white house. Like the schoolhouse, Lezin's house had a gable that split the pitched roof.

Mercedee walked to the door and knocked. They listened, but there was only silence. She knocked again. Still nothing. She walked along the front of the house to a window and looked in. She could see no one. Clara walked to another window.

"Do you see anyone?" Mercedee asked.

"No." Looking in the window, Clara asked, "Is there anyone else here with Lezin?"

"Yes, his wife, Marie Elizabeth." Mercedee's shoulders drooped, and she wiped her eyes. "I don't know where they would be."

Clara walked over and rubbed Mercedee's arm. "Is there anyone else we could see?"

"Yes, several other relatives live along the road, but I don't know any of them. I hope Lezin has told his cousins and uncles that Mamma and I are here." Mercedee walked away from the house to a drive that led past another house, one belonging to Uncle Augustin Potier, and to the Belleville Road. Across the road was a house owned by Pierre. Just north was Adolphe. At each house, the result was the same, and no one could give them help to get to Yarmouth the following day. Adolphe and his wife, however, offered them sandwiches, which they accepted with thanks.

Back at the rowboat, they traded off paddling, tired and weary from the earlier rowing. Disappointed, they walked down Chemin des Bourque to the convent.

Once there, Mercedee and Clara sat down to their dinner and explained to the girls and nuns that there were no horses to be had.

"Why don't you try in Tusket?" suggested Sister Mary Anne. "It's only a couple miles from here. Look for Mr. Browne. And the Surettes are repairing their boat. Perhaps Evangeline could help you. You should be home for beads if you don't get a horse."

"Thank you, Sister!" Mercedee cried.

She and Clara gulped down their dinners and hurried out of the dining room. Skipping down the steps leading out of the building, Mercedee said, "I don't even remember what we ate. I'm so worried about my Mamma!"

The long walk to Tusket proved as fruitless as the trip to Belleville, with no horse or other way to get to Yarmouth. As they wearily retraced their steps to St. Anne's, Mercedee said, "I can't give up! I must get to Concession. Perhaps if I can get to Yarmouth this afternoon, I can catch the coach this evening. Let's go on to Eel Brook again. It's not far on the other side of the convent, but maybe someone will help me."

"But Sister didn't say we could go. She'll be furious with us if she finds out."

"You go back, then. I'll continue on by myself. I can't give up yet." Mercedee strode ahead.

"All right. You know I can't let you go by yourself. However, I know we'll be in trouble!" Clara grumbled.

Two hours later, the weary but jubilant girls burst into the convent kitchen with their news. The startled nun glanced up.

"Sister, we got a horse! We met my uncle, Mr. d'Entremont, at the Eel Brook Post Office. He said he's going to Yarmouth tomorrow. He'll be passing here at six tomorrow morning with his mount and will take me to Yarmouth!" Mercedee paused, waiting for a reaction from the stern nun. Seeing little, she looked into the pan the nun held over stove. "Oh, look, you're making molasses candy! Can we have some before supper?" Mercedee bubbled.

"You found a man with a horse? That's fine indeed, but we were so worried about you. Sister Carmel and the girls have gone to Tusket to look for you," Sister Mary Anne scolded.

"Oh no!" Clara cried. "I knew we should have asked permission to go on to Eel Brook. Now they're on a wild-goose chase."

"Yes," Sister Mary Anne said. "Since you didn't let us know where you were, you'll have to go find the girls and Sister Carmel and save them any more worry. Here. Have a bite of candy and hurry off with you."

"Ooh," Clara moaned. "We've already walked so many miles and rowed two more. My feet are so tired."

"No complaining, Clara. It was your fault you didn't come by here before you went on to Eel Brook. Now you must go." Sister Mary Anne raised an eyebrow at Mercedee then turned toward the stove. "You can have supper when you've returned." She paused then turned back to them with a porcelain plate.

"Here's some bread for the trip." She set the plate on the counter, and the girls gratefully took a slice.

"Thank you so much, Sister Mary Anne." Mercedee sighed.

"Yes, thank you," Clara said.

"Let's go, Clara," Mercedee said. "Maybe they haven't gotten too far. It's almost dark, and it'll be chilly soon. Let's hurry."

Mercedee picked up a handful of sweet candy and hurried out the door with Clara trudging behind, her pretty face etched with gloom. An hour and a half later, the two exhausted girls with aching feet finally knelt to say their rosaries under the beautiful high ceiling of the chapel. The quiet peace filled Mercedee's tired body and comforted her anxious thoughts. Her earnest prayers and hopes winged skyward into the cool, damp Nova Scotia night.

Silently, she and Clara trod to the convent and headed for the kitchen. "Oh, this truly is a blessing," Mercedee said upon seeing two plates of food with cloth over them.

"I'm so very thankful," Clara said.

They picked up their plates, silverware, and a glass of water and dropped into chairs in the dining room. They quickly ate their dinner and coaxed their legs to ascend the stairs one last time. Finally in their room, they had just enough energy left to change into their nightgowns and fall into a restless slumber.

Mercedee stirred in her sleep and dreamed that she opened her eyes but could barely see a farmhouse through a thick fog. Moving closer, she made out the sharp gable on the side of the house and moved toward the front door. The door opened as Mercedee reached it, and her Tante Monique said, "Hello." Her round face was white with dark, piercing eyes. Mercedee walked past her into Mathilde's house in Concession. Her mother's sisters—Adelaide, Placide, Seraphie, and Marie Anne, a nun at the St. Vincent Academy in Halifax who took the name Sister Mary Rosalia—watched her silently. Then she passed her uncle Lezin and her father's sister, Aunt Moll, whom she'd stayed with in Digby. Mercedee walked on past them in a surreal procession to an open bedroom door with diffused light shining in through a window. Inside the room was her mother's bedroom of the house where they had once lived in Melrose Highlands north of Boston. Her mamma Agnes lay on the bed in a white dress with her eyes closed. As Mercedee moved closer, Agnes whispered her name.

"What is it, Mamma?" Mercedee asked softly as she sat on the bed beside Agnes. She leaned down near her mother's pale face. It wasn't unlike the many times as a child that Mercedee would lay beside her mother and hug her, praying that the wheezing in her chest would stop and that Mamma Agnes would be able to get out of bed and play with her, go for a walk, or visit Papa in Boston.

But Mamma couldn't do those things. Instead, they would sit, and Agnes would read books or tell Mercedee stories. If her mother's breath was strong enough, they might sing, although it usually ended up with Mamma starting the song and Mercedee singing the rest as Mamma started coughing or had to stop and lie quietly.

Mercedee lifted her mother's head, slid her arm underneath Mamma's neck, and pulled her emaciated body close. "I'm here, Mamma. I'm here. What do you want to say?"

2 SORROW

Sunrise, June 6, 1892

"Mercedee! The sun's coming up!" Clara called out, causing Mercedee's eyes to flash open. "You were dreaming."

"I'm quite glad that was just a dream. What time is it?" Mercedee gasped, trying to sort the dream from reality. "I was indeed in the midst of a terrible dream. I hope it wasn't a premonition."

"Well, it's almost seven o'clock," Clara said with a sense of urgency.

Outside their second-story window, the sun crept over the trees, sending rays of light and the shadow of St. Anne's Church steeple across the bay. The light brought Mercedee out of her groggy state with a start. She sat up in bed and glanced at Clara, who was on one elbow, looking back.

Almost on cue, the bells from St. Anne's sounded. Mercedee counted seven chimes, and her eyes opened wide. She threw her blanket back and jumped up, dashed to the window, and peered out toward the small barn. "Where is he? I don't see anyone. Did I miss him? Someone would have surely awakened me if he had come by." Mercedee returned to her bed and sat down, rubbing her feet, which were still sore from the long walks the previous day.

"Who?" Clara asked.

"Mr. d'Entremont, who promised me he would come at six with a horse to take me to Yarmouth."

"Of course," Clara said.

"And here it is seven o'clock. Unless I'm very lucky, he's come and gone, and I'll never get to Yarmouth in time for the nine o'clock train to Concession. Please, will you come with me to see how I'm going to get to Yarmouth?"

"Oh, Mercedee. My feet are so sore from yesterday, and if I go all the way to Yarmouth, how will I get back?" Clara sighed.

"All right. I understand." Mercedee's own aching legs and feet complained after the previous day. She dressed quickly and fixed her hair. She poured water from a pitcher into the bowl, splashed her face, and dried off with a towel. She picked up her bag and walked past her bed.

"Thank you for your help yesterday." Mercedee smiled at her friend.

"You know you don't need to thank me," Clara said.

"I suppose, but thanks anyhow. Get some rest, and I'll see you soon." Mercedee walked out the door.

She headed down the hallway to the stairs and descended to the kitchen to see if she could get an early breakfast and some food to take with her. In the kitchen, she was surprised to see Kitty talking to Sister Lucilla across the counter. When Mercedee entered, Kitty turned.

"Good morning. You're up early too? You must be tired after yesterday," Kitty said.

"Yes, I'm stiff." Mercedee stepped up to the counter next to Kitty. "But I'm also in a hurry to get to Yarmouth and take a train to Concession. I have to get there to see my ailing mother, you see."

"Well, I'm up early because I have to get to Yarmouth today too. I need to see my aunt Evangeline. Sister Lucilla here is helping me get an early breakfast and pack some food for the trip."

"Oh my," Mercedee said. "That's precisely what I was hoping to do. May I join you? I could help."

"Of course," Kitty said.

"But how are you getting to Yarmouth? I've been trying to find a way but have found nothing short of walking."

"Sister Lucilla just told me that Mr. Frost, the repairman, is going to Yarmouth today." Kitty gestured across the counter at Sister Lucilla. "If we ask, he'll most certainly give us a ride in his wagon."

"Yes," Sister Lucilla said. "Mr. Frost should certainly have room for another in his wagon."

"What tremendous luck!" Mercedee said. "May I have some early breakfast too?"

"Of course." Sister Lucilla smiled. "Pick up an apron, and we'll be done in no time."

"We should go by Sister Mary Anne's room and make sure she knows what we have to do and that she approves," Kitty said.

"I appreciate that." Sister Mary Anne's voice came from behind them as she entered the kitchen.

"Good morning, Sister Mary Anne," Mercedee and Kitty said in unison.

"You have my blessing." The sister walked closer and looked at them. "This is a trying time. Do what you can, and my prayers are with you. I recommend that you go out the back door and around the left side of the building. Mr. Frost is getting an early start pruning one of the bushes. I could hear the shears outside my window. You may convince him to leave early in his wagon. Tell him I said it's all right and that he should. His other tasks can wait."

"Oh, thank you dearly, Sister," Mercedee said.

"Yes, thank you," Kitty said.

"You're welcome, dear girls. Now, you should be going as soon as you can finish breakfast. And Sister Lucilla, would you please pack them something for lunch?"

"Yes, we shall," Kitty replied, and Sister Lucilla nodded as Sister Mary Anne left the room.

Sister Lucilla fried bacon and eggs in a skillet on a wood-fired stove as Mercedee and Kitty prepared their lunch. After eating, they put their lunches in their travel bags, thanked Sister Lucilla, and hurried out the back door. The yard overlooked the bay and the causeway on the Main Post Road to Tusket.

Mr. Frost was a seemingly odd and crotchety man in his late forties. He had worked at the convent for many years, and his legend grew as students told stories about how mean and mysterious he was. The tales were amplified by the fact that few students ever spoke with him. Mercedee and Kitty were nervous as they walked down the steps from the back door and skirted the convent building to where Frost was busy. From around the end of the building, they heard shears snipping.

Mercedee and Kitty peeked around the warped, weathered siding at Mr. Frost. Under his floppy hat, his hair was a mix of black and gray. His work shirt had frayed holes in the elbows and was worn under dark suspenders and tucked into weathered work pants. He was snipping winter-killed branches from bushes along the end of the building. Kitty and Mercedee glanced at each other as they slowly approached him. Mercedee cleared her throat and inhaled.

"Good morning, young ladies," Frost said before Mercedee could speak. "What can I do for you?" Frost clipped a twig from a bush. He tossed the wilted leaves onto other branches in a wheelbarrow sitting to his right. He straightened and faced the girls. He pushed his hat back from his forehead and raised one bushy, grizzled eyebrow, deep wrinkles evident above it as he looked at Mercedee. His cheeks were covered with white stubble.

Mercedee swallowed her nerves. "Mr. Frost, my name is Mercedee Meehan, and this is Kitty Hughes. Sister Mary Anne has given us permission to ask you for a ride to the train depot in Yarmouth. You see, it's a bit of an emergency, as my mother in Concession is gravely ill."

"Your mother?"

"Yes."

"Well, that is unfortunate. I'm very sorry to hear. I do need to make a trip to Yarmouth, and I can see from your bags you're planning to get there soon." Frost, who had fished for years before taking the maintenance position at St. Anne's, rubbed his chin and his weathered cheek. "And you have to go straightaway you say?" He squinted into the low morning sun.

"Straightaway would be perfect." Mercedee started to feel anxious. "Sister Mary Anne told us to tell you that she's in agreement with taking off as soon as you see fit."

"The both of you?" Frost glanced at Kitty.

"Yes, I need to get to Yarmouth today as well," Kitty said meekly.

"I'm sorry," Mercedee said. "I should have included Kitty."

"No need to apologize. I don't see why I can't head on into town right away," Mr. Frost said as the girls let out a sigh of relief. "Let's get the buggy from the barn and get on the road. No reason standing around talking." Mr. Frost set his clippers on the mass of stems and withered leaves in the wheelbarrow, wiped his hands on his overalls, and turned toward a small white building a short distance to the south. "Right this way."

"Oh, thank you so much," Mercedee said as she and Kitty followed him across the yard with their bags.

The trio reached a small barn where a mule stood at the end of a rope tether, already wearing a bridle for traveling. A buckboard wagon sat parked near the building. "Help me hitch the wagon up, Miss Meehan, and we'll be on our way," Mr. Frost said.

Mercedee and Kitty looked at each other with wide eyes, having never done anything with a mule or wagon before. Mr. Frost grabbed the mule's tether line and led the mule toward them.

"What do you want us to…?" Mercedee's voice trailed off.

"Hold on to the reins." Mr. Frost handed the narrow leather straps to Mercedee.

She put down her bag and grasped the reins, hoping the mule didn't decide he had anywhere better to go.

"And don't let the old mule go anywhere."

Mercedee held the reins nervously. *And just how do I do that?* Fortunately, the mule stood patiently as Mr. Frost grabbed a nest of straps from the wagon and walked over to the mule. He quickly placed a padded strap around the mule's chest, another over the shoulders, and a third over the back. Then Mr. Frost placed a strap over the mule's hindquarters and another behind his back legs and under the tail. He walked to the wagon and picked up one of the two rods that protruded from the front before lifting both.

"Grab that one," Mr. Frost told Kitty. "Help me roll the wagon over to the mule." Kitty tentatively helped, and soon the small wagon with one bench and a cargo area was behind the mule.

"Hold that rod up for me," Mr. Frost ordered. He watched Kitty as he slowly released his own, transferring the load to her. She struggled to hold the rod in one place, and Mr. Frost hurried to attach his rod to the straps. With the rod secured, he moved to Kitty's side. With a sigh, she released the rod to Mr. Frost and stepped back. When he finished hitching up Kitty's side, he set the girls' bags in the back of the wagon.

"Thank you very much, Miss Meehan and Miss Hughes." Mr. Frost took the reins from Mercedee. He walked to the side of the buckboard and offered his arm. "All aboard!"

The girls steadied themselves on his arm as they climbed into their seats.

"Go ahead and scooch on over so there's room for me." Frost followed them up onto the buggy and sat down on the left side. He snapped the reins, and the dark-brown mule begrudgingly started the wagon rolling around the building toward the Rocco Point Road. At the road, they turned left then left again on the Main Post Road to Tusket and then on to Yarmouth.

Mr. Frost kept the mule moving at a brisk walk across the causeway. Mercedee reached into her pocket for a handkerchief to wipe her nose.

"I hope your mother is all right," Mr. Frost said in a gruff but soft voice.

Mercedee quickly crumpled her handkerchief in her hands. "Me too." Through the corner of her eye, she glanced at the older man.

"I know it's tough when you have hardly anyone left," Mr. Frost continued. "I only have my wife, Carolyn. The sea took both of my brothers."

"Oh?" Mercedee said. "That's sad. Is your wife glad that you're working on dry land now? She must be."

Frost looked across the bay. "Hmm. I reckon she is. I know I am. I don't think I could hoist the ropes any more in any case."

They continued northwest past the tidal marsh, where a couple of men in the marsh hayfield were digging brooks to drain the receding tide. The marsh grass was up to their shins, and in another month, they would cut it for hay.

"Thank you again for making the trip early," Mercedee said.

"No trouble," Frost replied.

"It's really a nice trip. We didn't know if you would. I mean, we didn't, um…"

Frost raised his eyebrow and glanced over at Mercedee. "You know, sometimes things work out if you just say hello."

"I reckon you're right." Mercedee gave him a hint of a smile.

An hour and a half later, the wagon pulled in at the train depot at the north end of Yarmouth. Mercedee hopped down from the wagon and grabbed her bag from the back before Frost could get out.

"Thank you so much, Mr. Frost," she said.

"You're certainly welcome, and all my best to you and your mother."

Kitty made her way to the front seat next to Mr. Frost as Mercedee said, "You've been a wonderful friend. Thank you for your help. Maybe we can go rowing again soon."

"I pray for you and your mother," Kitty said.

Mercedee stepped up to the wagon, and Kitty leaned over the edge, and they hugged.

"Thank you." Mercedee sniffed. "Now you'd better go see your aunt. I'll see you when I come back." With her handkerchief, Mercedee wiped a tear from her eye as she turned toward the depot.

A couple of people at the window were purchasing tickets, so it was a few minutes before Mercedee could purchase a ticket on the 3:15 p.m. train. She looked at a clock on the front of the depot building, and it read 2:45 p.m. *The train should arrive in a mere thirty minutes.* She tried to muster a smile as she waved at Frost and Kitty. On seeing that Mercedee had her ticket, Frost flicked the reins, and the mule started the wagon rolling down Water Street toward the center of Yarmouth.

That thirty minutes seemed like an eternity as Mercedee waited. She watched a well-dressed older man waiting for the train. He rubbed his white handlebar mustache and pulled his watch from his vest pocket, where it connected to a gold chain. He noted the time and sighed as he returned it to his vest pocket. She suspected he was going to Digby or Halifax for business, certainly not wondering if his mother were doing well. She looked at the depot clock again. *The train is already ten minutes late!*

The afternoon sun was getting hot on Mercedee's forehead, and she weaved through passengers to the shade of the sharp-gabled station house. Reaching the shade, she heard the clacking of the train coming from the Yarmouth pier. A few seconds later, it blew a deafening whistle blast. As the train rolled to a stop on the far side of the depot, Mercedee looked at the clock again—3:15.

When the train stopped, Mercedee followed others and boarded. Travelers spread out along the train, forming lines at the ends of the passenger cars. Mercedee followed a woman in a dark-green dress up the steel steps and through a narrow door into a carriage. She dropped onto a bench seat with thin padding and set her bag on her lap. The bag was bulky, so when no one sat in the seat next to her, she put it in the empty seat.

Before long, the conductor—wearing a black suitcoat, pants, and round hat—came through the car, and Mercedee held out her ticket. The conductor read the destination and punched a hole in the ticket. "Church Point Station will be reached in about forty-five minutes."

"Thank you," Mercedee said. *If he's right, I'll reach Church Point Station at about four o'clock. It's a fifteen-minute walk to Concession and Mathilde's house. If Mamma makes it to dinnertime, I'll see her again...*

The train lurched, picked up speed, and pulled out toward Concession. The steam locomotive whistled its lonesome wail as the hisses and puffs echoed off the front of the station.

Mercedee looked ahead at the coach. A sign above the door read *Yarmouth and Annapolis Railway*. As she watched the trees and fields move past her window, Mercedee hoped against hope that her mother was alive and well. Many thoughts cascaded through her mind during the hour and a half that it took to traverse the thirty-odd miles to Concession. Darling Mamma needed her.

***

June 6, 1892, Concession, Nova Scotia

Mathilde Potier sat on a chair beside the bed in her house in Concession and dabbed bloody discharge from Agnes's chin with a white cloth. As she leaned over her sister, the loose joints in the wooden chair creaked. Agnes was staying with Mathilde while Mercedee attended St. Anne's, and she had been getting progressively weaker over the preceding weeks.

Mathilde looked upon a thin woman whose eyes were hollow and cheeks gaunt. She had been fighting tuberculosis for more than fifteen years, a desperate marathon and much longer than virtually anyone at the time had lived with the disease. But even as she grew weaker and more emaciated, Agnes's dark eyebrows and oval face radiated a certain beauty as she lay on the feather bed with her eyes closed.

Mathilde cared for Agnes as well as she could, which was little beyond comfort since there was no cure. All she could do was help keep Agnes's airway clear and try to give her water, soup, or whatever food Agnes could eat between bouts of coughing. Over the past few days, Agnes had begun raising a lot of blood, indicating the infection was damaging her lungs and bronchial tubes. Mathilde was with Agnes nearly all the time, helped by her younger sister Adelaide.

Agnes's coughing had stopped for the moment, but Mathilde wasn't sure if it was because Agnes was feeling better or if she was too weak to continue. Watching Agnes's chest slowly rise and fall, Mathilde held her sister's head up and put a cup of water to her parched lips. Agnes took a sip. The cool water no doubt soothed her raw and irritated throat.

With closed eyes, Agnes whispered hoarsely as Mathilde laid her head back onto the pillow. "Do you think Mercedee... got the letter?"

"I'm sure she will have received the letter," Mathilde said softly and reassuringly. "I'm sure she's on her way."

"I didn't want to alarm her, describing my condition." Agnes paused. "But I was so hoping she would come. I know that it's over this time. It's finally over." Agnes tried to suppress a cough but couldn't. She barked then grimaced in pain. Mathilde lifted Agnes's head and held the cloth over her mouth. When the cough was over, Agnes fell back against the pillow, breathing shallowly with a wheeze and a rattle.

Mathilde stroked Agnes's dark, gray-streaked hair.

"Don't talk. Just rest."

Agnes ignored her and continued, gasping in short breaths as if searching for optimism. "Maybe... if I tell Mercedee that I'm fine, I'll make it until she's done with studies."

"Maybe the Lord will have mercy and you'll make it," Mathilde said with a heavy heart.

"Did you get out my blue dress and white blouse?" Agnes wheezed.

"Yes, my lovely sister. They're on the table."

"If I'm gone before Mercedee gets here, will you dress me in it?" Agnes sighed.

Mathilde held Agnes's hand in both of hers. "Yes."

"So that Mercedee will remember me looking like a strong woman?"

"You know I will. You'll be beautiful."

Agnes looked up into Mathilde's eyes and tried to speak.

"Hush." Mathilde softly put her finger over Agnes's lips. "Do you know what I'm going to do?" She smiled at Agnes. "I'm going to put you in that dress right now so you can see yourself. And if Mercedee arrives, she'll see you too."

Agnes nodded.

"And if you feel better, you can take it off." Mathilde feigned an optimism that she didn't possess.

"Adelaide, please come and help me," Mathilde called over her shoulder.

Mathilde and Adelaide undressed Agnes and wiped her off with a warm, wet washcloth. That relaxed Agnes, and she dozed. Before long, they had dressed her in the white blouse and pulled the nice dark-blue dress up to her waist. The dress had once made Agnes look like a strikingly handsome French Acadian woman with smiling dark eyes. But the form-fitting lower sleeves had become loose and the belted waist two holes tighter. Agnes lay there with her eyes closed, touching the fabric with her fingers as Mathilde brushed her hair and pinned it back. Adelaide quickly left the bedroom.

"You look so nice. You really do," Mathilde said.

Adelaide came back in with a small mirror and held it up in front of Agnes. "Agnes, dear. Open your eyes if you can."

Agnes parted her eyelids. She struggled to focus on the mirror as if finally seeing herself.

Agnes took several shallow breaths and tried to fill her lungs with enough air to form words then whispered, "Thank you, my sisters. My wonderful…"

As Agnes's voice trailed off, Mathilde said with tears rolling down her cheeks, "My brave and strong sister. You're the strongest person I've ever known." Mathilde repeated the last sentence in French and added, *"Je t'aime. Je t'aime."* Agnes labored to breathe, and the hint of a smile crossed her face. Mathilde wasn't sure if Agnes was awake, but the vague smile said that Agnes had heard her. Mathilde kissed Agnes on the forehead. Adelaide stood in the doorway with her hand over her mouth and tears welling in her eyes.

"Au revoir, ma sœur. Au revoir," Mathilde said.

The room grew completely silent for a long moment. Adelaide walked quickly out of the bedroom, saying she was going in search of a handkerchief. Mathilde put Agnes's lifeless hands on her waist and dabbed tears from her sister's eyes.

Once Adelaide returned, Mathilde stood and looked at her. They hugged for a moment, sobbing.

Footsteps came across the kitchen. "Is Agnes gone?" asked William's sister Moll, who had come from Digby upon hearing that Agnes was especially weak.

"Yes," Mathilde sobbed. She looked at a clock on the kitchen wall. "Four o'clock in the afternoon, June 6 of 1892. Our little sister Agnes went to heaven."

***

Mercedee emerged from her daydream, startled by a loud train whistle as the coach lurched and slowed. Out the window was the sign for the Little Brook station. It wasn't much, just a platform no more than ten feet long for

56

passengers to step on, and it connected to a small building with an oversized roof that sloped off gently to each side. The village of Little Brook was about a mile northwest of the station and Concession was the same distance southwest.

A conductor came into Mercedee's coach from the rear and walked on through, calling out, "Little Brook Station!"

Mercedee wasted no time. She picked up her bag and walked to the doors at the end of the coach. When the train stopped, she pushed the door open, skipped down the metal stairs, and stepped onto the weathered boardwalk. The station was on the northwest side of the tracks, and Concession was southeast, so she had to wait for the train to move. It pulled out, and Mercedee walked down the three stairs to the dirt and gravel along the tracks. She stepped over the rails and headed down a worn path to a road that connected Church Point behind her to Concession ahead. Forest flanked the road, and several houses were on long, rectangular cleared fields.

Mercedee paused, set her bag down, and looked for a familiar face, but the dusty road was empty. Realizing that no one would have known that she would be on that particular train, she picked up her bag and walked quickly toward Tante Mathilde's modest farm about a quarter mile down the road. As fear and concern for Mamma fueled urgency in her mind and pain in her heart, Mercedee walked quickly and deliberately.

Now what? A thin French-looking man stepped from a yard and set a course that would intersect Mercedee's path. She tried to avoid him, but he walked along beside her and spoke words in French that translated to "Are you coming here to see the lady who passed away?"

Mercedee stopped abruptly and looked into the man's eyes, shocked. Her heart sank. She'd grown up speaking French before she learned English and asked, *"Est-elle morte?"*

The man replied, *"Oui."*

Mercedee teared up and pushed him away. She hurried down the road. He stopped and stood with his hands on his hips and looked after her with sad eyes.

"I'll believe it when I see her!" Mercedee called to no one in particular as she strode away.

He called out his condolences. *"Je suis vraiment désolé."*

Not yet, Mamma. Mercedee sobbed and switched the heavy bag to her other hand. *It can't be true.* She walked on, ignoring her tired feet and arms. She could still see Mamma Agnes's kind eyes from the last time they'd spoken and could hear her frail voice, weak from the ravages of the horrible disease. Mercedee had hugged Mamma for so long and promised to come back to Concession in the spring and take care of her. And yet there she was, racing down the dusty road for perhaps one last hug.

The path from the station led to Mathilde's house on the east side of the road. Mercedee crossed the intersecting road and headed to a gate in a low, tattered fence surrounding a small yard in front of a rectangular house with a gable in the middle that extended over a porch. Two dormer windows were in bedrooms on either side. Behind the house, a barn sat on the edge of a long field carved out of the forest. A mule and a couple of milk cows grazed in the lush grass. Mercedee searched the house and picked up her pace.

Nearing Tante Mathilde's house, Mercedee hoped against hope. She searched desperately for a window, yearning to see Mamma waving to her. But her heart sank as she saw Tante Mathilde and Aunt Moll coming out of the front door and across the porch. Mathilde returned Mercedee's gaze, swiftly descended the steps to the yard, and went to her. Mercedee stopped at the edge of the road as Mathilde got closer. Mathilde and Moll wore black dresses. Mercedee felt the crushing realization that the worst had indeed happened.

As they approached, Mercedee stood, stunned and unable to speak.

Tante Mathilde sighed. "I am so sorry. Agnes is in

heaven."

"My mamma? She is—?" Mercedee stifled a sob as she looked into Tante Mathilde's eyes.

"Yes. She's gone," Tante Mathilde whispered, clearly drenched in sorrow. Mercedee dropped her bag in the dirt, weakly embraced Mathilde, then nearly collapsed onto her, completely spent.

Tears stung Mercedee's eyes, and her heart threatened to fall from her chest. She couldn't believe what she had heard. *Mamma, she thought miserably, I kissed you goodbye just two months ago, and for the first time, you didn't cry, but I did. You stood at the window and waved, and I sent you kisses and pretended that I wasn't crying, but I was. Mamma, you can't be dead!*

Mercedee had always dreamed that Mamma would get better. She had made secret lists of the things they would do. The places they would go. The days they would spend reading and laughing. In the back of her mind, she knew those things were unlikely and tenuous at best. Still, she held hope that there was a chance. But that chance was gone. Really gone.

Mercedee and Tante Mathilde finally separated, and Mercedee turned to Aunt Moll.

"I'm so sorry, dear Mercedee." Aunt Moll gave Mercedee a hug. "Less than a year's time has passed since you and your mother were with us in Digby."

"Yes." Mercedee sobbed as they separated. "That was so much fun. But it can never happen again."

Moll looked at Mercedee and dabbed a tear. "Not in the same way, but I hope you can still spend time with me."

"Yes, yes, of course."

"Let's go inside," Tante Mathilde said.

Aunt Moll picked up Mercedee's bag, and they slowly walked across the yard on a cobble path to the porch. Raising a foot to the first step, Mercedee suddenly stopped. "No!" She buried her face in her hands, and Tante Adelaide looked from a window. "She can't be dead!"

"It'll be all right, Mercedee." Tante Mathilde led her up

the steps and into the house.

"Greetings, Mercedee," said sixteen-year-old Peter, standing next to his father, Uncle Avite, who sat. "I'm so sorry your mother passed away, and I'm sorry I wasn't at the station to meet you and walk you to the house."

"Thank you," Mercedee sobbed to Tante Mathilde's only son. "Thank you, and it's quite all right. You had no way to know which train I would arrive on."

Mercedee stepped toward her uncle. "Hello, Uncle Avite."

Mathilde's husband seemed unsure of what to say but stammered, "My condolences to you, young lady." Avite and Peter watched Mercedee and Mathilde walk slowly toward a door from the kitchen to a small bedroom.

Adelaide turned from the window, and together, the three of them walked into the front bedroom, where Agnes Eleanor Potier Meehan lay wearing her favorite blue dress and white blouse, her hair carefully arranged and her pale, sunken cheeks adorned with a bit of rouge to hide the pallor of death.

"Mercedee," Mathilde began with tears streaming down her cheeks, "your mother left you a blessing and one for your father. And she wanted to have on her blue dress for you so she would look familiar and presentable. She was so ill and suffered but was strong to the very end. Now she's with God."

Mercedee bent over her mother's form on the bed and touched her cold hands. She slowly sank to her knees and buried her face in the folds of the blue dress and the familiar quilt that her mother lay upon. She remained there for the longest time, sobbing miserably. What she had feared for so very long had finally come to pass.

The following days were a blur for Mercedee as friends and family gathered to pay respects. Several relatives crossed Eel Lake from Belleville, including Mercedee's uncle Lezin. The following day, a wagon arrived with a wooden coffin that they carried into the house. They laid Agnes in it, still wearing her blue dress and wrapped in her favorite quilt.

Early that morning, Mercedee had set out and found white lilies. She picked a large bunch and returned to the house. She wove the stems together and made a mat in the shape of a cross just the right size to fit on top of her mother's coffin and placed the flowers there.

Several men carried Agnes and her coffin to the carriage that was slowly guided by a man from Church Point who was wearing a black jacket and top hat. Uncle Avite, Tante Mathilde, Peter, Mercedee, and Tante Adelaide followed the wagon west on the road. Along the way, other friends joined them, creating a sizable procession to the train station, where many people gave their condolences and hugs then turned back. The family continued on, walking several miles to the St. Marie Church at Church Point.

The walk was long but gave Mercedee time to think. She missed her father, but William was unable to make the trip from Boston. Peter walked alongside her as they followed the funeral wagon. They were a distance ahead of the family when Peter spoke.

"I'm sorry your father couldn't make the boat yesterday. It would've been wonderful to have his company."

"I really miss him, and I know he's grieving. He would be here if he could. Thank you for your kind words. I hope to see him soon." Mercedee wiped a tear from her eye. "Can we go to the cove and row one day? Peter, you're the best cousin ever."

Peter smiled as if embarrassed. "Yes, we'll go every chance we get!"

***

Tante Mathilde noticed Mercedee and Peter walking some distance ahead and said softly, "Our little sister is gone."

"Yes." Tante Adelaide pushed a shock of gray hair from her face and paused to rest. "William didn't do right by Agnes. He should've been here."

Tante Mathilde turned to Tante Adelaide and tightened

her lips, accentuating the wrinkles in her weathered face. "He did what he could. How could he have supported her and Mercedee if he had traveled with her to Georgia? Agnes had to move to more favorable climates, you know."

"But you must know how I feel about speculators," said Tante Adelaide, always the curmudgeon.

"Yes, I do." Tante Mathilde started walking toward the church. "But how you feel doesn't change the facts or their situation."

"Speculators risk their family's security with every deal," Tante Adelaide continued. "If William had lost everything, then where would young Agnes have been?"

Tante Mathilde looked into Adelaide's face, but Adelaide turned away. "William did what he could, and he gave Agnes everything he had. And now he'll give Mercedee everything he can. I can't judge him because I don't know how hard his line of work is or how difficult it would be to change at this stage of his life."

"But Agnes was—"

"I know. She was our little sister, and that's why you hold William to a higher standard. But please don't take it out on Mercedee. She didn't choose this situation. Others chose it *for* her. In any case, would you please wait until after the funeral to start on William?" Mathilde turned, and they continued in silence behind the distant figures of Mercedee and Peter, who were much farther down the dirt road.

Peter and Mercedee reached the hamlet of Little Brook and waited for Mathilde, Avite, and Adelaide.

On arriving at Church Point, Mercedee stopped and looked across the grass at the cemetery, where fresh soil formed a mound beside a hastily dug grave. The wagon was near the grave, and two men set the coffin on a tarpaulin next to the grave.

After the family members regrouped at the cemetery, a priest joined them for a service to lay Agnes to rest. It was a peaceful day at St. Marie's Church Cemetery on the north coast of Nova Scotia overlooking the Bay of Fundy. Gulls hovered over the nearby shoreline, hanging on the westerly wind and looking for a snack. Sun filtered through maple trees that shaded the cemetery. After the service, two workers shoveled soil onto the flower cross and casket, slowly filling the grave. It was quiet aside from sniffs and sighs and the clinks of shovels sliding into dirt and dull thuds of soil and rocks landing in the dark grave.

After several minutes, Mercedee walked to the road and on across to a path that led to the shore. The cool wind brushed her face as she headed through the low brush. The walk was refreshing, and the sun pierced her sorrow. *If only Mamma could have shared this moment, she would have loved it.* Mercedee reached a grassy clearing with a plethora of flowers. The lupines offered pinkish-purple towers of tiny flowers standing above thick green leaves. Other areas were covered with white daisies, their petals contrasting with the green below and their yellow centers looking up at the sky. Mercedee left the path and meandered through the meadow, picking flowers and several tall grass sprigs. She assembled them into a small bouquet and headed back to the path before turning left to the cemetery.

Ahead, Mercedee saw Tante Mathilde, Tante Adelaide, and Peter coming up the path, obviously having followed her when she left the funeral. Mathilde carried a basket with the food they had packed earlier that morning. Peter walked behind them with his hands behind his back.

"Tante Mathilde, I'm going to the cemetery to place these flowers on Mamma's grave and fix it nice for her. I'll come back as soon as I've finished." Mercedee looked away quickly to hide the tears flooding her eyes.

Mathilde and Adelaide nodded as they passed her on the path, then they looked down to where the trail dropped off the bluff to the rocky, sandy shoreline.

Mercedee walked quickly to the road then to the cemetery as workers smoothed the soil mounded over her mother's grave. They pounded a simple wooden cross into the sod. Like many of the simpler monuments there, the three-foot-tall white cross had the name painted on the horizontal piece in black paint that resembled calligraphy: Agnes Eleanor Potier Meehan.

One worker stopped and looked up at Mercedee, rubbing his hand through his slicked-back hair. "I'm sorry for your loss. I wish you the best."

"Thank you so much." Mercedee sniffed, looking at him through tear-swollen eyes.

Both workers walked toward St. Marie Church, an enormous structure with twin steeples that towered over the cemetery and scattered buildings.

Mercedee bunched the stems of her bouquet and dug a small hole in front of the grave marker. She made the hole deep enough to reach moist soil to help keep the flowers from wilting right away. She placed the flowers in the hole and packed soil around them. "Mamma, here are some flowers that I know you'll like. I wish I had a vase to put them in with water so they'll last longer, but I don't."

Mercedee got up and dusted off her skirt. She stood there, completely alone in the cemetery except for the spirit of her mother. She looked at the mound of soil and the cross. "Goodbye, Mamma." She adjusted the grave marker so it was straight. "Goodbye."

Mercedee walked to the road one last time and crossed to the path to the shore. Her stomach reminded her of how long it had been since she had last eaten and the toll that walking all the way from Concession had taken on her. She moved quickly along the path, climbing slightly toward the low bluff, back into the coastal wind, and toward Tante Mathilde, Tante Adelaide, and Peter.

Tante Adelaide looked down the path and saw Mercedee coming. "Mathilde, what are you going to do with her? With Mercedee. Will she end up living with you and Avite?"

"I don't know about that. William will find a way to get her enough money to go to school. If only her papa could have come to the funeral." Mathilde sighed. "You know he's her only family."

"I think that is dreadful. Surely, William could have gotten the money from somewhere if he truly cared about Agnes and Mercedee. For him not to come when his dear wife was dying and then when she was laid to rest... mark my words. William will rue the day he decided to stay away!" Adelaide swept a stray lock of curly gray hair from her forehead and looked at Mathilde then at the waters of the Bay of Fundy.

"Now, please don't judge William too harshly," Mathilde said. "Moll said he couldn't catch the last boat because the notice wasn't delivered until it was too late. Steamships take at least two days from Boston to Yarmouth. And you know his business has been very bad in these hard times. He has to sell some land or woodland or something."

"I don't know how you can excuse him. His place is here with his daughter and poor dear wife. You've had to shoulder all his responsibilities. You've had to comfort his daughter and provide for her, not to mention the cost of the funeral. You and John can't afford to pay for all these expenses. I think you've done more than he could have expected. The casket was quite dear. Now, I suppose he'll want you to buy a headstone too. He won't appreciate all the time you spent caring for Agnes all these months," Adelaide said.

"Please stop this! You mustn't carry on so. Agnes is our sister. I wouldn't let her die alone. Where's your Christian charity? Besides, we received a postal from Monique yesterday. She says she's sending some money to help with the expenses. And Moll will too."

"Did Monique send any money?" Adelaide asked curtly. She was always skeptical of Monique, who ran a small dress shop in Orange, New Jersey. "If you ask me, William will send Mercedee to live with Monique like he did Ferdinand. One would think that William would have his children stay with him at least part of the time instead of being the seldom-seen father raising his children by postal."

"Now, Adelaide, Monique hasn't sent money yet, but

she did say she would next week. And how's a man of his age living in the middle of Boston supposed to take care of a teenage daughter all by himself?" Mathilde looked past Adelaide at a figure coming from the cemetery. "Hush now. Here comes Mercedee. She's coming up from her dear mother's grave. I hope she'll start to smile again soon."

"Tante Mathilde," Mercedee said as she approached, offering flowers in extended hands. "Look at the flowers I found in a meadow when I was coming over from the cemetery. My papa wrote that these are asters." Mercedee separated several round purple flowers from her small bouquet, much like the ones she'd left on Mamma's grave. "Papa said he used to pick them for Mamma from wet fields near Digby. I'm going to press some of these and send them to him." Mercedee sniffed and looked at the small flowers in her hand. "I also put some on Mamma's grave."

"Those are quite pretty, my dear Mercedee," Mathilde said.

"May we have our lunch now? I'm quite starved," Mercedee said. "We could walk over to the shore and watch the gulls while we eat." She didn't wait for an answer but walked to a wagon trail leading to a high point on the bluff. On the point, several large rocks appeared to be makeshift chairs. She sat, still fixated on her flowers.

Adelaide and Mathilde had watched Mercedee stroll away then stood and followed her. After a few steps on the path, Adelaide spoke. "You will certainly have your hands full with that girl. What will happen to her now?"

"I don't know, really. Mercedee could stay with us for a while, but we can't afford to keep her forever, and Lord knows William can't afford the tuition to keep her at the convent school. He still owes for last term." Mathilde stepped onto the road ahead of Adelaide and walked across to the path. The wind picked up out in the open and blew their dresses.

"Agnes was so concerned about having to bring Mercedee here and spend time with her before she died."

Mathilde paused. "That would have been terrible, what with her raising blood so often and coughing so terribly." Mathilde's voice turned soft as she spoke more to herself than Adelaide. "Oh, she suffered and didn't want Mercedee to see her that way."

"You just have too kind of a heart, sister," Adelaide said. "William must accept his responsibilities. Look at that dress Mercedee has on now. It is two inches too short. If she keeps growing like that, and she will, she'll end up close to six feet tall. Who would want to hire such a gangly, awkward girl?"

"She's a sweet girl. You mustn't be so harsh. And you should notice that she's rather agile for a tall young girl," Mathilde said. "Mercedee's a big help with the cleaning when she puts her mind to it. She's not much help with cooking, but she's lived in hotels most of her life. You can't fault her for that."

"Well, I think you should pack her bags up and send her to William. He would finally have to take care of her then."

"Yes, yes, but I can't do that. He doesn't know what she needs. I'll see if I can help her repair her dresses, perhaps add a ruffle or two. Monique said she's sending a cape we can dye and lengthen. It won't be too much work." Mathilde sighed, wringing her hands. "Mercedee will have to give up on school for this term and stay here." She stopped and faced Adelaide. "You know, she's fourteen years old now. She can help me with the house and maybe do some cleaning for the ladies in Concession, perhaps even here at the school at Church Point. She can make some money and help with her keep."

"That would certainly help," Adelaide said.

"Don't forget that she's your sister's daughter, and she took care of her mother starting when she could walk. Now hush, here she comes," Mathilde whispered.

The two stopped where the grass turned to dirt, the landscape dropped a few feet to a gravel berm, and sand formed the thin, smooth beach along the tidal flat of St.

Mary's Bay.

A chilly breeze drifted off St. Mary's Bay, and small waves broke on shallow water some fifty yards out. A long, narrow peninsula that began to the northeast and paralleled the coast for some distance protected the bay from storms on the Bay of Fundy to the north. In the distance, beyond a small island, a fishing boat moved slowly on the water. Even in mid-June, the breeze from the Bay of Fundy was cool and moist.

"Tante Mathilde," Mercedee called as she walked up from the beach. "Look, I've found some more lovely flowers. I'll show them to Peter." She held up a small bunch of yellow and purple flowers and gestured toward Peter, who was walking alone on the sand just below them.

"You should get your lunch now, dear. You may also be interested that I have a postal for you from Tante Monique in New York." Mathilde held out a small envelope.

Mercedee eagerly took the envelope. Instead of walking toward Peter, she headed off to the edge of the grass and opened it, facing the bay with wind blowing her hair and ruffling her dress. She carefully opened the flap and turned away from the wind so she could unfold the letter.

Mathilde and Seraphie spread out a wool blanket and set the picnic basket down. As Mercedee stood some distance off reading the letter, Adelaide wrinkled her nose and snorted. "A postal from Monique? Now there's another wicked woman. What's she hatching?"

"She wants Mercedee to write to her. I'm sure she thinks Mercedee will inherit Agnes's share of the woodlot and would love to get her hands on it. According to our father's will, Agnes got a nice sum of money and part of the timber. Monique can always smell money. Well, I won't let that happen if at all possible." Mathilde's voice was stern.

Mercedee finished reading and walked toward Mathilde and Adelaide. Reaching them, she took a deep breath and smiled. "I'm so happy I'm here with you, Tante Mathilde. The air in Concession is so pure and clean compared with

Boston with all of the smoke and dirt. I love Nova Scotia."
She looked across the bay. "I would like to stay here with
you forever. Tante Monique wants me to go and stay with
her in Orange, New Jersey, but I don't want to go. May I
stay with you?"

"Yes, of course you can, child. You can stay as long as
you would like. But you need to think about continuing your
education if your father can help with the finances."

Mercedee and Mathilde chatted as they ate, and Adelaide
interjected critical statements, prodding Mercedee to find a
way to stay with William in Boston. When they finished their
meal, they packed the basket and walked through the bustle
of the festival at the university then to the old church.

As they passed the cemetery, Mercedee paused, looking
across the field of headstones and at the small mound of
fresh soil over Mamma's grave. Tears welled in her eyes.

Mathilde said, "I miss her, too, my dear, but Uncle Avite
will be expecting us home soon. Let's move along."

"Yes. Yes." Mercedee said under her breath, "I miss you,
Mamma."

As Mercedee started walking, Mathilde was at her side
and said, "We also need to pick up your trunk. Sister Mary
Anne at Eel Brook sent a postal that she shipped it, and by
my estimation, it should be at the Little Brook Station. I
heard the train whistle some time ago, and I'll bet they
dropped it off at the station house." Mathilde took
Mercedee's hand, and they walked along the windswept
road back to the junction at Little Brook then turned left
down the road to the station and Concession.

As Mathilde had presumed, the trunk was in the small
station house.

"I'll help you with that," Peter said. He was a quiet
teenage boy a couple of years older than Mercedee.

Mathilde held the station-house door open, and
Mercedee and Peter picked the trunk up by the handles on
each end. It wasn't a big trunk and not terribly heavy. Peter
led the way out of the station house and down the three

steps from the platform to the dusty road. They headed once again toward Mathilde's farmhouse. Although the trunk wasn't that heavy, it did fatigue Mercedee and Peter's arms, so they walked briskly and took a couple of rest breaks.

It wasn't lost on Mercedee that the box contained nearly her entire life. That wasn't anything new, but it was different since Mamma was gone. Mercedee didn't even know if Papa was living in an apartment or house in Boston. She always sent letters to his office in the Boston Globe Building, which was on Newspaper Row in downtown Boston. She had never actually seen his office or where he lived.

On reaching Mathilda's house, Peter led her and the trunk upstairs to the room she had shared with her mother the summer before. They set the trunk down in front of a small chest of drawers. Peter smiled and said he was going to do the chores. "Thank you, Peter," Mercedee called after him. "I'll come help when I have unpacked." She liked spending time with her cousin.

The small bedroom had a slanted ceiling from the sloping roof, and a narrow dormer window cut through it. The small bed had a tubular metal headboard and footboard. A chair and small desk sat by the window. Everything in the room showed years of wear.

Mercedee sat on the bed, still feeling her mother dying in the room downstairs, and ached with the loss and emptiness. She finally rose and made her way downstairs, where Tante Mathilde and Tante Adelaide were fixing a shepherd's pie in a large cast iron pot. Uncle Avite sat on a rocking chair in the common area, looking out the front window, and Peter sat in an upholstered chair while reading a book.

"May I be of assistance?" Mercedee asked Mathilde, who was chopping carrots.

"Yes." Mathilde looked up. "Please fetch some wood from the stack on the back porch so that we can heat up the stove."

"Of course." Mercedee made her way through the small, crowded kitchen to the back door. She picked up several pieces of wood from the stack under an eve and carried them inside. The shepherd's pie smelled delicious as it cooked in the oven.

After supper, Mercedee picked up the last letter her mother had written her and slowly climbed the creaky stairs. She went to the room she had shared with her mother. Once inside, she sat on the bed. The dim twilight came in through the window and created twig patterns on the wall.

Mamma had suffered but had loved her to the last. Mercedee could still hear Mamma's soft but raspy voice struggling to speak from the years of infected cough, telling Mercedee that they would all be together someday. Suddenly, Mercedee felt terribly alone. Utterly alone.

She pulled out the desk chair and sat in front of the window. She leaned her elbows on the desk and looked out at the sky, trees, and field behind the house. It was evening, but in June, Nova Scotia daylight didn't fade quickly. Her window faced east, and the sky was progressively turning dark blue. Mercedee remembered the years of moving back and forth—summers in Melrose Highlands, hotels in Boston, and winters in hotels in Georgia or North Carolina. When Mamma was well enough to keep a home, they might stay in Melrose Highlands all year, but Mamma's good health never lasted.

Mercedee looked at her trunk. It had been her home to an extent, and she had been packing and unpacking it all the time. One of the bright spots was summertime in Melrose with Charlotte "Lottie" Kilgore. Lottie had once been her neighbor, and they'd had fun playing with their dolls. The dolls had names, and Lottie and Mercedee were their aunts. The two girls were the best of friends, and they wrote letters when Mercedee moved away. The last time was when Mamma had gotten quite weak, and they went to Papa's sister, Mary Ann "Moll" Fowler, in Digby, a port town on the Annapolis Basin.

Mercedee rested her chin on her palms. She gazed out the windowpane through uneven, rippled glass and watched the twinkling lights of stars growing brighter in the darkening sky. She thought of her father in Boston, alone in his room. *I wonder why Papa didn't come to the funeral service. He said he couldn't catch the boat, but he could've come later. I would have loved to have seen him. If he were here, I would feel so much better. We could talk about Mother and our loving family. I wonder if he cares about me. Ferdinand didn't come either. Of course, he's just my half-brother and not really Mamma's child, but she was so good to him, and his mamma was already gone for such a long time. Well, I don't care! I loved her, and she left a blessing for me.*

The room grew dark, and Mercedee changed into her nightgown. She turned the blankets back and crawled under then curled up and clutched her pillow. Tears spilled out from under her dark eyelashes as she whispered, "I'll never forget my dear, kind mamma. I never will!"

Finally, she drifted off to sleep.

3 A NEW OPPORTUNITY

The days following Mamma Agnes's funeral, Mercedee felt more at ease but haunted by her uncertain future. She shared breakfast and helped with the dishes. She sat on an upholstered chair in the living room and repaired her only spare dress with a needle and thread. She rarely got new clothes and always tried to make them last as long as possible while not appearing tattered or too small, which was a constant problem for a growing girl like Mercedee.

"That's nice stitching on the hem." Mathilde looked over Mercedee's shoulder at the length of fabric her niece had added around the bottom of her spare dress. "You could make a fine seamstress someday if need be."

"Thank you, Tante," Mercedee said. "I don't know if I'd like to do this all day, every day, though." Mercedee tied the thread and trimmed it with her teeth. She pulled the metal thimble from her finger and put it and her needle into a small box of sewing supplies, then she snapped it shut and relaxed into the chair.

"That does get tedious. But at the least, you would get paid for it instead of just trying to keep your clothes presentable." Mathilde smiled and put her hand on Mercedee's shoulder.

"Ah yes, but Tante, the world is too big and interesting to sit inside and stitch day after day." Mercedee looked out the window, holding the dress over her arm. "Don't you feel that way sometimes? If I can get more education, perhaps there are other opportunities out there."

Adelaide spoke up from across the room. "Seeing the world would certainly be nice. But you must do something to earn your keep in the here and now." Her taunt was met with a scowl from Mercedee. She wasn't paying rent, and there was nothing she could do without support from her father, so she helped Mathilde around the house as much as possible and left the arrangement up to her aunt's discretion. Mercedee certainly didn't appreciate Adelaide's snide remarks.

"Certainly, Tante Adelaide, but there must be something other than—"

Mathilde interrupted. "Oh, Mercedee, you have your whole life to travel about, but here's something germane to your immediate future. I just received a postal for you from your father."

"Oh, good!" Mercedee jumped from the chair. She reached for the small envelope Mathilde was offering. Mercedee pried the flap up with her finger and slid a letter out. She slowly sank back into her chair at the dining table, spread the paper with her hand, and read in silence, hovering over the letter.

As if running out of patience, Mathilde broke the silence. "Is there news? Can you tell me why he's writing?"

"Yes, Tante." Mercedee's eyes continued to dart back and forth following lines of the letter on the table. "Papa says that he collected a note from one of the men who owes him money, and he sold a piece of land." She glanced up at Mathilde. "He's made arrangements with my Tante Marie Anne—Sister Rosalia—at the Mount St. Vincent Academy in Halifax, and I can attend for the 1892–'93 school year. Oh my." Mercedee continued to read.

Mathilde leaned over Mercedee's shoulder. "And he

enclosed money for the train and to ship your trunk?"

"Yes." Mercedee held the currency in her hand as she reread the note.

Adelaide strolled over. "Well, it looks like William has finally—"

"Mercedee." Mathilde spoke up, cutting off Adelaide and squeezing Mercedee's shoulder. "Let's finish the dresses. The term at Mount St. Vincent will begin before we know it."

Mercedee lowered the letter and looked ahead as Mathilde continued, "This will be a great new start. Mount St. Vincent is run by the Sisters of Charity, and Tante Sister Rosalia is there. They'll take good care of you."

"Oh my." Mercedee pulled a separate piece of paper from behind the letter and scanned it.

"What is it?" Mathilde moved closer.

"It's a document from the academy. A list of the items I'll need during the year." Mercedee paused. "This is all a bit overwhelming."

"Well, pray tell what the list includes, dear," Mathilde said.

"The list says that I'll need four changes of linen, four woolen garments, and three black dresses. I'll also need a dressing gown, dressing case, six towels, and two bath towels." Mercedee looked closely at the paper.

"They certainly expect a lot," Mathilde said, clearly aware that the meager living that she and Uncle Avite were able to scratch out with their farm wouldn't afford nearly the extra funds required to purchase all these things.

"And I'll need table service of six serviettes. Two knives, two forks, a spoon for dessert, soup, and tea. And one work box." Mercedee dropped her arms to her sides and looked at Mathilde. Tears filled her eyes. "There's no way I can come up with all of these things. I have no money, and Papa didn't include that much extra."

Mathilde embraced Mercedee. "It'll be all right. It's only July. We can work on it. You're a good worker. You can sew. It's not impossible."

In her chair by a window, Adelaide scoffed and picked up a book of Longfellow poems from the end table.

"Oh, thank you so much, Tante." Mercedee hugged her aunt. "I'll do everything I can. For my mamma. Even though I feel so alone, I still have her memory and you, Tante Mathilde." She pulled away, folded the papers and bills, and slid them back into the envelope. "This will be fine. It will be better than Eel Brook."

Mercedee clutched the letter and envelope to her chest as she walked to the stairs. She turned back to the room. "Now if you'll excuse me, I need to write my papa a most grateful thank-you letter." She started up the stairs with a bounce in her step.

"And Mercedee," Mathilde called across the room, causing Mercedee to pause, "when you're finished with the letter, we should look at the cost of the school and see how much surplus your father sent. If there's enough, we'll plan a trip to Yarmouth to pick up material for dresses."

"There are a lot of chores this time of year. Don't forget that," Adelaide said, freezing Mercedee as she lifted a foot on the first step of the stairs.

"Yes, we'll remember," Mathilde replied, walking to the kitchen.

Mercedee shot a glance at Adelaide. "Have I not done plenty of chores?" She continued up the stairs.

"You know that young people who get handouts don't find their own way." Adelaide looked back at her book.

Mercedee frowned and ignored Adelaide. She walked on up the creaking wooden treads of the stairs and turned down the short hall to her borrowed bedroom.

"That is quite enough my sister. Quite enough!" Mathilde snapped. She picked up a glass of water and walked to the front door. She continued to the porch and sat down on a wooden rocking chair with a cushion hanging over the dowels of the backrest.

**

After breakfast, Mercedee helped Adelaide with the dishes then walked into the living room and looked out the window. Mathilde was talking to another woman on the edge of the road near the front yard gate. Noticeably younger than Mathilde, the woman wore a nice dress and had dark curly hair. Curious, Mercedee exited through the front door and crossed the yard.

Turning, Mathilde said, "Here she is. This is my niece, Mercedee."

"Greetings, Mercedee," the woman said.

"Mercedee, this is Mrs. Doucette. She lives in the house just down the road there." Mathilde pointed at a house similar to hers on the other side of the road and a short distance away.

"It's a pleasure to meet you, Mrs. Doucette." Mercedee smiled.

"And you, Mercedee," Mrs. Doucette said. "Your aunt was just telling me that you may be attending Mount St. Vincent Academy this fall."

"Why, yes," Mercedee said. "I hope to."

"Well," Mrs. Doucette said, "Mathilde says you're in need of some supplies for living on your own at the academy."

Mercedee looked quizzically at Mathilde then at Mrs. Doucette. "I do indeed need a few things."

"Before you say anything, and I say this because you may be like your Tante Mathilde and not ever want help"—Mrs. Doucette smiled at Mathilde—"we have a few extra things that may help you out. Just some extra forks and spoons and serviettes. They're doing us no good sitting in a box and not being used."

Mercedee saw something move and looked past Mrs. Doucette. A young girl emerged from the bushes in front of Mrs. Doucette's house and walked quickly toward them on the road. She carried a cloth bag over her shoulder.

"I don't know what to say except many, many times thank you," Mercedee said as Mathilde beamed.

"As I said"—Mrs. Doucette touched Mercedee's arm—"we're friends, and we knew your mother, dear young Agnes."

"Oh yes." Mercedee sighed as the girl approached.

Looking up at Mercedee, the girl took the bag from her shoulder and offered it to her.

"Please excuse little Elizabeth," Mrs. Doucette said. "She's shy around new people."

"Thank you, Elizabeth. *Merci*," Mercedee said kindly.

The girl shyly looked away. "You're welcome."

Mercedee bent down. "Your name is Elizabeth?"

The girl nodded.

"How old are you?"

Elizabeth turned side to side as if nervous and said, "Six."

Mercedee smiled, and Elizabeth finally smiled back, showing that she was missing a front tooth. "Would you like to come over and play tomorrow?" Realizing that she hadn't asked for permission, Mercedee glanced at Mrs. Doucette, who nodded her approval.

"Oui," Elizabeth said.

"Very good, then." Mercedee gave the small girl a hug.

After some more conversation, Mrs. Doucette and Elizabeth walked home, and Mathilde and Mercedee made their way into their house. Mercedee's stomach flipped and flopped. Only a few days before, she hadn't been at all sure about her future, and now she was going to a prestigious academy near the big city of Halifax, and a stranger was giving her items to help her cobble together what she needed to get in. It was almost too much. She took a deep breath and led Mathilde through the front door. She crossed to the kitchen table and took the items from the bag.

"That's very nice," Mathilde said, moving alongside Mercedee.

"Yes, indeed. This will take care of my table service and serviettes." She arranged the silverware on the table. "I'm so grateful. And thank you for asking her, Tante Mathilde."

Her aunt crossed her arms. "I didn't press Mrs. Doucette, to be honest. I told her you were going to the Mount, and she asked if you needed anything. She knew of the funeral and that your father is struggling. This is a small but sharing community, you know."

"Well, thank you anyhow." Mercedee returned the items to the bag. She carefully took them up to her room and put them in her trunk.

***

Later that afternoon, Mathilde rocked in a chair on the porch, squinting through the late-afternoon sun at a horse-drawn buggy coming slowly up the road from the southeast. As it approached, she recognized her husband and son. She watched as the single black horse plodded along, pulling the open-topped buggy to the edge of the yard framed by a weathered wooden picket fence. At the edge of the yard, a wagon path led around the house to the rear porch and then to a carriage house in a clearing carved out of the forest. Beside the carriage house was a dairy barn with stables for several horses. Adjacent to that was a small pasture with two horses grazing the thick grass that had enjoyed the wet climate, the June showers, and the warmth and sun of the first week of July.

As the buggy reached the wagon trail, Peter pulled on the reins and stopped the horse. Avite, a fit man of sixty-four, climbed down, pushed open a small gate in the low picket fence, and walked across the yard on a cobblestone path.

Avite watched as Peter urged the horse to pull the buggy around to the carriage house. He stepped onto the porch, settled onto a rocking chair next to Mathilde, and took a pipe from the pocket on the inside of his dark suit jacket. He swatted the pipe against his hand, dislodged the ashes, and shook them off the side of the porch.

"How is Mercedee doing? Still mourning Agnes, is she?" Avite scooped tobacco from a small bag into the bowl of his wooden pipe with its white ceramic mouthpiece.

"Still mourning, she is. My sister was all young Mercedee had." Mathilde rubbed her eyes and continued, "I've got some good news, though." She squinted at the sun shining below the porch eave and sparkling through the large maple trees on the far side of the road. "And some bad news."

"Oh my. Seems things always turn out that way." With this thumb, Avite packed the loose tobacco in the bowl of his pipe. "I'm always one for hearing the good news first, you know." He pulled his narrow-brimmed hat down, shading his eyes, and looked over at Mathilde.

She rocked back and raised her eyes above the shade of the porch eave. She opened her eyes wider, a burst of wrinkles radiating out from the corners of her eyes. "Well, she got a postal from her father. It seems that he sold a piece of land and has enough money to enroll Mercedee at the Mount St. Vincent Academy in Halifax for the coming school year."

Avite lit his pipe, blew smoke out of the end of the porch away from Mathilde, and looked her way. "Why, that's a fine development for Mercedee, it is. And your sister Rosalia will be close by to help at the academy."

"That's true," Mathilde said.

Avite paused and took another drag on his pipe. "I suppose there's a catch. Is William asking us to help pay for it or something along those lines? You did say there was an item of bad news."

"Well, not exactly that," Mathilde clarified. "But he sent a brochure from the academy, and they request that enrollees bring a number of items with them." Mathilde picked up the brochure from her lap and moved her finger down the page. "Here it is. Four black dresses, a white Easter dress, towels, a place setting of silverware, among other things."

"Oh my. I wouldn't think the poor girl has half of that in her worldly possessions. Am I right?" Avite held his pipe aloft and rested his elbow on the arm of the rocking chair.

"You would be right, Avite," Mathilde said. "The girl has

grown so fast that she has a hard time keeping dresses that fit." Mathilde wrung her hands in her lap and gave up trying to keep her eyes shielded as the sun dropped. She looked sideways toward Avite, who sat in the shade of a small maple tree growing off the corner of the porch. "I don't think she has more than two dresses and no other money that I know of."

"Did William send any money for travel or expenses?" Avite pulled the pipe from his lips.

"I'm not certain. He sent money, but I'm not sure if this is enough to cover the cost of the academy as well as the items they want her to bring. Certainly not all of it."

"I don't know how much we can help. Spent so much on seed this spring, and the market doesn't look great for crops. People just aren't moving to Nova Scotia like they had been." He chewed on the stem of his pipe for a moment and continued, "I'll have a look."

"Thank you," Mathilde said. "I have some scraps of fabric and some old dresses. We'll see what we can do. And perhaps Seraphie can help. Her dress shop in New York City is doing quite well."

"At the very least, Mercedee has some time to put things together." Avite put the stem of his pipe back in his mouth and looked across the road.

Peter sat in the buggy seat, guiding the horse to a large barn behind the house. As the horse reached an open barn door, Peter pulled the horse to a stop and hopped out to release the harness and bridle. He heard the back door of the house open behind him and glanced over his shoulder to see Mercedee bounding off the stone stoop and hurrying toward him.

"Hello, Mercedee." Peter looked down at his busywork. "It looks like you received some news from your father. Anything important?" Peter worked a buckle loose on one of the straps, and the horse shifted its weight.

Mercedee reached the horse's head and petted its long neck. "Why, yes. I received a letter from Papa, and he said that he finally sold a piece of land and has enough—apparently just enough—money to pay for my tuition at Mount St. Vincent Academy in Halifax."

Peter walked around Mercedee to take the bridle off the horse. "That sounds like some quite good news. Congratulations."

"Thank you." Mercedee sighed. "It is indeed great news. I wasn't sure what I was going to do."

"I've never been to Halifax." Peter patted the horse into the long, rectangular pasture surrounded by thick woodland. He and Mercedee carried the bridle to the barn.

Mercedee grimaced. "I've never been there either. I wonder what it's like." The barn smell—a combination of hay, livestock, leather, and wood—filled her nose.

"I don't have any idea. Maybe it's like Yarmouth but more boats, eh?" Peter chuckled.

"I hope you're right. I've heard Halifax is a bustling city. Sounds kind of scary."

"It couldn't be that bad, at least at the academy," Peter said. "We get letters from Sister Rosalia, and she seems very much at ease." He hung the bridle on a hook and turned toward the door.

"I am glad she will be there. She's my real family and so nice," Mercedee said as they headed toward the house. "Are you going to stay here and take over the farm?" Then she retreated. "If you don't mind me prying."

"Oh, that's fine, but I don't know if I want to try to make the farm work, really. The soil's not good enough to grow anything that you can sell. They grow a lot up in the Annapolis Valley, but it's colder here, and the best thing you can grow is pasture grass for grazing." He paused. "We feed ourselves with potatoes and carrots, things like that. And we have chickens behind the barn. We sell eggs locally and sometimes in Yarmouth."

"Yes," Mercedee said. "The farm doesn't sound lucrative."

Peter pointed at two cows in the pasture. "Those cows

provide milk too. Just for us. It seems the fishermen in Tusket are doing all right."

"But fishing is so dangerous, isn't it? Mr. Frost, who's a handyman at St. Anne's, said he was glad to get onto dry land before he was lost at sea."

"It sure can be dangerous. Some of the fishermen don't come back, but on the other hand, some men fish on the sea for many years." Peter sounded positive.

"My father owns a plot of land that has a lot of timber. That seems to be important."

"Oh yes, timber, especially hardwood, is valuable. Years ago, Avite cut the timber for this field. He and Mother made money on that, and we've been living on it. But the money's running out, and they're considering cutting some more, although there are only a few acres left."

Mercedee looked at the trees along the edge of the field. "It sounds like owning woodland is good, but you only get to cut the timber once."

"That's true. Working cutting timber and working at a saw mill is an opportunity. There are a lot of jobs right now. And there's a big cotton mill in Yarmouth." He paused and kicked a pebble across the barnyard as he walked. "I don't know. I think I'd rather get more schooling and be a reporter or something like that."

"Yes, that sounds more interesting," Mercedee said. "I hope I can find an adventure somewhere. I don't want to stay in one spot forever." She paused. "Not unlike fishing. An adventure every day."

"I can't argue with you there." Peter stopped near the back door. "Why are you nervous about Halifax? Haven't you been to bigger cities like Boston and such?"

Mercedee thought for a moment. "You're right. I suppose that big fancy academy is what makes me nervous. I've never been to a place like that."

"I can't imagine going to such a place. But you've been to many new places, and you did fine at St. Anne's, correct?" Peter held the door handle.

Mercedee said, "I believe I'm going to think about St. Anne's as an experience that I can use to prepare for the Mount."

The door opened, startling Peter, who jerked his hand off the handle.

It was Tante Adelaide. "Are you two going to help with supper or stay out there all night?"

"Sorry, Tante Adelaide," Mercedee said. "We were just coming in."

**

The next morning, the sun was especially bright through the kitchen window as Mercedee helped Tante Mathilde prepare breakfast. "Would you like some salt on those eggs?" Mercedee asked as Tante Adelaide sat down.

Tante Adelaide swallowed a bite of toast. "No, thank you. And thank you for helping with the cooking."

"It's no problem at all," Mercedee said, but her attention was on her other aunt, who was also sitting at the table. "Tante Mathilde, are you finding out anything about the money? I've begun a letter to Papa, but I don't know how to ask for more bills to help with the academy." Mercedee picked up Tante Mathilde's plate.

Tante Mathilde rustled a sheet of paper. "It says here that you'll need twenty-five dollars per term for board and instruction plus fees for bedding, laundry, books. Let's see. You'll need thirty dollars fifty cents for the year."

Mercedee looked in the envelope from her father. "Ten, twenty… there's a total of thirty-four." She looked at Mathilde. "Is three fifty enough to pay for all the extras?"

"We shall see what we can do. I have an old black dress that I don't wear anymore and some fabric stowed away." Mathilde walked into her small sewing room, and Mercedee could hear her rummaging through a trunk and sliding drawers.

Presently, Mathilde returned to the living room with a bundle under her arm. She sat in the chair facing Mercedee.

"It appears you've found a lot of fabric, Tante."

Mercedee looked on eagerly.

"Yes." Tante Mathilde took out a folded piece of dark fabric. "This is small, but we may be able to work it in." She handed it to Mercedee.

"This is an old skirt that we'll be able to take some pieces from, although it's quite worn." Tante Mathilde held up the long dark-green skirt by its waistband. She handed it to Mercedee, who folded it and put it on her lap.

Mercedee's eyes widened as Tante Mathilde held up another skirt, that one much smaller. "Do you remember this?" Tante Mathilde asked.

"Oh my." Mercedee choked back tears. "That's the skirt that Tante Seraphie gave me for my seventh birthday."

"Yes, dear," Mathilde said. "You wore it when you and—"

"Mamma visited you in the summer. Mamma was feeling surprisingly well. We had so much fun in Yarmouth and visiting Tante Moll in Digby." Mercedee glanced down as Tante Mathilde folded the skirt and looked on with sympathetic eyes.

"Hold those fond memories, dear," Tante Mathilde said softly.

Mercedee wiped her eyes. "May I see that skirt again, please?"

Tante Mathilde nodded and held the dress up.

"I have an idea," Mercedee said. "That dress is so small for me, and it's worn around the bottom. But with a trim and hem on the bottom, and taking it in around the midsection and waist, it would fit Elizabeth. Perhaps that would be a nice project. I could teach her how to sew. She's such a sweet little girl."

Tante Mathilde turned the dress and studied it. "Why, yes, I don't think we can use much of it for a new dress for you." She dropped the dress into her lap and looked at Mercedee. "When Elizabeth comes over to play, you could—"

With impeccable timing, a knock sounded at the door.

Mercedee got up, set the fabric and dress on the chair, and opened the door. "Hello."

Little Elizabeth held her head down shyly as the door opened, then she looked up when Mercedee spoke. Seeing Mercedee's face, Elizabeth smiled. "Hello."

"Please come in." Mercedee stepped back. "Have you ever sewn a dress?"

Elizabeth appeared to think for a moment. "No."

"Would you like to learn? We could make one just for you."

Elizabeth's eyes grew wide, and she smiled brightly as Mercedee led her into the house.

**

Over the following week, Mercedee worked on the dress with Elizabeth, took inventory of her trunk, and with Tante Mathilde, went through all of her fabric scraps, dresses, blouses, and shawls. They took one trip to Yarmouth, and by mid-August, they had sewn two dresses and two sets of linens. However, all of their toil notwithstanding, they had accumulated only about half of what the academy wanted. Yet that would have to do. Tante Mathilde had a couple of extra towels and pitched in with overnight supplies.

"Is that neckline still giving you trouble, Mercedee?" Mathilde had just walked into her sewing room next to the downstairs bedroom to see Mercedee leaning over a dress and blouse spread out on a sewing table.

Still concentrating on the collar, Mercedee said, "Yes, it feels a little tight at the top."

"I'm sure you'll be able to get the adjustment right." Mathilde looked over Mercedee's shoulder. "You may want to adjust the tuck by the edge."

"Oh yes." Mercedee took a seam ripper to a narrow row of stitching. She adjusted the tuck where Mathilde had suggested and sewed it up. After Mathilde left, she tried it on and exclaimed, "That's perfect!"

A knock at the front door echoed through the house. "Who in the world could that be?" Adelaide called from the kitchen.

Mercedee scrambled to take off the blouse and put her clothes back on properly before the others brought the caller inside. She buttoned the front as fast as possible and tucked her blouse in as she listened to voices in the living room for clues about who might be at the door. She dashed through the sitting room and across the living room just as Mathilde turned the brass handle, opened the door, and stepped aside.

There, framed in the doorway, stood a short, thin woman holding a suitcase and handbag. She sported a nicely tailored blue dress and light blouse with a narrow waist, puffed sleeves, small black buttons, and a high, thin white collar. She sported a fashionable hat over her neatly combed hair which was nearly gray. She raised one eyebrow over her serious, dark, and piercing eyes and looked up at the trio, who were wide-eyed and clearly stunned. She looked impatiently at the women standing in the doorway as if to say, "Well?"

"Seraphie!" Adelaide and Mathilde said in unison, welcoming their sister from New York City into the house.

"Come in, come in!" Mathilde said. "Let me help you with your bag."

"Thank you," Seraphie Wainwright said as she walked deliberately into the room, following Adelaide.

Mathilde stepped onto the porch and bent to pick up the bag then stopped. "Mercedee," she called back through the door. "Would you please help with this bag? I don't feel well."

"Of course, Tante." Mercedee headed past Mathilde to the bag. "What is it?"

"Oh, it's nothing, I'm sure," Mathilde said as she entered the living room with Seraphie.

"My goodness, sit down. That must have been a long trip," Mathilde said as Seraphie made her way to the dining table.

"I'm fine. I spent last night in Yarmouth because the

steamship arrived late in the evening. It wasn't a long train ride today." Seraphie liked to show off her active lifestyle.

As Seraphie set her handbag on the dinner table, Adelaide spoke up. "We didn't know you were coming."

"I received word from William that he had collected a debt from a client, and—oh, where's my brush?" Seraphie paused as she dug through her handbag then stopped and looked back up. "I heard that William was paying for Mercedee to enter Mount St. Vincent and decided right then that I was going to make it up here before she left."

"Just to see Mercedee before she left?" Mathilde asked as if confounded.

Mercedee looked on with wide eyes and raised eyebrows.

"I didn't come just to see her, although I certainly wanted to, but I plan to ride the train with her and see her to Mount St. Vincent. I also wanted to see Marie Anne—" She pulled a hairbrush out of her bag and said, "Oh, there it is." She stopped and touched her finger to her chin. "Or should I call her Sister Rosalia?"

"But there must be something else," Mathilde asked softly, not wanting to pry but still curious. "Coming all this way to travel with Mercedee?"

Mercedee looked, on hoping for more information as they all took seats at the kitchen table.

"Well," Seraphie continued, "you see, Sister Rosalia sent me a letter saying that William has been inquiring about the tuition and other costs at Mount St. Vincent. Now, I'm quite sure that you're aware that he has put some finances together, but he was asking Rosalia if he could get a bit of a discount or perhaps credit." Her voice trailed off as if she'd just realized that Mercedee was in the room and didn't want to alarm her.

"Yes," Mercedee said. "We received Papa's postal with money and the list of items from the academy."

"Right," Seraphie said. "From what I gathered from Rosalia—she's a bit concerned about how her Mother Superior will react if Mercedee isn't fully supported—I thought it might be prudent if I were there with Mercedee when she arrives to talk to Sister Rosalia about the financial side of things."

"Oh, thank you so much, Tante. I didn't expect any of this," Mercedee said.

"Of course not. I haven't seen your Tante Rosalia in ages, and we have catching up to do."

Matilde was relieved. She had worried about Mercedee taking off on such a long trip all by herself. Adelaide furrowed her brow, probably feeling that Mercedee was again getting undue attention. She inhaled as if to speak but mercifully delayed any comment.

"You didn't need to go to all this trouble, Tante Seraphie," Mercedee said. "I'll be fine. It seems all Mamma and I did was travel."

Seraphie put her hand on Mercedee's arm. "It's no trouble. I wanted to come. It'll be fun."

"We should get to dinner right away," Mathilde said as she followed Adelaide into the kitchen. "I was just simmering a large pot of *fricot*, and I think it should be just about done."

"I can hardly wait to taste it," Seraphie said. "I always liked your fricot, particularly your dumplings."

Mathilde smiled as she walked through the kitchen, past the stove on her right and a counter on the left. She walked out the back door and gazed at the pasture beyond the barn where cows and horses were grazing. Her vegetable garden shone green in the sun alongside the pasture. She picked up a piece of split maple from the woodpile on the porch and returned to the stove. She stoked the fire beneath the simmering fricot, a traditional Acadian stew with potatoes, onion, meat, and dumplings.

Seraphie followed as Mercedee carried her luggage to the empty bedroom off the kitchen.

"Would you like to see the dress I'm working on?" asked Mercedee.

"Certainly." Seraphie looked into the sewing room. "Is

that your dress and blouse on the sewing table?"

"Yes. I've been using some spare fabric Tante Mathilde found. It's been fun to try to find enough fabric to make puffed sleeves. I think it's coming along."

Seraphie, who owned one dress shop and was opening another, bent over the dress and blouse.

After a moment that tortured Mercedee's nerves, Tante Seraphie said, "Not bad. Not bad at all. And you certainly haven't had the best material to work with." She adjusted a sleeve. "You have a good technique."

"Thank you so much for noticing." Mercedee sighed, visibly relieved.

Matilde stirred a steaming pot on the woodstove and called over her shoulder, "Seraphie, you must be hungry. Mercedee, would you please help me slice some bread? We'll have dinner ready soon."

Seraphie and Mercedee walked into the kitchen.

"That fricot smells good. It reminds me of Mother Monique's recipe," Seraphie said.

"It's the old recipe, the way I make it anyhow, with a couple, dare I say, improvements." Mathilde continued stirring the pot. "How is Henry?" she asked. Henry was Seraphie's husband. "And are you teaching Agnes to sew?"

"Henry's doing well. As is Aggie. She's young but learning to stitch, albeit slowly and with great reluctance. She doesn't see herself as a future seamstress." Seraphie moved into the kitchen and took a taste of the fricot. "That's good. It certainly reminds me of Mother."

"Thank you so much," Mathilde said. "I'll bet it's hard to come by real Acadian dishes in the big city." She looked up at Seraphie, and they smiled. "And how's the dress shop doing?"

"Very well, actually. Business is brisk," Tante Seraphie walked to the living room and sat on an upholstered chair. "The economy is bustling right now in New York City, and New Jersey and Connecticut are growing in population."

"Very well indeed," Adelaide said.

"And how is Monique? Have you seen her?" Mathilde asked. Monique, their other sister, was two years younger than Seraphie and was a feisty, petite woman who was providing a home for Ferdinand, William Meehan's older son.

"I haven't seen Monique in some time, but I do get a letter from her here and there. She's as steamy as ever. You know they have that large new house in Orange, New Jersey, and she runs her own dress shop now..." She left further commentary about Monique unsaid.

Adelaide pulled out a chair and sat at the table with one of the bowls of fricot in front of her. "Is Ferdinand still living with them? Monique must be happy about that, because of her feelings for William."

Mercedee raised an eyebrow at her aunt.

"Actually," Seraphie subtly corrected, clearly aware that Mercedee was in the room, "Monique and Ferdinand share a bit of frustration with William, although it's certainly more Monique's disposition, so they could be considered peas in a pod to a certain extent."

"Oh?" Mathilde pried.

"Hmm…" Seraphie sounded cautious. "How should I say this? Monique doesn't like to wait for William's finances to come through to pay for Ferdinand's board, and Ferdinand must mostly hear Monique's point of view, which I'm sure she doesn't temper." Although Seraphie seemed to soften her remarks for present company, some aspects of the volatile relationship between Monique and William inevitably came through.

"That notwithstanding," Seraphie continued, "I hope Monique doesn't expect William to compensate her forever. After all, Ferdinand is past twenty years old now and has finished at Boston Tech. He pays a fee for room and board at her place in Orange, so she's happy to have him. As long as she gets some money from someone, she's fine. But I'm not privy to their arrangements."

"And her son, Phillip? How is he?" Adelaide asked as

Mercedee quietly moved two bowls of hot fricot to the table.

"I haven't heard any recent news, so I assume he's fine. I suspect he's nineteen now." Seraphie joined Mercedee in the kitchen. "When do you leave for Mount St. Vincent?"

"The day after tomorrow." Mercedee carried the plate of bread, a saucer with butter, and four small white plates to the dinner table. She filled two more bowls from the pot simmering on the stove.

Mathilde wiped her hands on a dish towel and dropped it on the counter. She carried the bowls of steaming fricot to the table and placed them next to the spoons. They all took seats at the table and waited for Mathilde to say grace.

After taking a spoonful of the fricot, Seraphie said, "The dumplings are perfect."

"Thank you," Mathilde said.

Seraphie turned to Mercedee. "I hope you're learning Acadian cooking from your tantes."

"I certainly am, Tante Seraphie," Mercedee replied.

"Well," Seraphie said thoughtfully, "day after tomorrow. I see that I got here just in time."

4 OFF TO MOUNT ST. VINCENT ACADEMY

"The train is coming, Mercedee," Tante Mathilde called, squinting down the tracks from the Little Brook Station.

Mathilde and Seraphie flanked Mercedee, who held her handbag and a cloth sack with food for the trip. Peter stood nearby, beside the station house, with Adelaide. Mercedee's trunk with all her possessions sat on the platform, hauled from Mathilde's house by Peter. In the distance, the image of a black steam locomotive of the Yarmouth and Annapolis Railway penetrated the shimmering morning light. Its short smokestack belched black smoke that rose upward and dissipated above the trees. The locomotive grew slowly larger, and Mercedee grabbed Seraphie's hand with excitement.

The train slowed to a stop. The porter, standing on a step and holding a handle on the rear of a freight car, saw the luggage on the platform and swung down to load the waiting trunks. Peter signaled him to load Mercedee's trunk.

"Remember to always keep your bags with you. And you'll get off at the Four Mile House Station just before Halifax. Sister Rosalia will be waiting for you." Mathilde's voice hid her trepidation at her impetuous niece going all the way to Halifax.

"I'll be very careful, Tante Mathilde." Mercedee took a deep breath, trying to hide her butterflies. "I won't lose my bags. You must know I have been doing this all of my life." Mercedee glanced at her aunt. "And thank you so much for everything you've done for me."

Mercedee wiped a tear from her cheek with the back of her hand and hugged her aunt one last time. Mathilde stood on tiptoe, reaching up to kiss Mercedee's cheek.

"Hurry now. The train will be leaving soon." Seraphie walked toward the open train-car door.

Mercedee handed the porter money, saying, "My trunk is going to the Four Mile House Station, near Halifax." The porter nodded and wrote on a tag as Mercedee turned to Mathilde and walked toward the train-carriage door. The porter put the trunk on a cart and wheeled it toward the baggage car.

"Perhaps we'll see you again for the holidays," Mathilde said.

"I'm already looking forward to telling you about the first term at the Mount."

"Now, Mercedee, the train ride is long, even with the new route with the connection through the Annapolis Valley. Fortunately, you won't have to change cars before you get to Halifax..." Mathilde's voice trailed off, and she paused, looking into Mercedee's excited but apprehensive face. Mathilde searched for something to say that Mercedee would take with her as a warm memory of the past months. Her voice finally pierced the noise from the hissing train. "You may be able to get some dinner in Annapolis Royal or Kentville. Just don't venture too far from the train station. Do be careful."

"For the last time, I'll be all right, Tante." Mercedee sensed Mathilde's concern from her wrinkled brow, showing the many years of living in southern Nova Scotia. As Peter returned, Mercedee pulled away and walked to the train-car door with him. She hugged him and whispered, "I wish you the best in your quest to become a reporter or whatever you decide. You must write and tell me what you do. Promise!"

Peter let out a rare laugh and promised to write. He couldn't refuse his vivacious cousin. She had more wonderful ideas than any of his friends, and he would miss her humor, sparkling wit, and daring escapades. "You have to write to me so that I know where you are. And next summer, we'll have even more fun if you're not married or a nun." Peter laughed.

"I'm only fifteen years old, Peter. I'm not going to get married anytime soon."

They chuckled, and Peter dropped off the platform. Mercedee gaily waved goodbye.

"Give Sister Rosalia my love," Mathilde called out as Mercedee greeted a train conductor and porter. Mercedee paid the conductor, received a ticket, and followed Seraphie onto the train.

A summer breeze ruffled Mathilde's gray hair and long flowing skirt as she watched the conductor close the doors and signal the engineer to depart. Presently, the locomotive hissed and pumped. A series of clanks ripped from the locomotive to the rear as the couplings between the carriages engaged, and the train slowly moved from the Little Brook Station. It slowly picked up speed and moved northeast toward the coast and the town of Digby. Mathilde and Peter ambled down the tree-lined dirt road to Concession. Only birds chirping and voices in the distance interrupted the stillness. Mercedee's exit had left a noticeable void in their environment.

"Rosalia will be good for your cousin," Mathilde said, though more to herself than Peter as he kicked a small stone down the road. Momentarily, she whispered, "She's carrying more than just her bag and trunk. I'll pray for her often."

Mercedee entered the train car from the rear and worked her way forward as the train lurched into motion. She and

Seraphie found empty seats among the few scattered passengers. She sat down next to Seraphie and held her bag on her lap, as did her aunt.

The train slowly pulled out of the station. Then the rhythmic pulsing of the steam pistons grew faster as it began its long journey along the coast. The Yarmouth and Annapolis Railway steam locomotives were narrow gauge and managed only about eighteen miles per hour. The trip from Church Point to the Mount St. Vincent Academy would take ten hours.

They first crossed farmland, bridged rivers, and dipped through broad, shallow, wet swales. In places, the track followed a narrow slice carved from the thick forest, and in other places, it raised above the water of marshes on built-up soil or low trestles. The north Atlantic seaboard climate was comfortable in late August, and farmers were busy cutting hay while dairy cows grazed along with horses.

After a couple of hours, the train reached Digby, a small but bustling port and trading center in the sheltered Annapolis Basin off the Bay of Fundy. Many steamship passengers who traveled up the Bay of Fundy from the United States and across the bay from New Brunswick boarded the train in Digby to continue south to Halifax.

"How are you feeling?" Seraphie asked, appearing to notice Mercedee's faraway gaze at the passing landscape. "I know it goes without saying, but this must have been a hard year."

"Yes, it was. And is. I feel so alone. I never wanted to imagine Mamma being gone, even though she struggled so all those years. As far back as I can remember, really." Mercedee paused. "But I feel like I'm old enough to face a rather empty world. Hopefully, I can manage at Mount St. Vincent and have more opportunities."

"You are strong to continue. I'm glad to hear you're optimistic. I hope your father can continue his good fortune," Seraphie said reassuringly, although Mercedee read doubt in her voice.

"So do I, Tante Seraphie. So do I." Mercedee scanned the passengers on the other side of the train car, mostly seeing the backs of heads.

"You know," Seraphie said, "losing your Mamma was hard for all of us sisters. She was the youngest, the baby. She was only a few years younger than I, but I still felt that I needed to watch out for her."

Mercedee shifted her gaze to Seraphie. "I didn't know that. Mamma didn't talk much about her younger days."

"We lived in Belleville, where our father had built a home and had some land and woods. He passed away when your mamma was only four years old. It was exceedingly difficult after that."

"How did you get by?"

Seraphie patted the bag on her lap. "I should say it was harder on the younger ones. Placide was fourteen, Marie Anne—or Rosalia —was eleven, Monique was nine, and I was seven when our father died. The others were older. Adelaide was eighteen, Lezin was twenty, Marine was twenty-one, Mathilde was twenty-four, and Leonisse was twenty-five. So, they all had jobs or were married and helped take care of us."

"That was a large family. Ten children. I have no real brothers or sisters. That's hard to imagine." Mercedee looked straight ahead, wondering what it would be like to have such a family. And to lose a father so young. "Mamma didn't talk much about all of her siblings."

"Agnes, Monique, and I went to Digby and lived with Mathilde. Mathilde later moved to Concession. Our mother wasn't well and had to rest to take care of her depression. Lezin stayed in Belleville with Mother, and she married Mr. Bourque." Seraphie paused. "Your father attended our church, St. Patrick's Parish in Digby. William and his mother came, and later William came with his wife, Adela."

Mercedee looked at a large barn next to a farmhouse they were passing. The land dropped off to the north toward the Bay of Fundy. Several farmers were trying to hook a team of horses up to a farm implement. "Did the Meehans live in Digby too?"

"The Meehans actually lived in Annapolis Royal—some still call it Port Royal—over on the east end of the bay where the Annapolis River runs in," Seraphie said. "William's father, Michael, owned an inn and some land there, and the inn did well. Unfortunately, Michael died when William was fifteen. William was the eldest of eight children. Life was hard, and although Michael had amassed assets, William's mother, Mary Mourine, got almost nothing from his estate. William did have an uncle, also named William, who managed Michael's affairs, but I don't know how they got by. The family all moved to Digby, and I suspect William and the older boys helped support the family."

"Did Adela die when Ferdinand was born?" Mercedee asked.

"No, she died giving birth to another child when Ferdinand was two years old. The child perished too. William and Ferdinand then went to live with his mother, Mary, in Digby," Seraphie said.

"That's what I thought. Mamma didn't talk about it."

"William worked by buying and selling real estate and later moved to Boston. He felt he could make more money there and support Ferdinand in Digby." Seraphie paused as if not wanting to judge William in front of Mercedee since the girl had lived with her mother for much of her life.

"That sounds rather familiar." Mercedee sighed.

"It was at least ten years after Adela died that William courted your mother," Seraphie finally said.

"Yes, Ferdinand is much older than I. He lived with us in Melrose Highlands before he went to live with Monique in New Jersey. He's quite independent."

"William paid Monique for Ferdinand's keep while he was at university. I don't know how much, but knowing Monique, she probably thought it wasn't enough."

"How did Mamma and Papa meet?"

"If I remember correctly, it was at a picnic in the summer

of 1876. William would periodically come back to Digby to be with his mother and Ferdinand, and William ended up knowing Agnes through the church. I know he spent time with Agnes at the picnic. We knew that he wanted to court her, but she was shy. Agnes was almost twenty-seven, but William was much older than she. He must have been forty-two or forty-three. Monique was very doubtful of William's motives." Seraphie looked out the window.

"I knew that William was a speculator, and his income wouldn't be dependable, particularly during the financial panic of the 1870s. But Agnes had never had a relationship, and William was somewhat established. His dealings in Boston were a far cry from eking out a living in Digby. I didn't know if Agnes would ever find a happy relationship until William. She seemed very taken with him, and they were married the following June."

"Mamma told me they were married in Boston."

"Yes. Agnes took off with William, and they lived in a hotel. He had an office in Boston as he does now, and they were married there."

"But Monique didn't like him? Did she not approve of the marriage?"

"I don't think she trusted William, and it wasn't lost on her that they were not married in St. Anne's or St. Agnes's Church near Belleville. She wasn't irked because he was Irish and not Acadian. It was that her little sister was going to marry him. You see, Monique and I were married and doing well. We were planning to move to New York. And our little sister was taking up with a speculator. And an Irish one at that."

Seraphie glanced at Mercedee to see if what she was saying shocked her. "I'm sorry. I didn't mean it in that way. I'm speaking of what Monique seemed to be feeling. And the Potier family are Acadians. We were in Nova Scotia long before the Irish arrived."

"I understand," Mercedee said. "But Mamma loved him."

"She did. And he loved her. He did everything he could. And there were no overt hard feelings. At least that I knew about." Seraphie continued, "Monique also thought William should have found a wife and raised his son, Ferdinand."

"It sounds like it was difficult for everyone," Mercedee said. "I know that Papa tried to take care of Mamma and me, and most of the time he was able to provide financially if he wasn't there in person. Mamma was so sick that she couldn't stay in the cold country in the winter."

"William tried dreadfully hard. And I feel he doted on your mother. He's worked hard to support her and her poor health. He always had a new venture that was going to make a fortune, but things like that are risky. He bought into an iron mine near Torbrook, which is near South Mountain, east of Annapolis Royal," Seraphie said as the train lurched and rattled. "Iron mines and the blast furnace in Londonderry were producing steel and buying iron ore from mines around Nova Scotia. Torbrook seemed sure to be a boom, selling ore to the Londonderry blast furnace, but the ore didn't make good steel, and all the Torbrook mines became worthless."

Mercedee looked out the window as the train chugged past Digby. She tried to catch a glimpse of her Aunt Moll's farm, where she and Mamma had stayed one summer before. Aunt Moll was her father's sister, and she had been kind to them. The farm was on the west side of town but just out of view. *I must come back and see Moll sometime.*

Before long, the train emerged from thick woodlands to the north. The engineer gave a loud whistle as the train crossed busy streets. On the left, ships sat in the Annapolis Basin while dockworkers unloaded merchandise cargo and loaded agricultural goods and wood products.

The port had a small warehouse, a broad wooden platform that extended right up to the train tracks. Visitors parked wagons in the back, away from the tracks, and people crowded the platform. Other travelers stood under the station roof to escape the sun, and still others waited in line to buy tickets.

The train stopped, and Mercedee and Seraphie got off to visit the lavatory. They held their bags secure in front of them as they negotiated a path through the people entering the train carriage as they exited and then the crowd in and around the station.

Boys in newsboy hats, ragged shirts with suspenders, and knee-length pants called out, offering newspapers. One lad held up a copy of the *Digby Weekly Courier* in front of Seraphie and cried, "Newspapers! Hot off the press!" Seraphie nudged him aside and led Mercedee into the cool of the station.

On the way back to the train, Seraphie purchased a copy of the local paper.

"Thank you, ma'am!" a newspaper boy said as he folded the paper in thirds and handed it to her.

"Phew!" Mercedee gasped as they boarded the train. "The Digby station is mayhem."

"Yes. It was quaint and quiet when I was young."

After pulling out of Digby, the train rolled south then eastward around the south side of the Annapolis Basin and on to Kingston. Mercedee was deep in thought, wondering how the school year would go. The Mount was a much more prestigious and challenging school than St. Anne's. With limited funds and supplies, she was already starting behind.

After Kentville, Mercedee looked about the carriage at the other passengers. The coach wasn't full, and many seats had only one passenger. Something familiar caught Mercedee's eye, and her gaze fixed on a girl wearing a bonnet two rows in front of her. She stared with interest. *Who is she? She looks awfully familiar.* But Mercedee couldn't see enough of the girl to place her. As the girl turned and looked out the window, Mercedee saw her profile and instantly sprang up and out of her seat. "Clara! Clara La Brun!"

The girl turned around and looked shocked, but when she saw Mercedee's face, hers lit up. "Mercedee?"

"Clara, what are you doing here? Don't tell me that you're going to Mount St. Vincent too!"

"Where else could I be going, silly?" Clara laughed. "This is the train to Halifax."

"This is wonderful! Come over and sit beside me. I can't believe how cute your bonnet is!"

Clara rose from her seat and picked up a black satchel. She moved quickly from her seat, and the two girls embraced.

"It's so good to see you," Mercedee said. "Meet my Tante Seraphie, who came up from New York City to travel with me to Mount St. Vincent."

"How do you do, ma'am?" Clara said as Seraphie stood.

"Pleased to meet you, Clara. How do you know Mercedee?"

"We were both at St. Anne's last year," Clara said.

"Yes. We had many adventures." Mercedee laughed. "Tante, may I sit across the aisle with Clara?"

Seraphie nodded, and the two girls plopped into the seat. Seraphie sat down and unfolded her newspaper.

"I am so glad to see you!" Clara said. "Your father must have found the funds so that you could go. I didn't think I would ever see you again."

"Just barely. Papa sent me just enough money. With the help of Tante Mathilde, I scraped together supplies," Mercedee said.

"It's wonderful to see you. I'm going to St. Vincent because my mother wants me to have some *manners and refinement*. After all the capers we pulled at the convent at Eel Brook, she would have done better to have kept me at home."

Clara and Mercedee laughed.

"I had a lovely summer, but not one of my friends has any imagination," Clara said. "Not like you do. How's your papa? Have you seen him lately?"

Mercedee's dark eyes clouded. "No, I haven't seen him for three years, since Mamma and I came to Concession. He hasn't been able to come to Concession because of business." She looked at her hands. "He did make enough money to pay for a year at the Mount, though."

"You know"—Clara lowered her voice conspiratorially—"your Tante Moll lives next to us in Digby, and I heard her tell my mamma that your father was losing money on his property ventures, something about silver prices, and he's nearly penniless. Can you imagine how I felt when I heard that? I just cried with sorrow for you!"

Mercedee's eyes widened. "So that's what Tante Adelaide was talking to Tante Mathilde about! They sure became quiet when I walked in. They were talking about me going to work to pay for room and board. Tante Mathilde told her to stop talking nonsense because she wouldn't hear of it. Tante Adelaide certainly looked guilty. Then Papa's letter came, and Tante Mathilde told me I was to come to Halifax. I didn't know what was wrong."

"Well, he must not be in that much difficulty," Clara said.

"Yes," Mercedee said thoughtfully, "he said in the letter that he collected debt on a property. I hope Tante Moll is misinformed." Mercedee teared up thinking about her father in distress and her mamma gone.

The train lurched on uneven tracks as Clara put her arms around her friend and gave her a handkerchief to soak up her tears. "It's all right. He must not be as poor as they said, or he wouldn't be able to send you to the Mount. I'm certain they were wrong."

Mercedee gazed out the window at the thick vegetation broken intermittently by glimpses of spectacular cliffs and the brilliant water of the Bay of Fundy as the train clacked down the coast. "Whatever am I going to do?" Then with characteristic practicality, she straightened her shoulders and raised her chin. "I'll have to take care of myself. I can become a governess or a seamstress, or perhaps I'll become a Sister of God. Peter always teased me about that, but he said I was so irreverent that the church would fall down."

"Mercedee," Clara said in a low voice. "The last time I saw you, you were trying to get to Concession to see your mother. You left with Kitty. Did you…?" Clara stopped speaking as Mercedee looked down at her bag and dabbed her eyes with her handkerchief.

"I'm sorry." Clara sighed.

"It's all right. You need to know," Mercedee said as she wiped her nose. "When I got to Tante Mathilde's house, Mamma had already passed away."

"I'm so sorry."

"We had a nice funeral at Church Point, and being with my family helped a lot. I knew Mamma didn't have much time left when we came to Nova Scotia. I guess her time had to come." The tears stopped, and Mercedee looked out the coach window.

"Did you get the cards we sent from the convent?" Clara asked softly.

"I did." Mercedee wiped her eyes with her handkerchief. "Your card helped. Thank you."

"We'll have fun at the Mount, though," Clara offered.

"Yes, we will. It'll be so nice to be with you there. I'm certain that we'll never cause any trouble." Mercedee wiped her eyes again and broke into a smile.

Clara chuckled, obviously relieved that Mercedee was unable to be morose for long. Clara chattered about their friends and escapades.

Mercedee laughed but was thinking about her poor papa and their financial state. She remembered the doctor bill for Mamma's care that Tante Mathilde had sent Papa. Each visit was five dollars, quinine pills were fifty cents each, and the witch hazel, emulsion, iodine, malt elixir, pancreatic medicine, glycerin, and creosote that the doctor had used to treat her mother had added up to a whopping $23.25. Has Papa been able to pay the bill? Dr. Elderkin came from Weymouth Bridge to treat Mamma. He was a sad little man who must have known that Mamma had little time and no hope. Mercedee resolutely put the sad thoughts aside and turned to meet the new challenges and adventures ahead.

"I hear the Mount is very large. Many girls come from all over Nova Scotia and Newfoundland and even New Brunswick and Boston," Clara said. "Kind of scares me."

"Me, too, Clara. I wish I had seen this place before starting school."

"And I'm sure the sisters are very strict."

"I don't know," Mercedee said thoughtfully. "We didn't have any trouble at St. Anne's. Nuns are nuns. I know how to handle them." She chuckled.

"No trouble?" Clara whispered. "Sister Carmel whipped us."

"Well…"

Clara whispered more softly, "You told her not to whip kids."

"Oh yes," Mercedee whispered with her head lowered. "I asked her if being a convent was an exception to the law."

Clara nodded. "What did she say to that?"

"She said, 'I don't think it's anybody's business what I do.' I didn't say anything after that." Mercedee glanced across the train car at Seraphie, who looked over the top of her newspaper with the hint of a frown.

Claire giggled and covered her face with her hands. "When you tossed a rock near Sister's feet when we were walking along the lake, I was sure you were going to be in trouble. But you calmly explained that it was a frog. And you looked so innocent!"

"Yes, that was a fancy trick! Sister almost dropped her reticule trying to get away from the edge! And putting a pill bug in Emma's lunch bag was worth it to see her howl!"

"You're so intrepid! I would never have done that." Clara wiped the tears from her cheeks. "I hope we find some friends who will share our adventures."

Mercedee's eyes shone with mischief. "I've been keeping a list of ideas. It has to be secret. I've always wondered what's in the books the nuns keep in their private study. How can we decide if we want to become nuns if we never get to see their directives? Maybe we can figure this out."

The train slowed as the conductor announced, "Windsor."

Mercedee jumped up, clearly startling her aunt, who had been reading. "Tante Seraphie, can we get some lunch? I'm starving. There's a snack house there." Mercedee pointed at a stand next to the station.

Seraphie closed her book and picked up her reticule. "Come on, girls. Let's get a drink and a sandwich. We have a few minutes."

The girls bounded off the train. Mercedee chose a paper-wrapped sandwich and a lemonade and showed Clara her choice. "Here. This looks like a good lunch, and no crickets!"

Mercedee laughed as Clara carefully checked her sandwich for surprises.

Clara grinned. "I know all about your tricks!" Clara lifted her skirts and stepped back onto the train.

Seraphie shook her head at the antics of her niece and took her seat across the aisle. The train whistle echoed across the wooded hills as it picked up speed and left the station.

Mercedee munched her sandwich then said, "I hope we can be in the same dorm, Clara. You're my best friend, and even though we make new friends, we'll always be close. You won't have to worry about other girls because we will be together."

Clara wiped her mouth with a small serviette. "Oh, thank you! I feel so much better now. We'll be a best friends' circle."

"Well, maybe at a big academy like the Mount, the sisters will be nicer," Mercedee whispered.

Clara nodded. "It'll be fun, I'm certain."

As the afternoon passed, the sun cast beams into the car as the train rolled through tree shadows. The route dropped from rolling upland hills into a basin filled with a bay to the left and more rolling hills to the right. The track was on the water's edge, and farther south, it merged with two other tracks. Noisy steam freight trains and one passenger train passed them, headed north.

"Four Mile House Station!" The conductor's voice boomed through the coach as he walked down the aisle, and the train slowed to a stop. The girls jumped up and searched the bay out the windows. Seraphie's eyes snapped open. She had been dozing with her head against the window.

"Come, Clara!" Mercedee called. "This is our stop." Both girls grabbed their handbags and cases and followed Seraphie down the aisle to the door at the end of the car. They stepped onto the small platform and breathed in the cool, humid air of the basin mixed with coal smoke. In a long hiss, steam from the locomotive swirled around in the breeze. Several other passengers also quickly exited the train. A porter delivered Mercedee and Clara's trunks to the platform from a freight car.

A uniformed conductor walked out onto the platform and bellowed, "All aboard for Fairview, Armdale, and Halifax!" The doors closed as he stepped back onto the train. The locomotive whistled twice, and it leaned into the line of carriages with a slow pulsing of the steam pistons. It gradually picked up speed and left Mercedee, Clara, and Tante Seraphie in sudden calm with only the echoes of the locomotive in the distance and empty tracks and water opposite the small station building. To the west, trees covered rolling hills. Scattered fields and farmhouses littered the landscape.

Mercedee looked around to find Mount St. Vincent. Tante Seraphie picked up her case and motioned toward the station house. "I'm sure Sister Rosalia will be here soon. We should move our trunks over there." She pointed at the corner of the platform.

As Mercedee and Clara dragged their trunks toward the station, the door opened, and Sister Rosalia hurried out. She wore the traditional coif and head covering with a hand-carved rosary and silver cross on her chest.

"Sister Rosalia!" Mercedee dropped her bag and stepped forward. She threw her arms around her aunt in an enthusiastic embrace. "I'm so glad to see you, Sister. This is my friend Clara La Brun. Clara, this is my aunt, Sister Rosalia. She's my mother's sister."

Sister Rosalia's kind eyes settled on Clara and Mercedee. She had been a well-respected nun at the academy for twenty years.

Sister Rosalia turned to Clara. "I'm very pleased to meet you, Clara La Brun," she said with a sweet smile. Then she put her hands on her niece's shoulders. "My, my, Mercedee, you have so grown since I last saw you."

"Oh, I don't think I'm that tall." Mercedee was uncomfortable with the attention and turned to look at the fishing boats returning from the Atlantic and crossing Bedford Basin. "Look at the beautiful evening and ships on the bay. Is this Halifax Bay?"

"That is Bedford Basin, an extension of Halifax Bay. The city is around the point over there." Sister Rosalia gestured to her right.

Sister Rosalia paused as Seraphie walked up beside Mercedee. The sister took a second look and gasped. "My sister Seraphie. I didn't know you were coming. So wonderful to see you." She stepped forward, and they hugged.

"It's good to see you, too, Sister," Seraphie said.

"May we get supper? I'm famished!" Mercedee put her hand over her mouth. Her nervous energy had gotten the best of her.

"Dear Mercedee, you must learn temperance." Sister Rosalia sounded much more like a finishing school sister than an aunt.

"She will. I'm certain," Tante Seraphie said.

"I'm sorry, Sister," Mercedee said humbly.

Sister Rosalia continued, "We'll have plenty of time to explore the bay and Halifax. You've been on such a long train ride. Now get your bags from the platform, and we'll go to the Mount. It's not far, just up the road." Sister Rosalia pointed at the uplands framed by pink and orange clouds of the sunset. "I brought a buggy. It's right over there." Sister Rosalia headed toward the station door.

Mercedee and Clara picked up their bags and trudged behind Sister Rosalia. Tante Seraphie followed with her handbag and suitcase. The foursome walked past a vacant dust-covered counter and old postings, to the exit door. They lugged bags down the steps to a plain-looking horse-drawn buggy. After Sister Rosalia helped them load their bags onto it, they retrieved the two girls' trunks. With everything loaded, Rosalia climbed into the front seat and took up the reins. Mercedee sat beside her and Clara, and Seraphie sat on a second bench behind them. The two girls took long, exhausted breaths.

Rosalia snapped the reins to nudge a short, sturdy old brown horse and guided it down Bedford Road. The girls looked around with wide eyes at the water of Bedford Basin, dark in the twilight and shadow of hills to their right. Several train tracks followed the road on the left, and houses, woods, and fields were visible on the right as the buggy rocked along. In less than a mile, they arrived at a street to the right that paralleled the road. Rosalia turned, and they followed the road around a bend and through a stand of trees.

As the wagon emerged from the trees, Rosalia said, "You'll soon see the academy motherhouse. There's a little farm behind the motherhouse. We walk on the paths in the park on nice weather days and normally get in many lovely walks. We have a nice saltwater bathing house on Minard's Basin, with a high fence and a rope to hold onto so there's no danger—"

Then both girls gasped as the motherhouse of Mount St. Vincent Academy came into view.

The castle-like motherhouse loomed four stories tall with dormer windows and two immense dormitory wings. Mercedee and Clara gawked at the fairy-tale building. Spires scraped the sky at three intervals, and as the girls watched in awe, the setting sun illuminated the cross atop the spire over the entrance. The cross glowed in the orange light of the sunset peeking over the low hills.

"Oh, I've never seen anything so beautiful," breathed Mercedee. "Will we really be able to live here in this magical place?"

"I'm just speechless!" added Clara. "How will we ever find our way around in this castle?"

The buggy slowly crawled the length of the building and toward the center rotunda. They passed the four-story left wing and neared a small decorative roundabout in front of the stairways.

Sister Rosalia glanced at Mercedee, her face transfixed on the building. "Seraphie, have you ever seen the Mount in this spectacular light?"

"No, I haven't. The light is amazing. I think I see princesses waltzing in the ballroom," Seraphie replied.

"Really, Tante. Really," Mercedee said. "Oh, Clara, we're going to love it here."

Clara closed her mouth and rubbed her eyes. "I'm so happy we're here together. I would never find my way around such a magnificent place."

As Sister Rosalia pulled the buggy to a stop in front of the rotunda, two nuns walked out to meet them.

"Welcome back, Sister Rosalia, and welcome to our two new students," Sister Caramella said with a warm smile. She adjusted her wire-rimmed oval spectacles on her narrow face.

"Thank you, Sister Caramella," Sister Rosalia replied as she and the girls climbed down from the buggy.

Tante Seraphie picked up her purse and stepped down on the other side of the wagon. "Sisters, this is Mercedee Meehan and Clara La Brun. They were both at St. Anne's school in Eel Brook near Yarmouth last year. Mercedee and Clara, meet Sister Caramella and Sister Michaela, Sisters of Charity, Halifax."

"Pleased to meet you," the girls chorused.

Sister Michaela nodded, a hint of a sneer on her heavyset face. "Pleased to meet you," she said dryly.

Sister Rosalia turned to the two girls as Seraphie rounded the wagon. "Now, I came and picked you up in the wagon because you had bags. It's normally only a two-minute stroll to the station, and we walk when we need to take the train to Halifax."

"Yes, Sister Rosalia," the girls said as they retrieved their bags and trunks.

Rosalia handed the reins to Caramella and gestured behind her. "This is my sister Seraphie Wainwright. She's traveled from New York City and will be visiting while Mercedee gets settled in."

Seraphie exchanged greetings with Sister Caramella and Sister Michaela and put her bags on the low step.

"Caramella, will you please take the buggy around to the stables while I get our guests situated?" asked Sister Rosalia.

"Yes, Sister Rosalia," Sister Caramella replied and led the horse around the building.

Rosalia led the way through a lovely rotunda that welcomed visitors. Seraphie held her bag in one hand and one end of Mercedee's trunk in the other, and Mercedee held her bag and the other end of the trunk. Sister Michaela helped Clara with her trunk. They passed under the rotunda, and Mercedee stared up at the spire and then at the stairs winding above.

"Tante Seraphie, have you ever seen anything so grand? Look at the towers going all the way to heaven!"

"Watch where you're going," Tante Seraphie told Mercedee, who was looking up at the archways. "We don't want you to have a great fall before you even find your room."

"Yes, Tante."

Once inside, the girls and Seraphie found themselves in a richly furnished high-ceilinged parlor. They moved past a greeting room and an open area. An archway to the right led to the left, and sweet choir voices echoed through large doors of a concert hall. A wide stairway lay directly ahead.

After entering the hallway, Sister Rosalia stopped and the group set down the trunks and tried to catch their breath. Seraphie put her hands on her hips and exhaled. She was a diminutive woman but strong and healthy for her forty-five years. Her eyebrows were dark, but wisps of hair escaping from under her hat showed streaks of gray.

"We're standing in the main building, where the sisters, Reverend Mother Berchmans, and the chaplain, Father Develyn, live." She pointed ahead. "The Reverend Mother has an office over there." Then she pointed ahead and to the left at a door with a brass plate with the words Reverend Mother in script. "Your quarters and classrooms are upstairs, on the third floor, in the north wing. You'll be in the Immaculate Conception Dormitory. I'll show Seraphie to a guest room here in the main hall. And the abbey is through the archway to the left."

"Clara and Mercedee"—Rosalia turned toward them—"it's September 5, so lectures and lessons begin in one week. You need to be busy becoming familiar with the academy and meeting sisters and other students. You'll also need to organize your attire and class materials. Use your time wisely."

Another nun approached from the long hallway. She was a thin young woman with a kind face and apprehensive smile. "Hello, Sister Rosalia. Are these two new students?"

"Yes." Sister Rosalia gestured to the two girls. "This is Mercedee and Clara. Mercedee and Clara, this is Sister Marianne. She'll show you to your rooms and give you a tour of the student wing of the academy building. Sister Michaela, please help the girls find the dining hall. They're very hungry after the long train trip."

"Yes, Sister." Michaela gave Mercedee a measuring look.

"Thank you, Michaela." Rosalia continued, "Mercedee."

"Yes, Sister Rosalia."

"Tomorrow morning, come and pick up your books

right after vespers. You'll need your reader, practical methods book, scholar's companion, and your catechism. Oh, and this goes for Clara too."

Mercedee and Clara stared at Rosalia, looking overwhelmed, as if trying to take it all in.

Rosalia continued, "In the afternoon, you'll need your literature, history, science, and grammar books. These are fifty cents each." She rubbed her chin. "Let me see. You'll also need three notebooks, paper, pens, and ink. And oh yes, a music book, pencil, and an eraser."

"Thank you, Sister Rosalia." Mercedee struggled to memorize everything Rosalia had listed.

"Hurry now. Dinner is in thirty minutes." As the girls departed, Rosalia turned to Seraphie, who had been watching with her bags. "I'll show you where the guest room is, and we can get some supper."

Sisters Michaela and Marianne helped Mercedee and Clara with their trunks through the main building to the stairway in its center. Additional stairs were located at the far end of both wings. They climbed up two floors then entered the north wing along a large hallway. Their footsteps were sharp on the hardwood floors and echoed from the high ceiling. Ornamental lamps lit the walls, which held small alcoves filled with biblical statues. Michaela led them in silence to a large door standing partially open on the right. The door had a brass placard that read Immaculate Conception Dormitory. Another door on the left had the label St. Vincent Dormitory. It was eerily quiet except for low voices and subdued laughter coming from inside the Immaculate Conception dorm.

Sister Michaela said, "This is where you sleep." She opened the door, and they entered then walked through a row of beds covered with white sheets. Each bed had one nightstand and a dresser. A white curtain surrounded each bed and could be pulled for privacy. Muted voices came from different directions, and a small group of girls sat on a bed several bunks away. There were few empty beds, and

Mercedee was glad to see that their beds were adjacent.

"The kitchen is in the basement, and dinner is in thirty minutes," Sister Michaela said. "Freshen up and come downstairs. Talking isn't allowed on the stairs. When you finish dinner, unpack your trunks. You'll take them all the way to the bottom floor and stow them in the storage room. We've assigned each of you a space on the shelves. You may place your trunks where your name is posted."

Wide-eyed, Mercedee and Clara looked at Michaela.

"Sister Marianne knows where your shelf spaces are and will help you find them. Do you understand?" Michaela asked.

"Yes, Sister Michaela," Mercedee replied as the nuns left the dorm.

5 SISTER MICHAELA AND THE BOSTON GIRLS

Mercedee and Clara looked at the room of bunks, and Clara said, "I'm glad we have these bunks by the windows. We can walk down this aisle to easily reach the door. I'm sure we'll be coming and going quite a lot."

"I love the windows so close. We can see Bedford Basin from here." Mercedee was feeling that her time at the Mount could be a good experience. She had her friend Clara and a week to learn what she needed to know about the coming school year.

As Mercedee and Clara walked to their bunks, a shrill voice with a mocking tone came from a bed on the side of the room. "What have we here?"

They turned toward the girl's voice.

"Aren't you two a sight? A beanpole in a tattered dress and a walking mushroom. You two must be fresh from the backwoods!" The insult came from one of four girls in a group of beds across the large room.

As Mercedee and Clara made eye contact with her, the blond girl who had poked her head through the curtains over her bunk pulled her head back and drew the curtain.

Mercedee at first thought the comment was a joke but quickly realized what a hurtful insult it was. Her anger grew as the words fed the insecurity she had carried with her into the elaborate and majestic motherhouse. She boiled over.

"Well, then, just who are you, Miss Smarty Pants? If we're from the backwoods, then it's a lot better than your home in Rudeville!" Mercedee growled. She scowled at the truly rude welcome she had just received. She looked down at her dress, which was certainly more backwoods than urban sophistication, and her heart sank. But no sooner had her words faded than the door opened again, and in walked Sister Michaela.

"Who said that?" Michaela looked directly at Mercedee, who couldn't hide her guilt and looked back at Michaela with her mouth open. "That is no kind of language to be used in the Mount St. Vincent Academy, Miss Meehan," Sister Michaela said sternly as she approached Mercedee and Clara.

Mercedee felt herself falling out of Michaela's favor, and the very long day was becoming substantially longer. "But I was simply replying to—"

"Mercedee"—Michaela closed the distance between them—"I'm surprised to hear such unfriendly words from you on your first day. We have a code of conduct here at the Mount. Anne is a kind and generous girl, and you should greet new people nicely. You will stay here in the dormitory and pray for forgiveness for your unseemly behavior. Perhaps missing dinner will curb your tongue."

"Um, yes. Yes, of course, but you see—" Mercedee stammered, trying desperately to state her case.

"Good. Perhaps the Lord will grant you forgiveness while Clara fetches dinner. Consider how you should treat others kindly on an empty stomach." Sister Michaela hurried to the door. As if on cue, Anne reappeared from behind her curtain, smiling smugly.

"But that isn't what happened…" Mercedee sighed as the door closed behind Michaela. Her words dissipated in the large room.

Mercedee realized that Anne had played her, and she had fallen right into Anne's trap. In Michaela's eyes, Anne was still a little darling, and Mercedee was the mean girl. Mercedee could feel that Michaela didn't like her from their first meeting. She wasn't sure if Michaela treated all new students that strictly or if Michaela knew that Mercedee was Rosalia's niece and wanted to prove that Mercedee wouldn't receive special treatment. Mercedee had to quickly learn the tricks other students played on newbies so she could keep Sister Michaela at bay.

Mercedee silently sneered back at Anne and walked to her bunk with Clara. When they pulled aside their curtains, their beds were open to one another. Tears welled in Mercedee's eyes as she dropped onto her bed. Clara sat beside her.

Mercedee whispered vehemently, "Anne is mean. Mean and awful. I'll find a way to make her sorry. Just wait!"

"Bite your tongue!" Clara whispered back. "I'm sure she's just testing the new girls. Trying to put us in our place. You'll only make things worse if you try to get even. It's what she wants."

"I'm well aware," Mercedee replied softly. "Anne has undoubtedly done this before, and I'm not going to make it easy for her to get me in trouble again."

"I'm so sorry you can't have dinner, but I have some rolls and cheese in my bag," Clara said.

Mercedee took a deep, soothing breath to calm her temper as Clara continued.

"I know you. You'll think up a great trick to play on this nasty Anne, but please be careful. Sister Michaela doesn't look like she'll forget. You don't want to run afoul of her again."

Mercedee looked at her shoes. "I also have some bits of food left over from the lunch I ate on the train." She glanced at Clara. "But that was a most harsh welcome for us. We were ambushed on our first day. This isn't at all fair. I'm starting to miss Concession and St. Anne's. I already feel very out of place here."

Anne's voice rose above the whispers again. "Mercedee and Clara, Sister Michaela's new peeves! She'll make you miserable!"

"Perhaps, oh kind and generous Anne"—Mercedee replied sarcastically, just loud enough for Anne to hear in case Michaela was lurking outside—"I will give you nothing but kindness from now on."

Mercedee and Clara smiled at each other as they heard whispers from Anne and her friends.

***

Rosalia led Seraphie to the center of the main building and the stairs. They climbed two floors to the nun dormitories on the south side. Rosalia followed a hallway to several guest rooms.

"That was nice of you to accompany Mercedee from Mathilde's in Concession, Seraphie," Rosalia said as they walked down the hallway.

"Thank you," she replied.

"I assume you weren't just wanting to make sure that Mercedee made it here in one piece," Rosalia said.

"You're right, and astute as always," Seraphie said as Rosalia opened the door to a guest room. They walked into a living area with an upholstered chair and couch.

Rosalia lit an oil lamp and led Seraphie farther into the room, past a painted portrait of Pope Pius IX and a round table against the wall with an open Bible on a stand. She opened a door and turned to Seraphie. "This is the bedroom." She moved aside as Seraphie carried her suitcase in and set it on a twin bed against a wall. Rosalia turned on a lamp on a desk. At the end of the room, a window provided a view of a lawn and trees that were starting to show the reds and yellows of autumn.

"Thank you, Sister Rosalia." Seraphie looked around the room. The smell of burning kerosene and mustiness filled her senses.

"I appreciate you providing me accommodations with no advance notice. I care deeply about making sure Mercedee gets here and situated without any problems…" Seraphie sat on the bed next to her suitcase and faced Rosalia, who stood in the doorway.

"But?" Rosalia asked.

"But I also must tell you that I corresponded with William, and he did collect payment from two men who owed him money on properties. I don't know all of the specifics, but he doesn't have all that he was promised in the deal."

Seraphie rubbed her hands together. "You see, 1892 has been a better year for him, but he still needs to settle another account to have all the funds." Seraphie folded her hands in her lap and looked at Rosalia.

Rosalia folded her arms across her black gown. "How much money did he send?"

"There's enough for tuition," Seraphie replied.

"And supplies and books?"

"He's several dollars short. But he says he'll send more before the midyear holiday." Seraphie's concerned look showed that she wasn't convinced that would actually happen.

"I can start an account for now and settle it as William is able," Rosalia said. "Are there any other sources of funds?"

"I don't know of any. My dress shop in New York is doing well, and I may be able to help, but business can be fickle. I'm hoping 1893 will be much better for business in New York."

"Well, it appears that Mercedee is covered for now. But if the economy isn't good this next year and William's deals falter, Mercedee could be left in the lurch. The Sisters of Charity can help students in financial trouble. I can see what's available, but this puts me in an awkward position with Mercedee being my niece."

"Of course, Marie Anne. I can see how that would be

difficult for you. Hopefully, your superiors will show understanding if they know that Mercedee has just lost her mother," Seraphie said.

"I'll try, but I can't make any promises. It will also help if Mercedee excels and doesn't get into any trouble."

"Yes, I'll remind her to be on her best behavior."

Rosalia paused. "Good. Well, thank you for coming. It's always good to see you. And thank you for telling me about William's finances in person." Rosalia turned toward the bedroom door. "However long Mercedee can attend will be good for her. I hope she doesn't end up adrift."

"I as well." Seraphie rose from the bed.

Rosalia clasped her hands and walked into the living area. "You must be hungry. Would you like to go to the refectory and get something to eat?"

"Yes. Yes, please." Seraphie followed Rosalia out of the room, turned off the lamp, and closed the door behind her. Several nuns greeted Rosalia as they passed and walked down the long hallway. Their shadows moved along the wall as they passed sconces with ornate globes on rods suspended from the wall on either side. The hall was quiet except for low murmurs and the taps of their feet on the waxed hardwood floor.

Rosalia, walking with her hands clasped behind her, broke the silence. "I'm sorry I couldn't be there for our poor sister Agnes's funeral. That poor girl. I prayed every day for her last spring."

"It was very sad," Seraphie said. "Such a long fight for survival with consumption. I received a letter from Mathilde with the bad news. I suppose we all knew she could only endure for so long."

"Yes. She survived much longer than most who are afflicted." Rosalia paused near the doors to the lavatories. "Do you need to take a lavatory break?

"Oh yes. Thank you." Seraphie walked quickly and disappeared into the lavatory.

As Rosalia waited in the common area, she heard Sister

Michaela and Caramella coming down the stairs from the dormitories. Michaela was speaking as they left the stairway toward the sisters' quarters. "She just arrived and is already calling another student derogatory names. It was utterly uncalled for."

"Excuse me for eavesdropping," Rosalia said, "but who are you talking about?"

Michaela faced Rosalia and said matter-of-factly, "Miss Meehan."

"Oh." Rosalia sighed as Michaela and Caramella continued down the hallway.

Seraphie came out of the lavatory and heard the talking. "What was that about?"

"Oh, nothing important," Rosalia said. "I'll catch up with them later."

Rosalia and Seraphie went to the stone stairway and descended three floors to the basement. On leaving the stairs, they crossed a large common area with doorways to the storage room and recreation room.

Entering the refectory where food was served, Seraphie spoke up. "Mathilde told me before I left Concession that Agnes had sent Mercedee a letter informing her that her mother wasn't doing well," Seraphie said sadly. "Mercedee tried to arrange transportation from St. Anne's Church in Eel Brook but faced much difficulty. Unfortunately, she arrived just after Agnes passed away."

With a cafeteria-style serving area, the refectory was large enough to seat at least a hundred girls. It was past normal dining hours, but a long counter held containers and covered plates with bread, cheese, and a pan and a warmer with leftover portions of roast beef. Seraphie put a roll, some butter, and a piece of beef on a plate and poured a glass of water from a pitcher on the table. She picked up her food and a fork rolled in a serviette and followed Rosalia to a table at the edge of the room.

"Oh my. Very sad indeed," Rosalia said as Seraphie bit into a dinner roll. "The poor girl wasn't afforded the chance to say goodbye to her mother. Was William apprised of his wife's condition?"

"I'm not sure how much he knew. Agnes wrote to him when she could, but he didn't travel much. Apparently, there's always so much to do in Boston." Seraphie paused. "Mathilde said that Agnes's condition declined rather quickly."

"And William didn't come to Concession for the funeral?"

"No. No, he did not. Mathilde sent several posts as Agnes's condition deteriorated, but William said he couldn't travel and couldn't come to the funeral at Church Point. He had his excuses. He told Mercedee that he couldn't get a ticket on the steamer in time, but we all can make excuses, can't we?" Seraphie crossed her arms. "He's lived in Boston for Mercedee's entire life, in absentia for all intents and purposes. I'm sorry. Knowing that little sister Agnes passed away without her family was difficult, and I do get emotional."

"Yes. But we must be strong. And Mercedee must be strong. Our Lord is watching over her." Rosalia put her hand on Seraphie's shoulder. "Was Mercedee strong after her mother passed?"

"Mercedee was quite strong, judging by what Mathilde passed along. And I don't think she expected William to be there. She hasn't seen him for what must be at least three years. Of course he may not have had the funds to make the trip. He has been struggling financially for at least a year." Seraphie took a bite of beef, swallowed, then continued, "But I was there, as was Mathilde, who had looked after Mercedee while she was at St. Anne's, and Adelaide was there as well as Mathilde's son, Peter."

"Well, that was fortunate," Rosalia said.

Seraphie finished her roll and beef, took a sip of water, and continued, "And Mathilde kept Mercedee over the summer. Mathilde told me she wasn't sure what Mercedee would do with no money to return to St. Anne's, so it was a godsend when the postal came from William saying that he had arranged the funds for tuition."

Seraphie put her fork and serviette on her plate, and they pushed their chairs back. They placed their dishes on the counter and walked toward the door.

Rosalia clasped her hands behind her and looked down as they walked. "I hope William can afford to keep Mercedee here. She needs it. Otherwise, what will she do? Find a husband in Digby? Or a fisherman in Tusket?"

"That's an option, but there are others, and I hope it doesn't come to that," Seraphie said as they exited the refectory and made their way toward the stairs. "I must believe that William will be able to keep Mercedee in school."

***

Mercedee took the last of her clothes out of her trunk and put them in a drawer in a small dresser, not much bigger than a nightstand, next to her bed. She carefully folded her dresses and tried to store them in the drawers without crumpling and wrinkling. She wondered how girls with larger wardrobes would manage. Clara also finished unpacking and sat on her bed, facing Mercedee through her open curtain. She reached into her bag and pulled out a tin the size of a pie pan and handed it to Mercedee.

"Thank you so much. I'm so hungry. You should head down to the refectory and get some dinner," Mercedee said.

"I will. I'll also see if I can sneak you something when I return." Clara got up and closed her curtain then walked to the door. On her way out, she glanced cautiously at Anne and her friends.

Mercedee pried the lid off the tin with her fingernails and picked out a roll. The first bite was delicious but dry, and she looked around for a water pitcher. Seeing none, she put the lid on the tin and got up to explore the hallway. Outside the dorm, Mercedee found lavatories to the left, toward the main building, and the doorway to the St. Vincent Dormitory across the wide hallway. To the right was the hallway and the stairway at the north end of the motherhouse. She decided to try the lavatory.

Walking down the hallway, Mercedee heard footsteps in the stairwell up ahead. Her heart jumped at the thought it could be Sister Michaela. She slowed her pace and looked around apprehensively. A girl's head appeared, rising with each stair as she climbed above the horizon of the top step. As she appeared, Mercedee could see that the girl was a bit shorter than she was, had chestnut-brown hair, and wore a brown dress, a white blouse, and black leather shoes. The girl looked quizzically at Mercedee, and as she approached, she seemed to notice that Mercedee appeared confused. "Hello. Can I help you find something?"

"Hello, and yes. My name is Mercedee. I just arrived. I'm looking for a drink of water. Is there a fountain about?"

"I'm sorry for not introducing myself. My name is Bell Condon. The lavatories are over there." She gestured to her left. "There's a drinking fountain right outside the door. But if you want a big drink, you'll need to go down to the refectory and kitchen."

"Thank you," Mercedee replied. "Are you in the Immaculate Conception dorm? I just moved in there with my friend Clara."

"No, I'm across the hall in St. Vincent."

Bell and Mercedee spent an awkward silent moment, and Mercedee started to walk slowly to the bathroom doors. "It sure is quiet here," she said, subtly urging Bell to walk with her.

"It's early in the year," Bell said, "but in the next few days, many girls will arrive on the train, and it'll be very busy."

"Oh yes. I'm glad I was able to unpack with no one else in the dorm." Mercedee chose not to let on about Anne. She could sense Bell relaxing.

Mercedee reached a drinking fountain near the bathroom door and took a sip. "Ah, that's nice water. My mouth was so dry after eating a roll." She started walking back toward the dorms, and Bell followed. "Would you like to come in and talk while I finish my snack?"

"Sure." Bell sounded timid. "But some of the Boston girls are here, and I hope I don't have to talk to them." She lowered her voice to a whisper. "One word of advice. Don't let anyone see you with food up here. It's not allowed."

"Oh yes. I shouldn't have blurted that out," Mercedee said softly. "Sister Michaela has already disciplined me, and I can't get dinner from the refectory."

"Sister Michaela? You just arrived. My goodness," Bell said.

"I know now what Michaela is like," Mercedee said in a low tone.

As they neared the doorway to the Immaculate Conception dorm, Mercedee stopped and asked, "Boston girls?" Then she reached for the door handle.

"That would be—" Bell was cut off by Anne and two other girls who pushed the door open and barreled through the doorway.

The girls were chatting and walking quickly, and Mercedee was unable to avoid Anne, who was at least six inches shorter. Anne struck Mercedee's hip and bounced into the hallway, nearly falling to the floor. Mercedee stepped back to let the other two girls pass.

One girl said, "Are you all right, Anne?" then turned toward Mercedee and growled, "Watch where you're going, you big clod!" The girl had dark hair and wore an expensive dress.

Mercedee put her hands on her hips. "Well, if you girls hadn't rushed through—" She caught herself and calmly continued, "Excuse me. These doorways are just too small. I sincerely hope you're all right." Mercedee's apology dripped with sarcasm, and she left them, disappearing through the door into the dorm.

Anne and the other girls scowled as Bell, looking at her shoes, followed Mercedee.

As Mercedee reached her bed, she opened the curtains

and plopped down. "Have a seat, Bell." Mercedee suddenly enjoyed the quiet of the dorm without Anne and her lot there. "Where are you from, and why are you here a week before everyone else? I took the train from Concession, which is out by Yarmouth, with my aunt Seraphie."

"I'm from Newfoundland," Bell said somberly as she sat on the bed next to Mercedee.

"Where in Newfoundland? And what's wrong?"

Bell looked at her hands in her lap. "I'm from St. John's. This last July, nearly the whole city burned. It was horrible."

"Oh my." Mercedee sighed and put her arm around Bell's shoulders. "Is your family all right?"

"Our family home was spared by the grace of God. Most of the city and all of the commercial sectors were completely destroyed." Bell paused, still looking at her hands. "Fortunately, we live on the west end, the only part of the city still standing. The large Anglican cathedral burned as well. The west end is mostly Catholic, including my family. The rest of the city is protestant. We don't get on so well with them, and this fire could make things quite a lot worse."

"That's horrible. Is that why you came to the academy early?"

"Yes, I've been here one week already." Bell glanced at Mercedee. "My father operates a fish-processing business. It's on the waterfront and was damaged. Several of his employees lost everything, and their families are living in our house. My father asked the Mount if I could come early, as there's no room there. I just hope his business can be recovered and he can afford my tuition and expenses."

"I hope so too. And I commiserate. My father is struggling to pay for me to attend," Mercedee said.

"Yes. My father is battling with his insurance firm. So much of the city was completely destroyed that many people are trying to get insurance firms to pay out so they can rebuild. The insurance firms are putting the people into difficulty."

"Is Anne from Newfoundland too?" Mercedee asked. "I don't mean to change the subject, but…"

"No. Anne and her friends are from Boston. They have their own little clique. They don't like me and the other girls from Newfoundland. They call us Newfies and country girls. They think we're unsophisticated."

"Of course. That's why you called them the Boston girls," Mercedee said softly.

"I assume that Anne got you in trouble with Sister Michaela?"

"Yes." Mercedee thought for a moment. "I see…" This was welcome information about the factions that existed at the academy and explained Anne's derogatory greeting. The Boston girls were looking for an easy target. Bell was not going to stand up to them. Mercedee made up her mind to show them that she was not one to mess with. "Who are Anne's friends?"

"The dark-haired one is Gertrude. She goes by Gertie, and the light-haired one is Bridgette."

"I see. Are there other Boston girls who came early?"

Bell looked at Mercedee. "Several, and these girls tell the others what to do. But don't worry about them. I just stay out of their way."

"I won't. Worry about them, I mean, although it's not my nature to just stay out of their way." The sound of someone coming interrupted Mercedee's thought, and she looked up to see Clara step into the curtain opening. She held a serviette-wrapped object.

"Mercedee—" Clara looked at Bell and stopped.

"Clara. This is Bell. Bell Condon. Bell, meet Clara. Clara's my friend from St. Anne's Convent School near Yarmouth."

"My pleasure to meet you, Bell," Clara said as Bell looked back shyly. "And I brought you something, Mercedee." Clara offered her the package.

Mercedee set it on her lap, and the serviette parted to reveal two dinner rolls and a piece of roast beef.

Clara lowered her voice and looked suspiciously at Bell then added in a whisper, "Finish this quickly and dispose of the serviette. We're not supposed to have food up here. I'm sure Sister Michaela will be up soon to check." She glanced again at Bell.

"I know," Mercedee said. "Bell told me of the rule against having food up here."

"Clara, I'll take the serviette when Mercedee is finished," Bell said. "I should also dispose of it before Anne, Gertie, and Bridgette come back. You know they'll run to Michaela if they find out."

"Oh yes." Clara looked at Mercedee, who nodded as if to say that Bell was a friend and took a grateful bite of the roast beef. "I take it that Anne, Gertie, and Bridgette are the girls who started this whole row?"

"Yes." Bell sighed. "Watch out for them. We call them the Boston girls."

"I'll stand and watch the door," Clara said, looking down an aisle between bunks at the wooden door.

"Thank you so much for the food, Clara." Mercedee swallowed and said in a low voice, "Bell has shared information on a number of things about life here at the Mount. I'll fill you in later. Bell is in the St. Vincent dorm across the hall."

"I've learned a few things about the kitchen as well. This is certainly different from little St. Anne's Convent School," Clara added.

"Yes, I'm sure it is," Bell said. "And I'll need to get back to my dorm, or I'll get in trouble. They'll be turning out the lights soon."

Clara looked at the door. "That must mean that Anne and the other two… you called them Bridgette and Gertie? Will they be back soon?"

"I'm sure they won't be gone long," Bell said. "As soon as you're done with that, I can take the serviette, and you can get ready for bed."

Mercedee finished the roast beef and one of the rolls.

She tucked the other into a drawer with her clothes. She folded the serviette and handed it to Bell. "Thank you so much."

"Yes, thank you," Clara said.

"You're quite welcome." Bell was comfortable with her new friends.

Bell retired to the St. Vincent dorm, and Mercedee and Clara finished the long day with one more grueling task. They had to move their trunks to the storage room. Working together, they carried one trunk at a time down the stairs to the entry area, where they met Sister Marianne, who showed them their respective shelf spaces in the storage room another floor below.

When Clara and Mercedee finally got to their beds, they fell asleep immediately. Mercedee awoke with stiff muscles and a newfound dislike for Sister Michaela.

***

The sun was still low in the chilly September morning sky, shining into the east windows of the motherhouse as Seraphie, Mercedee, and Rosalia stepped off the wagon and climbed the steps to the Mile House Station Depot building. The midmorning sun was warm, contrasting with the cool breeze coming across the Bedford Basin. They walked to the train platform. Mercedee carried Seraphie's suitcase. Presently, the ten o'clock train arrived from Halifax. It blocked the sun shining through the depot windows.

Mercedee bent slightly to hug Seraphie, who returned the embrace, then Rosalia gave her sister a goodbye hug.

"Thank you so much for coming here with me, Tante Seraphie," Mercedee said.

"You're welcome," Seraphie replied, "and be on your best behavior for Sister Rosalia, will you?"

Before Mercedee could speak, Rosalia said, "I'm sure Mercedee will do her best. And I also want to thank you for coming. It was wonderful to see you again."

"Mercedee, do you feel comfortable? Classes start tomorrow," Seraphie said.

"Yes, Tante. I've already made a new friend and met several of the sisters. It's a very nice place." Mercedee hugged Seraphie.

"I'm glad," Seraphie said. "Take advantage of this. You don't know how many chances you may get in life." Seraphie picked up her suitcase and turned.

"Safe travels," Rosalia called over the hissing locomotive.

"Goodbye," Mercedee called out.

Seraphie said one last *"Au revoir"* over her shoulder, walked into the passenger car, and disappeared down the aisle. Mercedee and Rosalia stood on the platform until the train pulled away, then they walked through the small station house to the wagon and the road to Mount St. Vincent Academy.

It was the first day of classes, and the Immaculate Conception dorm was abuzz with activity as forty-odd girls opened their curtains, got out of their beds, and dressed. Sister Michaela called out above the din, "Be dressed, washed, and assembled for breakfast by seven thirty. No exceptions." She walked across the hall to roust the students in the St. Vincent dorm.

There was a rush to dress and prepare to go to breakfast. Sisters expected girls to be in line on time and to walk down the stairs in single file without talking.

Mercedee sat on her bunk in her nightgown and took some clothes from her small chest and set them on the bed beside her. She picked up a brush and pulled it through her long deep-brown hair as Clara did the same on the adjacent bunk.

"We'd better get to the washroom." Clara gestured at the wall clock that showed ten after seven.

"Yes, it looks like there could be a rush to get in." Mercedee finished fashioning her hair into a bun on the back of her head. She picked up a small overnight bag and a towel issued by the academy and jumped up. "We had better go."

Clara was on Mercedee's heels as they joined numerous other girls headed for the washroom. Soon, the two girls walked briskly back into the dorm.

"I see that we have ten minutes. I think we'll make it," Mercedee said. But when she pulled back the curtains at her bunk, her skirt, white blouse, bloomers, and socks, which had been folded and stacked neatly, were scattered across her bed, and one sock had fallen down on her narrow ankle-length leather boots. She backed out of the curtain and turned to Clara. "Did you see this?" She gestured at her bed.

"Oh my." Clara looked past Mercedee, and Anne and her cohorts several beds away were laughing.

Mercedee said, "What in the—"

"Mercedee!" Clara whispered. "We need to get dressed. They're just going to get you in trouble."

Mercedee raised her hand. "Oh my," Mercedee said loud enough for Anne to hear. "What a terrible mess! I must be more careful with my things." She winked at Clara. "Just wait," she whispered.

Mercedee clenched her jaw and gathered her clothes. She glanced at the clock and dressed quickly. Clara finished dressing and picked up her bag. The girls hurried out the door.

Sister Michaela said, "It's time to go, students!" just as Mercedee and Clara reached the back of the line. The girls' close call clearly wasn't lost on Sister Michaela as she turned and led the line of girls to the stairway and down to the cafeteria.

Mercedee wanted to say something to Clara but held her tongue, knowing that the sisters forbade talking while walking to or from the cafeteria. Mercedee still had to reckon with Anne and the Boston girls. And the best way to make them pay was to find allies. Soon, she would try to find out who the Newfoundland girls were.

At the refectory, Mercedee and Clara put their schoolbag straps on their shoulders and carried their plates and tea from the counter, looking for a place to sit. Most of the tables were full or nearly full, and most of the girls sitting at them appeared to be already acquainted and having conversations. Mercedee looked for a table in the corner, and Clara followed her toward an empty place. A familiar voice cut through the din.

"Mercedee, over here!" Bell waved. She was at a table with other girls and a couple of empty chairs.

Mercedee and Clara made their way to Bell's table. They set down their plates and tea and put their schoolbags beside their chairs.

"Hello, Bell." Mercedee glanced at the three other girls at the table as she sat down. "I'm Mercedee Meehan, and this is Clara La Brun."

"These are my friends, Marie Duteau and Beatrice Lancaster." Bell pronounced "Marie" in the French style and gestured to her friends.

Clara and Mercedee sat down, and Mercedee asked Marie and Beatrice, "Are you both in the St. Vincent dorm with Bell, or are you in the Immaculate Conception dorm with Clara and me?"

Both girls started to talk at the same time then stopped, giggling. "Go ahead, Beatrice," Marie said.

"We're both in St. Vincent," Beatrice said. She was very neat and spoke with a British accent. Her hair was light brown and held back with combs. She wore a dark dress with puffy sleeves above the elbows and a high neck.

"And you're over in Immaculate with the Boston girls. Have you met Queen Anne?" Marie asked, her voice soft with a French inflection.

She had dark hair, olive skin, and dark eyebrows. Mercedee thought she looked like a long-lost cousin of the Potier clan.

"Have we ever." Clara rolled her eyes. "And *queen* is right."

"I feel like she and her friends are watching us whenever they're in the dorm," Mercedee added. "I declare that I'm going to find a way to put her and her ilk in their place."

"That won't be easy with Sister Michaela on guard duty. And Anne always seems to stay on Michaela's good side," Bell said.

"Yes, we noticed that too." Mercedee was quiet, deep in thought.

"Where are you from?" Clara asked the group.

Beatrice went first. "I'm from Fredericton, the capital of New Brunswick. My father is a manager at the large cotton factory in nearby Maryville. But most of my family lives in Cornwall, England."

"We like to tell her she should stop putting cotton in her ears when she can't sleep in the dorm," Bell needled.

"Oh, Bell, I have done nothing of the sort. But I do detest the whispering and carrying on." Beatrice nudged Bell, who was taking a bite of biscuit, with her elbow.

"And you, Marie?" Clara asked.

"Toronto. We lived in Montreal when I was young, and then my father had to move to St. John's, Newfoundland. We lived not so far from Bell's family." Marie paused and took a bite of eggs.

"Did your family lose anything in the fire? Bell told me it was awful," Mercedee said.

"Yes. We lost our house. We were able to move some things out as the fire spread into our neighborhood, but it was terrible. And my family is now living with another family while we try to rebuild. My father may have to move again if the insurance company won't pay." She sipped her tea and continued, "I do not like moving."

"Je vois ce que tu veux dire." Mercedee had said "I know what you mean" in French to commiserate with Marie. "My mother was sick when I was young, and we were always moving."

"I'm sorry to hear that." Marie sighed.

"Mamma left us last June," Mercedee whispered to herself, looking down and moving her eggs and bacon around on her plate with her fork.

"Sister de Sale is our main teacher. Is she nice?" Clara

interjected into what was becoming a somber moment.

"Oh. Yes," Beatrice replied, somewhat reserved. "She's fair. But like most of the sisters, you don't want to get on her bad side."

"Indeed," Bell added, "de Sale is far nicer than Michaela but not as nice as Sister Rosalia. Rosalia is the kindest."

"Well, Rosalia is—" Clara spoke up but stopped as Mercedee shot her a stern glance. "Um, Sister Rosalia met us at the train station on our first day here. Yes, she was genuinely nice."

"Oh yes, Rosalia is kind, but let me warn you," Marie said in a serious tone, "she'll make sure that you take all of your medicine if you catch a cold!"

Beatrice, Bell, and Marie broke into laughter as Mercedee and Clara tried to understand the joke.

A whistle carried across the dining room, and everyone directed their attention to Sister Michaela standing in the doorway.

"We need to go," Beatrice said, and the girls took a last bite and picked up their bags and plates.

En masse, the students filed to the counter and handed their plates and cups to kitchen staff. They then made their way to the door and lined up behind Michaela in the hallway. Michaela instructed them not to talk and to maintain a single file. More than sixty girls marched obediently up the two flights of stairs. There, they turned down the hallway that separated the classrooms for graduates on the left from student classrooms and the library on the right. Another library in the main building was reserved for the sisters.

Walking down the large hall with so many girls, Mercedee was apprehensive and pulled her schedule from her bag. Her hand shook as she read the schedule. Her first class was English, followed by geography, then lunch, and the afternoon classes included French and science. Her teacher was Sister de Sale, who was unknown aside from what Beatrice had commented about her over breakfast.

Bell appeared next to Mercedee as she walked down the

hall. "I have English class first. Do you?" she asked over the shuffle of numerous feet on the hardwood floor and nervous chattering.

"Yes," Mercedee replied. "I think the classroom is right over there." With her class schedule, she pointed at a doorway on the right that a number of girls were filing into.

Mercedee took a deep breath to settle her nerves, reminding herself that she had previously been in new surroundings with a new school, new classmates, and strangers, although St. Anne's was nothing like the Mount. It was nice to have Bell and Clara as old and new friends, but she could feel the divide between the moneyed girls from Boston and herself, the too-tall practically orphan in poorly fitting clothes, a girl who hoped her father could make a deal to pay for her class supplies. She swallowed, feigned confidence, and walked down the hall with Clara and Bell.

Mercedee led Bell and Clara into the classroom. Lamps glowed on either side of a slate board at the front of the room to augment the light coming in through a tall, narrow window. Lamps also flanked a desk and chair at the front of the room, and the tall, thin form of Sister de Sale. Windows at the back of the room looked out over the Bedford Basin and railroad tracks along the shore. Paintings of Jesus, Mary, and a pope from long ago hung above a steam radiator.

The room had twenty-four desks with a center aisle. Students occupied seats in the rear of the room, and the only two empty desks that were together were in the front row, directly in front of Anne, Gertie, and Bridgette. A third empty desk was in the second row on the aisle next to Bridgette. Clara and Mercedee sat in front of the Boston girls. Bell sat in the aisle seat beside Bridgette.

As the last students entered the room and filled the desks, Sister de Sale walked toward the door. Mercedee heard whispers and giggles from the seats behind her.

"Move over, Beanpole. I can't see the board," Anne whispered quietly, and her friends stifled giggles.

Mercedee clenched her teeth and quietly looked down at her desk. She and Clara traded glances, and Mercedee shook her head.

Sister de Sale closed the door and faced the class. "For those of you who are new to St. Vincent Academy, I am Sister de Sale, your teacher and mistress general of the academy. In this class, we do not talk, and we do not giggle. We pay attention, and we learn."

Mercedee opened her book with the hint of a smile at Sister de Sale's admonishment of Anne. Sister de Sale continued, "This class is English grammar and writing. I will provide you with daily in-class assignments and reading assignments that will require you to choose a book from the student library. The best way to learn to write is to read the great authors. Remember that the student library is only open on Sundays so extracurricular reading will not interfere with your classwork. You will need to plan and check out your books promptly."

As the lesson progressed and de Sale made reading assignments, Mercedee grew more comfortable with her teacher. Sister de Sale seemed matter-of-fact and not as harsh and demeaning as Michaela. She made Mercedee want to work hard.

"Now, class," Sister de Sale said as the lesson concluded, "your assignment for next week is to visit the student library, select a literary work, and read the first chapter. Next week, you will receive an assignment based on the reading." Sister de Sale walked to the door. "For new students, the student library is on this floor near the main building. The theological library is in the main building upstairs and is only for the Sisters of Charity. Class is dismissed." Sister de Sale walked to her desk, and students filed out into the hallway.

Leaving the classroom, Mercedee felt something odd on her head. She had put her hair in a bun on the back of her head, but it felt as if it were coming loose. "Bell, would you please look at my hair? Is something amiss?"

Bell moved behind Mercedee. "Why, it looks like the

ribbon has come loose."

Clara also moved behind Mercedee. "Yes, it's loose. I tied it for you myself, and it was in fine shape."

Mercedee faced the two as her hair fell down her back. "I'm sure you did. It must have come loose for some other—" Mercedee stopped short as, behind Clara and Bell, a short distance away, Anne, Bridgette, and Gertie stood laughing. Mercedee started walking down the wide hallway. She held her bag in one hand and, with the other, retrieved the loose ribbon that had held her hair together. "Let's go to the lavatory. My hair will be just fine."

"It was Anne again, wasn't it? She sat right behind you."

"Those Boston girls just never relent," Bell said.

"No bother," Mercedee said. "I won't give them the satisfaction." And with that, she walked into the lavatory. She stopped in front of a mirror and pulled two combs from her hair. As Clara and Bell looked on, she smoothed her hair back and placed the combs in her hair to keep it out of her face but allowed the hair in back to fall onto her high-buttoned blouse. Mercedee then smoothed her hair and said to the mirror, "Let's go to the library."

The girls walked to the hallway and on to the student library. Clara looked at Bell as they approached the library door. "How much time do we have before we have to be in geography class?"

"I believe we have an hour. We'll hear the clock tower chime," Bell said.

When they reached the library, the door was closed, and Mercedee spun around to face the other two. "I just remembered. We can't check out books until Sunday."

"Ah yes," Clara said. "Let's go downstairs to the recreation room instead."

The girls filed into the room and piled their books on a table and pulled out papers from the class. The recreation room had a hardwood floor, several couches, small tables, numerous chairs, and a piano. Lamps hung from the low ceiling, and afternoon sunlight came in through the short west-facing windows that peeked above the land surface, as the basement was only partially below ground. A door allowed access to the park behind the motherhouse, where girls attended physical education class three times a week when weather allowed.

Mercedee spoke up. "I'm going to somehow make Anne pay for this. She's going to rue the day she tried to hurt me. I might paint her eyebrows red while she sleeps!"

Clara and Bell laughed gleefully.

"We're going to have a wonderful year," Bell said. "I never had the gumption to get back at them."

Mercedee thought for a moment. "But it'll have to be perfect. The perfect insult. Everyone has to know about it, but we can't get caught by Sister Michaela. That would be worse than anything Anne could do."

"Yes," Clara said. "She would have the last laugh, and who knows what would happen to us?"

"Anne has been the instigator," Bell said. "And she's never been punished."

Mercedee said again, "It has to be perfect."

***

Classes continued, and Sunday finally came. After mass, Mercedee and Clara met in the main hallway and headed for the stairway where Bell was waiting. "Does the library have a good selection of current literature?" Clara asked Bell, who had been at the academy the previous year.

"Oh yes," Bell said. "It's quite good."

The trio made their way to the top of the stairs at the second floor and walked, panting, to the open library door. They paused to catch their breath, and Mercedee tepidly entered. A young nun sat at a desk in a small office that led to the library. Mercedee stopped in front of the nun and inhaled, but before she could speak, the nun broke the silence.

"Hello. You must be Mercedee. I'm Sister Josephine Precort, but I also go by Joe. I'm the reference librarian for the student library."

Sister Precort paused as Bell and Clara moved into the small office and peered into the library. "I'm in charge of keeping track of books checked out to students and making sure all are returned in good time and aren't damaged beyond normal use."

"I am indeed Mercedee Meehan, and this is my friend Clara La Brun, and do you know Bell?"

"Yes, I know Bell, and it's very good to meet you, Clara." Sister Precort took out a bound logbook, turned it around, and slid it across her desk toward the girls. "This is the checkout book. When you find a book that you want to check out, bring it to me and fill out these columns with your name, the book title, the book number on the spine, and the date. I'll initial that it's all correct." Joe leaned back in her chair. "Each book is due back in three weeks' time."

Mercedee, Bell, and Clara nodded, looking at the list of names and books. Mercedee noticed that Anne of the Boston girls had checked out *The Picture of Dorian Gray*, which had been published only a couple of years prior.

"You may check out as many as three books at once and will need to renew the books if you need more time," Joe continued. "If someone else wants the book while you have it, they may put a hold on it, in which case you can't renew it."

"I understand," Mercedee said.

"Yes," Clara agreed.

"The card catalogs are along this wall"—Joe pointed through the back door to the right—"and the stacks are on the other side."

Mercedee said, "Thank you, Sister Precort."

"Sister Joe is fine," Joe interrupted. "Let me know if you need any assistance with the card catalog or finding a book. And tell me if there are any books in the wrong place on the shelves. And of course, keep voices low in the library."

"Of course." Mercedee walked into the library with Bell and Clara in tow.

The girls saw stacks of bookshelves along one long wall,

and on the other were several collections of card catalogs with small, labeled drawers. Tall windows and yellow-tinted electric lights lit the room. Several tables and chairs were arranged in the center. A group of girls sat around one table, and a few other girls were sitting in chairs and reading.

Mercedee got to an empty table and laid down her writing pad. The three pulled out chairs and seated themselves. "I have an urge to read Mark Twain." Mercedee used a low library voice and smirked.

"Oh, that sounds like you," Clara said. "You're going to get in trouble."

"Yes, I don't think the sisters will like that, even if they have Twain's books here in the library," Bell concurred.

"You know I'm only half serious." Mercedee's voice grew louder. "But I'd love to be reading a book that Sister Michaela—" She stopped short as a nun's habit appeared in the doorway, and none other than Sister Michaela was looking straight at her.

Michaela walked slowly across the room to the girls' table and whispered to Mercedee, "If you don't hold your tongues and keep your voices low, you'll lose your library privilege and have no chance at succeeding in Sister de Sale's class." She pursed her lips and glanced at Bell and Clara, seeming to enjoy the awkward silence. "Am I making myself clear?"

"Yes, Sister Michaela," Mercedee replied softly, looking down at the table.

Michaela paused, and the girls' faces flushed. "Very well, then." She walked across the room and disappeared through the door.

The girls sat in tense silence for a moment, clearly not wanting to speak and wondering what to say. They hadn't been talking particularly loudly before. Mercedee looked at the door and, feeling sure that Michaela was gone, started to laugh but covered her mouth with her hand to remain as silent as possible. That triggered nervous laughter in Clara and Bell, and they also struggled to muffle the sound.

"Are you sure they don't have Mark Twain here?" Mercedee asked, and Bell rolled her eyes.

Clara whispered, "You should pick *Jane Eyre* instead."

"Hopefully, this is not your Thornfield Hall," Bell added.

Mercedee frowned, not having read the book. "Maybe I will. Sounds like my kind of book."

"You'll like it," Bell said. "I think I'm going to see if *Little Women* is available."

"I want to read Little Women too," Bell whispered. "But perhaps I'll check out *Pride and Prejudice* instead."

"It sounds like we've come to a conclusion." Mercedee glanced at the door to see if Michaela was still watching them. "But I also want to get Michaela somehow."

Bell shook her head. "I wouldn't try. She'll get you."

"Yes, Mercedee. You're begging for real trouble," Clara whispered.

"We'll see about that. Oh, and are there any good books in the sisters' library? The secret library that we aren't supposed to have access to?" Mercedee gave them a wry grin.

Bell looked concerned. "I think their library mostly has Catholic Church books. Probably all in Latin."

"Yes, Mercedee," Clara said. "I don't think you need to find out. If you set foot in there, you'll have more than Michaela after you."

"Oh, we'll see about that." Mercedee got up and walked toward the card catalogs.

***

"All right, students. It's been a week since your reading-and-writing-a-synopsis assignment. Leave your synopsis of chapter one from the book you have chosen to read on my desk. You may be excused." Sister de Sale pointed at the corner of her desk and stood behind it as the students filed out of the classroom, dropping their papers on the desk. As Mercedee passed and placed her paper on the stack, Sister de Sale said, "Mercedee, please stay behind. I need to have a word."

"Yes, Sister." Mercedee stepped out of line and waited in front of the wooden desk.

When the rest of the students had filed out, Sister de Sale picked up the papers and stacked them neatly in the center of the desk. "Miss Meehan, I am impressed with your hard work and demeanor in class thus far in the term."

"Why, thank you, Sister. Your words are much appreciated." Mercedee clutched her small bag and writing pad against her chest.

"Are you familiar with what we Sisters of Charity call the Child of Mary status?"

"I am not. Not that I can recall."

"Well, students who are exceptionally well-behaved, are performing well academically, and attend all ceremonies may become a Child of Mary." Sister de Sale's sincere look into Mercedee's eyes was more expressive than her typical matter-of-fact voice.

Mercedee blushed slightly and nervously replied, "Oh. I see." Her mind was a flurry of thoughts. A Child of Mary? That seemed contrary to every sign that she was getting from Sister Michaela. But then, she was doing well in Sister de Sale's class and enjoyed her as a teacher. The offer was still confusing, however.

"I know there are many adjustments that you'll be going through in your first term here at Mount St. Vincent, but if you continue to strive, obey all Sisters, and practice self-control, you may become a Child of Mary." Sister de Sale adjusted her glasses and clasped her hands.

"Well"—Mercedee was both touched and scared by the vote of confidence—"I don't know what to say." She paused. "But I will say thank you. I'll try very hard to become a Child of Mary."

"Very well, then. I've added you to the list of pupils who may attend a meeting this afternoon to hear how the Children of Mary are chosen and what is expected of you. Do your best, and remember, it's not easy, and not just anyone can achieve this. You must follow all rules." Sister de Sale paused. "If you have no questions, you may go."

"I have no questions right now," Mercedee said.

Sister de Sale was a woman of few words, and Mercedee liked that about her. She felt very special to be singled out as someone who could become a Child of Mary, although she wondered how many girls had been told that. Mercedee felt good about herself, but wondered if she could curb her impulses to get revenge and be a very good Child of Mary.

Sister de Sale said, "You should get on to your next class, then."

"Yes, Sister. Thank you." Mercedee walked out into the hall, where Bell and Clara were waiting.

As Mercedee joined them, Clara spoke up. "Is everything all right? I hope Sister de Sale isn't mad at you about something."

"No, no. It's nothing like that," Mercedee assured her. She lowered her voice as Sister de Sale exited the classroom behind her with a book and the stack of papers and walked down the hall toward her office and quarters. "Everything's fine."

"Oh, good," Bell said.

"Do you want to go downstairs and get some lunch? It'll start soon," Clara said.

"Yes," Mercedee replied. "I'm already hungry."

They walked down the hall in the same direction Sister de Sale had gone, past doors to other classes, small groups of girls talking, and a bulletin board with notices of events and ceremonies. At the end of the hall, Mercedee spotted the door to the sisters' library. Bell and Mercedee looked curiously into the library before they followed Clara down the stairs. They dropped off their bags and pads at their dorms then regrouped and skipped downstairs to the refectory.

After lunch, they stopped in the recreation room. Bell chose a small group of chairs in a corner away from girls milling about and seated at other tables. Bell was first to speak. "Mercedee, do you like Jane Eyre so far?"

"I do like it, although it's getting a little scary." Mercedee took the book out of her bag and put it on the table.

"I thought it was scary also, but I won't spoil it for you." Clara took a worn copy of Little Women out of her bag. "Bell, did you get Pride and Prejudice?"

Bell nodded and fished around in her bag, finally producing the book. "It was a good idea to come down here to read. Even with the noise, we don't have to worry about getting in trouble."

They opened their books to their bookmarks and sat quietly. The room was peaceful except for some murmurs from girls at other tables. After a while, the piano came to life, which raised everyone's heads. The song was a peppy version of "Buffalo Gals," sung by none other than Anne, Bridgette, and Gertie, and they were around the piano, facing the other girls.

"What are they—?" Mercedee clenched her teeth.

"Do they mean that—?" Clara asked.

"I think so," Bell added.

"Yes, they're calling us buffalo girls." Mercedee glared at Anne as the last notes of the chorus died.

The Boston girls giggled and skipped over to a table, chortling and talking as others looked on.

Mercedee looked down at her book. "It doesn't matter."

"Good idea," Clara concurred. "We should just ignore them."

"For now." Mercedee tried to ignore her embarrassment and anger.

The girls continued to read and take notes for their assignment until time for classes and returned to the second-floor classrooms. After the final class of the day, the girls quietly filed down the stairs to the refectory for high tea. Mercedee and Clara sat at a table and enjoyed the shepherd's pie served with tea.

Bell reached the table with another girl. "Mercedee and Clara, this is my friend Jean Freal. She's from Montreal."

"Hello, Jean. Good to meet you. I'm Mercedee Meehan." Mercedee gave her a measuring look.

"I'm Clara La Brun. Pleasure," Clara said.

Jean put her plate and teacup down on the table. "It's good to meet you, Mercedee and Clara. And thank you for letting me sit with you." She pulled a chair out, sat down, and adjusted a strand of straight hair that fell across her forehead. She had light skin and dark hair and eyebrows. She reminded Mercedee of her Potier side of the family.

"You're from Montreal, then?" Mercedee asked.

"Yes." Jean spoke with a French accent. "My family escaped from Nova Scotia to Quebec during *Le Grand Dérangement.*"

Mercedee raised her eyebrows. "Really? You're Acadian?"

"Yes."

"My ancestors were also in Nova Scotia before the expulsion. They evaded the British soldiers and were in hiding for years." Mercedee took a bite of her shepherd's pie.

"Really?" Clara said. "You never talked about it before."

"I suppose we were too busy getting into trouble at St. Anne's," Mercedee said with a smile that transformed into a melancholy face as she thought about Mamma Agnes. "But yes, my mother's side of the family is Acadian and hid from the British. Some say they got help from the Mi'kmaq indigenous people."

"That's interesting," Bell said. "My family came from Britain long after that."

"I feel for your ancestors," Jean said. "Life was very hard for the Acadians in hiding. And for those allowed to return. It was much easier for my family in Montreal."

"My mother married an Irishman, and I was born in the United States, so I'm part Acadian, I suppose." Mercedee suddenly felt less connected to Acadian history than Jean.

"You'll always have Acadian blood. It's a part of you," Jean reassured her.

"Yes. I think you're right."

"Mercedee," Clara said, "you never said what your conversation with Sister de Sale was about."

"I didn't want to really talk about it, but Sister de Sale was impressed with me in the class and said that I could possibly become a Child of Mary."

"Really? Is it so?" Bell asked. "That's an honor. It's very hard to become a Child of Mary."

"Yes," Jean concurred. "She must be impressed with you."

"Sister de Sales must see you with different eyes than Sister Michaela." Bell rolled her eyes.

"I'm sure that Sister Michaela sees everyone with different eyes." Jean laughed.

"I don't hold out much hope," Mercedee said. "This is probably for girls much better than me."

"You never know," Bell offered. "Be careful and follow all of the rules."

"That's what I'm afraid of," Mercedee said. "I usually break rules when I'm not breaking rules."

They ate without talking, and before long, Sister Caramella announced that the kitchen was closing and it was time to begin the orderly trek up the stairs to the dorms. A line formed, and the students returned their dishes to the kitchen and filed out of the refectory and up the stairs.

Mercedee was deep in thought about her family and wondering what it was like for the early Potiers. On the last of the stair landings before the top, something came to her, and she said, "Jean, I just remembered something my mother said that Grandfather Ambroise—" Then she caught herself and put her hand over her mouth. The words seemed to echo through the hallway forever as Mercedee realized her error. She had just broken one of the most important rules of the Mount: no talking on the walk to and from the refectory. Feeling both panic and fear, she looked at her shoes and kept walking, hoping against hope that her errant verbalization hadn't been noticed.

Mercedee looked up the last flight of stairs, and she saw over the heads of the other girls that Sister de Sale was standing there and looking down at her. Mercedee lowered her head and kept walking, hoping. But when she reached the top step, Sister de Sale pulled her aside.

"Was that you who spoke on the way up the stairs?" de Sale looked both stern and disappointed.

"Please forgive me, Sister. My mind was somewhere else, and I know it was wrong—"

"Hush, child. You know the rules. Continue on to your dorm."

Mercedee tried not to make eye contact with anyone as she walked down the hall to the dorm door, stifling a tear. She particularly didn't want to meet the Boston girls. On reaching her bed, she sat down and put her face in her hands.

"Are you all right, Mercedee?" Clara's voice came from the adjacent bed. She was obviously aware of what had happened.

Mercedee took a deep breath. "No. Not at all, really. I have to be, though. There's a meeting soon for girls who are eligible for the Child of Mary status. And I have to go, although I know I don't belong now."

"Don't despair, friend," Clara said "If one simple mistake is too much, then perhaps it's too much to ask."

After several minutes of nervous reflection, Mercedee got up from the bed and tried to compose herself as she walked to the stairs and down one floor to the meeting room. She stopped at the lavatory and adjusted her hair. She looked in the mirror into her own life. *There is no one else,* Mercedee thought to herself, her hands on the white ceramic sink. *I miss you, Mamma. Help me now.* She dabbed a tear from her cheek and forced a smile. She left the lavatory and joined several other girls heading to the same destination.

As she took a seat in the classroom, Mercedee's stomach clenched when she saw that the sole sister in the room was Michaela. *Maybe Sister de Sale didn't pass the incident on to Michaela?* Mercedee wondered as Michaela spoke about the virtue of being a Child of Mary and the responsibilities of maintaining such a high standard of behavior and moral standing. She went on about the devotion to self-control so much that Mercedee was sure she was telling them how to become a nun in the Sisters of Charity. She was becoming torn between the need for acceptance, the challenge of achieving the high bar of the Child of Mary, and the urge to flee that very controlling doctrine. She looked at her desktop and thought about the times she and Mamma Agnes had been free, back when Mamma was healthy enough to go for a walk, even a short one down the block. Or when Mamma would read her a story—

"But one aspiring Child of Mary feels she is more important than the standards."

Mercedee looked up from her daydream. She tried to remain calm as Michaela continued, "She thinks she is an angel and that she doesn't have to follow the rules."

Mercedee tried not to look around or blush. She could feel eyes upon her and wanted to hide under her desk or run from the room and the academy. She had never tried to make people think she was an angel. *What is Michaela talking about?*

"This girl does not follow Mary and speaks out of turn." Michaela looked around the room, her round face with its permanently sour expression framed by the nun habit. Michaela only glanced at Mercedee, and for that, Mercedee was grateful.

"This kind of behavior is not the standard of a Child of Mary." Michaela talked about adherence to the traditions of the Sisters of Charity and the importance of not missing any ceremonies.

"But just as the Lord accepts repentance, so do the Sisters of Charity."

The meeting adjourned with no other mention of the incident, allowing Mercedee's nerves to relax. She walked with other girls she didn't know and avoided eye contact in hopes that they didn't recognize her from her transgression on the stairs. Once out of the room, she made her way alone down the hallway and to the stairs.

How did Michaela even know about the incident on the stairs? Those sisters seem to be connected to telephones. As soon as something happens, they all know about it. She clenched her jaw. *Was Michaela just calling me out? Was she telling me to leave? Does Tante Rosalia know? Of course she does. Everyone does. Is this the end?* It was only a handful of words. Mercedee's mind was a maelstrom of anxiety.

She reflected on what had happened and couldn't believe Michaela was accusing her of thinking that she was an angel and could do no wrong. She grew angrier as she ascended the stairs toward her dorm. She resolved to make sure that the sisters knew she wasn't an angel. That she was not that girl. She wasn't a Child of Mary and didn't need the bridle of it, or the ridicule from that squat Michaela.

"How was the meeting?" Clara asked from behind her curtain as Mercedee sat down on her bunk.

"Fine," Mercedee said matter-of-factly. "It resolved quite a lot." She sat in awkward silence. "It'll be time for high tea soon. We should prepare."

"Yes." Clara glanced at Mercedee but remained quiet.

Before long, the sisters called the students to line up for high tea. Mercedee and Clara joined the line that moved slowly down the hallway. Bell came out of the St. Vincent dorm with Marie and Beatrice. Mercedee waved at them, and they responded, taking a place in line. Mercedee moved along in silence but wanted to scream. She wanted to show them all that she wasn't an angel, and that she was in no way a Child of Mary. But she did nothing except slowly make her way down the stairs to the refectory.

Mercedee, Clara, Bell, Jean, and Beatrice ate their meal with little talking.

Clara finally spoke up. "How are you, Mercedee?"

"I'm fine, actually. I've made up my mind. I'm not

perfect enough to be a Child of Mary, and I don't want to be." She took a drink of water and dabbed her lips with a serviette. "But I'm reading Jane Eyre and quite enjoying it."

"Oh yes," Bell said. "Jane is an orphan who meets—"

"Stop. I don't want to know what happens."

"Oh, of course. I'm sorry," Bell said.

"I'm only to where Jane has been falsely accused of starting the fire and has been sent to Lowood School for orphans. I like her. She will not be forced into submission," Mercedee said.

Mercedee Meehan

Agnes "Mamma" Potier

Sister Rosalia

Seraphie Wainwright

St. Anne's Church, 1890 looking east from causeway over bay.
Dark building far right is convent. Courtesy Argyle Township
Courthouse Township & Archives, Image P1983-37.

THE MOUNT IN 1894

Engraving of Mount Saint Vincent Academy Mother House, 1894,
Courtesy of Sisters of Charity Archives, Halifax, image #542.

Actual telegram sent to Mercedee from her
father William

Actual telegram reply from Sister Rosalia to
William Meehan.

6 REVENGE

"Bell, what is Beatrice upset about?" Mercedee asked when the girls met in the hall between classes.

"Gertie insulted her. Those Boston girls have really become belligerent."

Mercedee looked around to see if there were any Boston girls nearby but saw none. "What did she say?"

"Gertie called her an Acadian farm girl." Bell clasped her hands and waited for Mercedee's response.

"That's not surprising," Mercedee said. "I'm not sure if they're just trying to play a game or trying to get us to do something silly and get in trouble."

"Last year," Bell said, "they picked on girls who couldn't stand up to them. I think they're just mean."

They started down the hall toward the stairs.

"You know," Clara said, "I have an idea to get them back."

Everyone walked down the hall slowly until Mercedee's curiosity got the better of her. "What's your idea, Clara?"

"It's Sunday, so let's go in the library and talk about it there," she replied as they reached the door to the library.

They walked inside the library office, where Sister Joe Precort sat while going through a short stack of books.

"Greetings, girls. Is there anything I can help you with?"

"No, thank you," Clara said. "We'd just like to go in and read if that's all right."

"Yes. Certainly. Use the time to get ahead on your studies."

Clara, Bell, and Mercedee walked to a table at the rear of the library and near the windows. They were glad they had the place to themselves.

Clara looked at Bell and Mercedee and whispered, "I noticed that Anne puts her dress in the drawer by her feet. And she's a heavy sleeper."

"Oh yes," Mercedee said quietly.

"Here's my plan. One of us gets up early, before she is awake. We sneak over to her drawer and take her dress. We hide it on the empty bed by the window and pull the curtain so it is not visible. Then we scamper back to bed and pretend to be asleep. She'll be panic-stricken when she can't find her dress and can't get ready for breakfast." Clara raised her eyebrows and clasped her hands on the table. "What do you think?"

"It could work," Mercedee said. "But when should we try it?"

"How about Monday?" Clara suggested.

"Oh, wait," Bell said. "If I remember correctly, Anne's birthday is in two weeks. We can make that a birthday she'll never forget."

"Yes!" Clara whispered loudly. "Wonderful idea, Bell."

Mercedee looked at them as if she were a spy plotting a clandestine sabotage. "That's our plan, then. Put it on your calendar, and in the meantime, watch where Anne puts her clothes."

Mercedee, Clara, and Bell picked up their bags and left the library.

For the next week, they watched Anne store her things before bed, sneaking glances at her while other girls came and went to the lavatories. Anne had a routine. It would be easy to get to her dress, and although it was October, a bit of light entered the room before girls started to rise each morning.

"Are you ready?" Mercedee asked Clara quietly at breakfast.

"Yes. All set. Tomorrow is her birthday. I'll sneak over and get the dress, and you'll have the curtain pulled back at the empty bed near the window."

"Right," Bell said.

Voices drew nearer, and the three girls as well as Marie and Beatrice, who sat at the other end of the table, looked up to see Anne, Gertie, and Bridgette walking through the tables and talking loudly to their friends. They were handing out sheets of paper.

At a table close by, Anne said, "Oh, girls, get your best dresses and come to our ball in the main exhibit hall tonight after high tea. It's by invitation only, and here is yours." She gave them what looked like a hand-drafted fancy ball invitation and walked right by the table with Mercedee and the other girls before moving on to another table, also offering them an invitation.

Mercedee and her friends looked at each other, their faces laced with scorn. When Anne and the others sat several tables away, Mercedee broke the silence. "So. They're having a ball without us. Fine. But I think the worst of it is that Anne will have her dress put away, and it will be very hard to get our revenge."

"Yes," Bell said.

"Maybe there's an easier way to exact our vengeance." Clara took a bite of her meat pie.

"Let's meet at the recreation room tomorrow before lunch and see what we can come up with," Mercedee suggested.

"Good idea," Clara said. "Think hard tonight for the best idea."

"I will," Bell said.

"It's a plan, then." With a dinner roll, Mercedee wiped gravy from her plate. "The Boston girls won't get away with this."

Mercedee, Bell, and Clara finished their dinner and walked up the stairs to the main floor, past the entrance to the auditorium—where the Boston girls would soon be decorating and holding their ball—and on up the two flights of stairs to the dorms. Mercedee sat on her bed and unlaced her black leather boots, which were slightly small and needed polishing. They extended to just above her ankles, where her bloomers, which were normally covered by her dress, began.

"Are you going to turn in early?" Clara asked.

"I'm going to read Jane Eyre for a while and call it a night. We don't need those Boston girls and their fancy ball." Mercedee pulled off her boots and put them under the edge of her bed near the foot.

"That's a fine idea," Clara said, also working on her shoes then pulling a pin out of her brown hair to let it fall to her shoulders.

"Perhaps something in these books will help us with ideas," Mercedee said.

"Tee-hee. Yes, indeed."

The next morning seemed just like a normal day. Mercedee tried to ignore Anne and not get in trouble with Sister Michaela, but she also tried not to be an angel. She still fumed at Michaela because of her comment. Before long, Mercedee was heading into the recreation room again. She walked into the library and picked a table in a secluded spot, where she waited for Clara and Bell, who showed up in minutes.

"Over here," Mercedee whispered with a wave.

Clara and Bell walked over and pulled out chairs.

"Any ideas?" Mercedee asked.

Clara spoke first. "I propose short-sheeting her bed. My sister did this to me once. You go to her bed while she's in class and untuck the top sheet, tuck the bottom end under the pillow, and fold it back up so it looks normal."

Bell and Mercedee smiled as Clara continued, "When

she gets in bed, she only gets halfway in and runs out of bed."

"I like it," Mercedee whispered. "What do you have, Bell?"

Bell put her hands on the book in front of her and lowered her head with a wry smile. "I was thinking we could swipe some sugar from the refectory and put it in her bed. It's nearly impossible to get all of it out. She'd spend a miserable night lying on grains of sugar."

"Oh, that would really show her," Clara said.

"Yes," Mercedee agreed.

"But Mercedee," Clara said in a low voice, "by the look on your face, you have something even better."

"I don't know about that," Mercedee whispered, "but here it is." She looked around the room to make sure no one would overhear. "I like your ideas. They would make her night one to forget. But few people would know about the pranks. She's insulted us in front of everyone." Mercedee paused and looked around again.

"How's Anne been acting?" Mercedee asked, and Bell and Clara seemed to ponder that for a moment until Mercedee answered her own question. "Like a queen. A queen with subjects who follow her around like acolytes."

"Yes, Queen Anne indeed," Clara agreed.

"One way to insult her would be to sarcastically commend her for doing what she's doing," Mercedee whispered.

"But how do we let everyone know about it?" Bell asked.

"We write a letter. An insulting letter with sarcasm. Perhaps a critique of their little ball. It shall start, 'Dear Queen Anne.' The letter praises her for her wonderful kingdom but is also a critique of her royal ball. And we post it on the bulletin board so that everyone else sees it before she does."

"That's brilliant," Clara said hoarsely.

"Oh yes," Bell said.

"But wouldn't the nuns recognize our handwriting?"

Clara asked.

"They might," Mercedee whispered, "and that's why *we* write the letter. I'll write some, you write some, Clara, and Bell, you pen some too. That way it won't be obvious." Mercedee looked out the window. "And if Sister Michaela questions us and she asks me if I wrote it, I can say no. Because I did not. *We* did."

Clara whispered, "When we write our parts, we should cover up the other parts. That way, we can say we've never even seen it. And we won't be lying. I think it'll work."

"I'm in," Bell said.

"Good," Mercedee said softly. "I'll ask Sister Joe for an extra piece of paper and say I need to take notes on a book that I can't check out today. That way, the paper won't come from any of us."

"And we can meet here in the recreation room after lunch when most girls are going to class," Clara said.

"We should have plenty of privacy," Bell added.

"And we can post the letter on the bulletin board in front of the classrooms in the evening when no one is around." Mercedee looked over her shoulder one more time to scan the room. "Think of ideas for your part but don't tell anyone what they are. We'll meet Wednesday after lunch."

"Right," Bell and Clara said as one.

The trio put their things away and rose from the rectangular wooden table. They scampered out of the recreation room. They walked as quietly and calmly as possible to the stairs, but their hearts were racing. They would put the Boston girls in their place.

In the library office, Mercedee paused. "Sister Precort."

The young nun sitting at the desk was thumbing through a library-checkout logbook.

"May I have a sheet of paper for an assignment in Sister de Sale's literature course? I can't check the book out until Sunday, so I need to take detailed notes."

"Well, that is a bit unusual," Sister Precort said, "but yes. Just this time. Keep in mind that I can't do this regularly."

She opened a desk drawer, retrieved a sheet of letter paper, and handed it to Mercedee.

"Thank you so much, Sister Precort. I'm just behind in the class and would never have time to request a sheet from Sister de Sale. You have certainly saved me. Thank you so much."

"You're welcome. And please keep this to yourself."

"Certainly. No one will know." Mercedee slipped the paper into a large textbook, returned it to her bag, and walked out into the hallway to rejoin Bell and Clara. They walked to the stairwell and went to the dormitory floor while trying to keep their excitement under control.

***

Mercedee scanned the recreation room and chose a table as far away as possible from another group of girls discussing the upcoming Christmas vacation. She pulled a textbook in front of her and pulled out the sheet of paper. The thought of Christmas made her heart sink. That one would be her first without Mamma. Papa was in Boston, and it would be impossible for Mercedee to join him. She didn't even know if she would have money for train fare back to Concession. She would love to see Mathilde again.

Mercedee gazed out the ground-level windows at the field west of the academy. The afternoon sun was at a low angle in the southwestern sky. The sun's rays split around leafless branches and lit up the room. She longed to bound out the door and run up the rise to a beautiful view of the bay. She could twirl in the cold fresh air and feel the freedom and life of happier times. The light faded soon, and the room took on the yellow tint of the tungsten bulbs hanging from the ceiling.

Studying and reading in the open space of the recreation room was something Mercedee enjoyed. She dreamed of finishing her schooling and traveling. There were so many adventures to be discovered. Maybe in the West or the maddeningly busy cities like Boston or New York, where Tante Monique and Seraphie lived. Bicycles were for sale, and one could pedal all the way across Nova Scotia.

Mercedee never knew of a time when she and Mamma hadn't been on the move or when a move did not seem imminent. They'd had a house in Boston for a few years, but Mamma got sick again, and they moved into a hotel where Mamma could rest. Times were good then, and Mamma Agnes was healthy enough to stay in Boston for the warm summertime. That life was at once scary and free.

"Hello, Mercedee." Clara's words cut through Mercedee's daydream. "Bell's visiting the lavatory and will be here soon." Her eyes sparkled as they waited to begin their devious plot. Mercedee had such wonderfully evil ideas. Clara plopped her books on the table and bounced onto a chair next to her friend. She squinted into the sun as it illuminated the wall behind her.

"Oh, good. Here's my idea." Mercedee slid the piece of paper out from between the pages of her textbook and placed it on the tabletop between them.

"I have an idea too," Clara said. "I've been thinking about this a lot." From her bag, she took a case containing an inkwell and two pens. "But you go first."

"Shouldn't we wait for Bell? Oh, there she is." Mercedee looked past Clara to the doorway, and Bell was hurrying toward them.

"Hello." Bell reached the table and pulled out a chair beside Clara. "It looks like you're ready to go."

"Oh yes," Clara said as Bell sat down and put her small bag on the table. "Do you have any diabolical ideas?"

"Indeed, I do," Bell replied. "But you two first."

"Ha!" Clara chuckled. "That's what I just said to Mercedee before you got here."

"Then it's unanimous. I'll go first," Mercedee said with a wry smile. She looked at the other table of girls to make sure they were paying no attention. She lowered her head and spoke softly. "My idea is to continue with what we were talking about but make the letter an open letter to Queen Anne and her two ugly stepdaughters. A letter of sarcastic adoration."

Grins grew on Clara and Bell's faces as they lowered their heads with Mercedee.

"An anonymous letter, of course."

"Oh yes," Clara said. "My idea was much meaner but similar. I like it." She smiled.

"Yes," Bell said. "Queen Anne the Magnificent with her entourage of silly tarts."

The three of them laughed. "We can say how fine the ball was, in a truly awful sort of way."

"Oh, that's good," Mercedee said. "A letter to the malevolent and uppity queen from her loyal servants. You are the greatest ruler of all." And they chuckled again.

"But how will we write it so that they don't know that we're the authors?"

Clara tapped her chin. "We should use fancy calligraphy so no one can recognize our handwriting."

"Yes," Mercedee said, "and we'll each write different parts. Actually, let's narrate our parts and someone else write." She gave them a devious look. "That way, if anyone asks, you can say you didn't write it, because you only wrote part, and we can say that not only did we not write it, but we also didn't even see what we came up with."

"Now *that* is a plan," Bell said.

"Give me the pen." Clara unscrewed the cap on an ink bottle.

As Clara dipped the pen in the ink and turned the paper so she could write, Mercedee began to dictate, "Dear Your Highness, Queen Anne of Boston. From your humble, loyal, and lowly servants of Halifax. The unmatched beauty of your drippy nose, droopy eyes, and mussed hair gives us—"

"Slow down, slow down. I have to make this fancy," Clara said.

"Okay. I'm sorry, but I'm on a roll." Mercedee grinned.

"There. Now it's your turn, Bell." Clara passed the paper and pen to Bell, who dipped the pen in the ink.

"Ready," Bell said, "and don't forget Bridgette's thick glasses."

"Ha. Yes, good thinking." Clara narrated her part.

The composition continued until the page was full, and Clara drew a crown at the top and decorations in the margins. When the ink dried, Bell slipped the royal letter into her textbook, and they grinned at each other, barely able to contain their mirth.

Bell put her hands on the book and looked at the other two girls. "Tomorrow morning early, I'll go to the lavatory before everyone rises and sneak downstairs to the bulletin board. No one will be the wiser."

"This could be a wonderful Christmas break knowing that Anne is steaming the whole time." Clara smirked.

"That'll be nice. Oh, and Bell, be sure to hide the letter in case Sister Michaela is patrolling the halls at that hour. If you hear anything at all, just keep it hidden, and we'll post it another day," Mercedee said.

"Oh yes," Clara said. "You never know what Michaela will do."

"I certainly will. I know her all too well." Bell pushed her chair back and slipped the textbook into her bag.

The next morning felt like Christmas Day for Mercedee, her stomach knotted in anticipation. She and Clara remained calm as they emerged from their bed curtains and prepared for the day. Anne, Bridgette, and Gertie walked toward the door with their noses held high, and Mercedee relished the thought of the prank coming to fruition.

With their preparation complete, Mercedee and Clara walked casually into the hallway and lined up for the trek downstairs for breakfast. Mercedee spotted Bell, who was farther ahead in line and looking back at her. She didn't dare speak, but when Bell winked at her, she returned the gesture. Clara apparently noticed and looked up at Mercedee, giving her a silent, quizzical look. Mercedee smiled and nodded, and Clara struggled to remain quiet as the line moved like a silent snake winding its way down the stairs.

As they reached the first steps, the pace picked up, and Mercedee passed Sister Michaela standing watch by the banister. Mercedee returned Michaela's scowl with a tepid smile, tempered by her nerves and the fact that the nun was going to be investigating her most serious crime later in the day.

In the refectory, Mercedee and Clara joined Bell, Marie, and Beatrice at a table far from the Boston girls. They gave each other knowing smiles but said nothing, not wanting the others to know.

"Are you ready for the Christmas break?" Marie asked in her French accent.

"I am," Beatrice said. "I'll be so glad to be done with that geography class and spend some time in St. John's. My father wrote that they're making progress getting his business back up, and it'll be possible for me to go home."

"I'm looking forward to a break, although I'll most likely stay here. Perhaps explore Halifax. Unless the impossible happens and my papa sends me money to travel back to Tante Mathilde's for the holiday." Mercedee sipped from her glass of water and took a bite of eggs. She sat in silence, wondering ruefully whether she would be able to make the trip to Concession. She would love to share her first term at the academy with Mathilde and Peter, but she knew that wasn't likely. She barely had enough money to pay for the school year at the academy. She glanced at Marie and Bell.

"I'm going back to Fredericton for Christmas. Is anyone else traveling?" Beatrice asked.

Marie spoke first. "I'm staying here. In her last post, my mother said the work on the house isn't finished, and our section of St. John's is still in turmoil from the fire."

Bell swallowed a bite of food. "I think I'm staying here over break too."

Relieved, Mercedee added, "Well, it sounds as if we can keep each other company."

"This could be a rather fun holiday," Bell said.

"Yes, the possibilities are endless. Maybe we could go

skating on the pond. Without the Boston girls, we could have a real party!" Marie laughed.

"Now I kind of wish I could stay too," Beatrice said.

"And what about you, Clara? You haven't said anything," Mercedee asked her friend seated to her left.

"I think I'm going home," Clara said to her plate. "I got a post from my mother, and she's ill."

Mercedee frowned. "I'm so sorry. I hope it's not serious."

"Yes, what's her malady?" Bell asked.

"She didn't say. Mothers are never honest about how sick they are."

"So true," Marie said.

"Indeed." Mercedee nodded. "I hope all is well."

"I should think that my father would have sent a note if it was serious," Bell replied.

"That's probably true," Bell answered.

"I'm sure it is," Mercedee said. "And we had better finish eating and get in line to head back upstairs."

"Oh yes." Clara's gloomy face turned into a smile.

Mercedee knew how a mother's condition could be much worse than she let on, but she didn't say anything.

The girls finished their breakfasts, dropped off their plates, and walked across the refectory to the line forming in front of the stairs. Mercedee ignored the ever-present jeering from the Boston girls, biding her time in cool confidence, hoping against hope that someone like Sister Michaela hadn't seen the letter and taken it down.

Soon, they were marching up the stairs. Mercedee was on her best behavior and nodded to Sister de Sale as she passed her on the third floor. Girls streamed out of the stairwell and flooded the hallway, heading to their respective dorms. On reaching her bed, Mercedee gathered her class materials and leaned out to look down an aisle through the beds and at the smug Boston girls. She was looking forward to their retaliation. Anne and Gertie were talking as Gertie fixed her hair. Before the girls noticed, Mercedee leaned back and asked Clara, "Are you ready to go?"

"Wait just a minute. I seem to have misplaced my paper." Clare grinned and shuffled her papers until the Boston girls had left the room.

Mercedee followed Clara across the large room, dodging girls milling about their beds and stepping into the aisle. At that point, nothing seemed unusual. Even in the big hall, the normal number of girls were talking and heading toward the stairwell. Walking side by side, Mercedee and Clara looked around then at each other and shrugged. They descended the stairs with complete decorum and emerged into the hallway near the library. They saw a gathering of students and heard the hum of voices. They glanced at each other again and, that time, fought smirks. They went quickly down the hall, feigning curiosity as laughter spread through the crowd.

Reaching the group of girls at the bulletin board, they heard a girl reading the text aloud. Some girls laughed, and others said, "Oh my!" Another asked, "Who is Queen Anne, anyhow?"

Mercedee looked over the heads and saw Bell on the far side. She tapped Clara on the shoulder, and they moved over to Bell. When they reached her, they gave each other satisfied looks and acted as if they'd never seen the letter on the bulletin board.

Listening and watching, Mercedee, Bell, and Clara took in the commotion until a voice cut through the din.

"What is this?" It was Anne, and she and Gertie pushed their way through the crowd to the bulletin board. They stood and stared at the neatly penned and adorned letter.

"Let's go," Mercedee whispered to Clara and Bell. They nodded, and the three of them quickly slipped down the hall and into their first period classroom. Mission accomplished.

***

Anne glared at the letter, read it, and turned to look through the crowd. "Oh, I think I know who did this! Where *are* y—" Her words were cut off by the sight of Sister de Sale coming out of the nearby classroom and heading toward the bulletin board.

Sister de Sale walked along the wall, and the girls moved away to give her space. "What is all the fuss about, girls?"

"Anne," de Sale said. "Why are you so upset?"

Anne walked toward de Sale and pointed at the bulletin board. "That."

Sister de Sale turned and looked at the board then read the letter. "Oh my," she said softly through her fingers. She almost seemed to be hiding a smile. She unpinned the letter and took it down. "Tell me truthfully. Who is responsible for this?" She scanned the wide-eyed students, who stood silently. She looked through the crowd, but all the girls said nothing.

"This is humiliating!" Anne cried.

"Calm down, calm down." Sister de Sale put her hand on Anne's shoulder, but Anne turned away.

"It was them." She pointed through the crowd at where Mercedee, Bell, and Clara had been standing.

"Who?" Sister de Sale looked perplexed. "I don't see anyone."

"They were there. We know who did this," Anne said.

Sister de Sale looked at the letter again then at Anne. "The letter isn't signed, and we don't know who wrote it. Now, class will be starting shortly, so I advise you all to go about your business, and I'll consult the other sisters and see if we can get to the bottom of this."

The crowd dispersed with much muffled conversation and several girls stifling laughter. Anne stood there, fuming, with Gertie and Bridgette.

The tension was high that day in classes that Mercedee and the others shared with the Boston girls, but it only fueled Mercedee's feeling that she had indeed won the battle over Anne.

In the following days, Mercedee, Clara, and Bell went about their business without acknowledging that the prank had been perpetrated at all, but whenever they could, they would whisper to Anne, "Hello, your highness" or "Good morning, my queen" as they passed her in the hall or refectory and they were certain no one would overhear.

As days passed, it appeared the entire episode had blown over. But one week after the posting of the insulting letter, Sister Michaela intercepted Mercedee in the classroom hallway after her last class. "Please come with me, Miss Meehan. We need to have a word."

"Why, of course, Sister. Whatever is the matter?" Mercedee feigned ignorance as she followed Michaela past the student library to the main building, where the sisters allowed few students to go. They entered a doorway that led to the sisters' library and into a hallway that provided access to a row of offices. She passed Sister Rosalia's office, Sister de Sale's office, and went into another, larger room with a table. At the table sat Sister Rosalia, Sister de Sale, Sister Precort, and Sister Caramella.

Mercedee's heart skipped a beat. *Oh my.* She could feel her palms sweat as Sister Michaela asked her to sit in the empty chair. "Hello," she said meekly. "Is something wrong?"

The sisters looked at each other, and Sister de Sale produced the letter and placed it on the table in front of Mercedee. Sister de Sale was the first to speak. "Do you know anything about this?"

Mercedee turned the letter and looked at it carefully. "Why, no. I've never seen it before. Is this what someone posted on the bulletin board? If that's the case, then I saw it briefly while walking to class but never before that." She looked at the nuns.

Michaela frowned, de Sale showed no emotion, and Rosalia gave her a kind but measuring look.

"Honest," Mercedee added. She knew she wasn't lying because when the group drafted the letter, she was careful not to look at any part that she didn't write, and she never saw it when Bell packed it in her textbook.

"We know that there has been growing friction between

the group including Anne, Gertrude, and Bridgette and you, Bell, and Clara," Michaela said. "I suspect you did this."

"Honestly, kind sister, I didn't write it. I honestly didn't see it before it was posted."

Michaela's face reddened. "You know that this kind of gesture is subject to reprimand, but lying to the Sisters of Charity is grounds for expulsion."

"I'm certain that it is, but I'm also certain that this was not penned by my hand." Mercedee pointed to the last portion of the letter which had been written by Clare and calmly shot back. "I have never lied to you before, and this will not be my first time."

"Well." Michaela sat in tense silence.

Mercedee read the pause as a sign that Michaela had no evidence or testimony about who had written the letter. Michaela fidgeted, probably in frustration that Mercedee hadn't made any confession.

"There are many girls on my floor. I'm new here, as is Clara. We have no reason to start something with Anne and her friends. Please believe me. I didn't write this, and I don't know who wrote that." Again, that technically wasn't a lie because she didn't watch Bell and Clara and didn't know which of them had written which part.

Rosalia rubbed her hands together. "Mercedee, we don't want any friction among the students. As Sister de Sale has said, there are tensions between you and your friends and Anne and hers." Rosalia looked at Michaela, who clearly wasn't happy with the tone that appeared to be letting Mercedee off the hook.

"Help us find out what this was about," Rosalia said, "and if you hear anything, be sure to let us know. And talk with us if there are issues with Anne and her friends so that we can work with you before there's a confrontation." She and Mercedee looked into each other's eyes until Michaela's voice severed the gaze.

"And if I find out that you had anything to do with this, you will be expelled immediately." Framed by her habit,

Michaela's round face seemed to struggle to keep from bursting as the nun's anger grew.

"I understand," Mercedee said softly. "If anything comes to light or if there are any hard feelings, I'll come straight to you."

Michaela, Carmela, and de Sale rose and left Rosalia and Mercedee alone in the room.

Rosalia reached across the tabletop and took Mercedee's hands in hers. "Be careful. Don't get caught up in cliques and conflicts. It's not worth your time or energy. I've been here many years, and in these sorts of feuds, no one wins. Let us deal with these conflicts."

"I'll be careful," Mercedee replied. *It's Anne's play now. She'll be the one who suffers Michaela's wrath if anything new happens.*

"Christmas break will be upon us very soon. You should use that time to focus on your own studies and goals," Rosalia continued. "You're doing well in your classes. You can be proud of that."

"Thank you, Tante. Thank you." Mercedee broke their gaze and stood. Rosalia watched her walk out of the door. Mercedee was overcome with relief. She wiped her sweating palms on her skirt as she headed down the hallway.

Unless Bell or Clara slipped, there would be no repercussions for their prank, and hopefully, Anne had learned that she didn't own Mercedee and her friends. As Mercedee walked along the hall, she noticed that the door to the sisters' library was open. Stacks of books were back there, past a small office much like the office leading into the student library. And Sister Joe Precort was in that office. Apparently, she worked in both libraries. Mercedee paused.

"Hello, Sister Joe," Mercedee said, and Joe looked up. "Is this the sisters' library?"

"Hello, and yes. These are special books and collections that only the sisters get to check out."

"Fascinating," Mercedee said.

Noting Mercedee's interest, Joe continued, "Yes. These books aren't required for courses on the student level, and many are in Latin, so there's no need for students to use them."

"And you manage both libraries?" Mercedee looked past Joe and at the stacks.

"Why, yes. I spend most of my time with the student library, but I also make sure books are where they should be here. Most of the sisters take care of the books anyhow."

"I'm sure they do."

"Well, I need to go through this list of checked-in items, so if you'll please excuse me." Joe looked down at a ledger on her desk.

"Of course, of course. I'll be on my way."

"Oh, and Mercedee," Sister Precort said, "I believe you that you didn't write or see the facetious letter before it was posted, but I can't help wondering where the party who posted it, whoever they are, got a sheet of paper?" She wore a hint of a smile. "Paper is rather hard to come by."

"Hmm," Mercedee said as if thinking aloud. "That *is* a conundrum. Perhaps I should be reading Arthur Conan Doyle instead of Charlotte Brontë."

"No, Jane Eyre is much more entertaining. If I were you, I would stick to Brontë."

Mercedee grinned at Sister Precort and walked out of the main entrance and up the stairs to the dormitory.

"Where were you?" Clara asked on seeing Mercedee returning to her bunk.

Mercedee collapsed onto her bed and dropped her bag on the floor. She lay back on the mattress and sighed. "I can't talk about it right now." She rolled her eyes toward the area of the room where the Boston girls were.

Clara stood so she could see Mercedee's face. "Oh, all right. But please. Sister Michaela just took you away to the main building and you don't want to talk about it?"

"Everything's all right."

"Oh, thank goodness." Clara sighed with a long exhale.

"I have an idea." Mercedee rose onto her elbows. "We do need to talk, and we have some time before supper. So let's see if Bell is about and meet in the recreation room, where we can talk in private."

"Fantastic idea indeed," Clara said. "You rest, and I'll go over to the St. Vincent dorm to find Bell. I'm sure she's over there. I'll be back with her shortly, and we can go downstairs."

"Agreed." Mercedee lay back down on the bed.

A short time later, Mercedee, Bell, and Clara were at a table in the recreation room, far from the door and beyond earshot of two other groups of girls sitting and talking.

Clara was the first to cautiously speak. "What happened, Mercedee? Tell us all about it," she said quietly as Bell looked on with her eyes wide.

"Well"—Mercedee looked around the room—"Sister Michaela called me into the main building. It was a bit scary."

"I can imagine," Clara said.

"She led me down a hallway, past many offices. Finally, we reached a larger room, like a room for meetings. And inside were Sisters Rosalia, Precort, de Sale, and Caramella. And I sat before them." Mercedee used a confident tone, but she couldn't hide the fear she'd felt.

"Oh my," Bell whispered. "I've never known anyone called into the main building. I would have melted."

"Well, they sat there looking at me, and de Sale pushed the letter in front of me and asked if I wrote it," Mercedee continued as Clara covered her mouth with her hand. "I'm sure they expected me to crack open right there. I'm certain Michaela did."

"That must have been so frightening," Bell said softly.

"Oh, it was. But I didn't respond right away. And they just sat there. They didn't follow up with any other information, so I knew they didn't have any evidence or statements from anyone else, so I told them the truth. That I had never seen the letter in its entirety before and I had not written it."

"And that's true, just as we planned it," Clara said. "But

how did they not force you to give up Bell and me?"

"Because I told them right off that I didn't know who wrote what. And that was also true because I didn't know which parts you wrote, Clara, and which parts you wrote, Bell." Mercedee paused and again looked at the girls at the other tables, who apparently had no interest in the three of them. "And I was rather matter-of-fact. And they offered no other evidence, so they could do nothing to me."

"Brilliant," Clara whispered. "As you said, it was just as we planned it."

"Yes," Mercedee said, "but you two must be ever so careful not to let on to anyone, and if they call you in, you must stick to our story. I know Michaela doesn't believe me and would like nothing more than to prove that I lied and expel me from the school. She will if she can. I'm very worried because it'll be much harder for you two to deny any knowledge without lying since you did post it."

"Do you think they're satisfied?" Bell asked. "I'm not good at fibbing, especially to someone like Sister Michaela."

"It appears to me that they don't feel they have a case and are going to let it drop. I know Sister Rosalia and Sister de Sale feel that way. Michaela's hands are tied, but she'll be watching us like a hawk."

"I'm quite relieved." Bell sighed.

"The real victory here is twofold," Mercedee whispered. "Anne and the Boston girls know that we won't just submit to them and that we can be even cleverer than they are. Now it's their play. We can sit back and let Anne try to seek revenge on us. She can be the one getting into trouble. It's already been a full week, so the Boston girls know we're in the clear."

"Right," Clara said. "We just can't say anything to anyone."

"Agreed," Bell said.

"All right, then. Do you promise to keep this between us? Here. Hold hands in a promise ring." Mercedee held out her hands, and Bell and Clara clasped them.

"I promise," Clara said solemnly.

"As do I," Bell said.

They released each other's hands and exhaled.

"Good. I feel better." Mercedee's eyes twinkled, and the other girls smothered their laughter. "We did it!" Mercedee put her hands on the table, exhaling in relief. "Oh, and Bell, you'll be interested that I saw the sisters' library. The entrance is just inside the main building. Joe Precort is also the reference librarian there. I saw many stacks inside."

"Oh," Bell said, "I would so love to get ahold of one of the books from there, even though we're not supposed to check them out."

"Yes, I thought of you when I saw them. Sister Precort said that most of the books are in Latin, and we probably would never want them." Mercedee rested her elbows on the table and clasped her hands.

"I'd still like to—Oh no, look who found us." Bell nodded at the door as Anne burst through, followed by Gertie and Bridgette.

Anne stopped and scanned the room. Her hair was in a bun, and she wore a fancy dark ankle-length dress that hung below her perfectly tailored white blouse with puffy shoulders and a snug collar. Her gaze fixed on Mercedee, who sat tall and showed no concern for Anne at all. Anne led Gertie and Bridgette over to the table.

"You're in trouble, Mercedee," Anne said. "I told Sister Michaela that you wrote that insulting letter, and she's going to punish you."

"Oh really, your highness?" Mercedee calmly watched Anne's blood pressure rise. "For your information, I didn't have anything to do with the letter. So you should find Sister Michaela and apologize for your false accusation."

"You're not being truthful. And you will pay for this." Anne put her hands on her hips.

"As I told Sister Michaela during my interrogation—and you should know that your baseless accusations led to my sequestration and questioning—I did not write the letter and never saw it before it was posted on the bulletin board. And I did not in any way lie."

"Your interrogation? Sister Michaela took you to the main building?"

"That, she did. Along with Sisters de Sale, Rosalia, and Caramella."

"Oh."

"I told them the unvarnished truth. So no one in this room will pay for the letter, as I presume that no one will pay for the ball that you invited none of us to and flaunted in our faces." Mercedee leaned forward and raised her voice slightly. "In some ways, I wish I *had* written the letter, because you *are* acting like a queen. But I don't need a queen, and I don't care what you do or who you tell about the letter. You'll never know who wrote it or how it was posted."

Anne started to speak but was clearly aghast. She stood with her mouth open.

"My dear Anne, I would like to ask you to refrain from any further mocking or jeering of me or my friends. I will not hesitate to report any such behavior to the sisters, the very sisters who know that I am not responsible for the rather clever letter."

Anne's expression softened, and her shoulders drooped slightly. She was facing checkmate. She turned and walked to the door with Gertie and Bridgette close behind.

Once they were gone, Clara said, "I would say that went well."

And the threesome burst into laughter.

***

No posts came from Mathilde or Papa William in the final weeks of the term, and Mercedee realized that she would be spending Christmas at the Mount with Bell. Clara had to return to New Brunswick because of her ill mother, and most of the other girls had gone home.

Mercedee and Bell walked out into the winter sun around the convent gardens and talked about their plans. They laughed uproariously at the pranks they could pull if they got the chance. Mercedee's eyes twinkled at the thoughts of revenge and hilarity. During cold, wet storms blowing northward along the Atlantic seaboard, she spent her time reading and writing letters to her father in Boston.

Her father always professed his love for Mercedee and said that he hoped his latest deal would finally yield the payoff that would provide financial security for them. He promised he would have money and they would live together in happiness.

Mercedee stared through the dormitory window that thudded with the impact of large raindrops carried in from the Atlantic Ocean by gale-force winds. The windowpane was cold, but warm air rose up from a steam radiator to her right. The room was quiet. Bell was her only close friend who'd remained at the academy for the three weeks of solitude, and of the other twenty-odd students who stayed, Mercedee knew only Marie.

Mercedee was deep in thought and melancholy. The Christmas of 1892 was her first without Mamma Agnes. Her mind drifted back to the previous Christmas. She had made the short trip from St. Anne's to Concession, where Tante Mathilde was caring for her mother. Mamma was thin and weak but in good spirits. It seemed she would perhaps hold her own, and in Mercedee's most optimistic moments, she'd imagined Mamma improving. Maybe even making it to Church Point for Easter service.

"Mercedee, would you like to get some lunch at the refectory?" Rosalia's soft voice broke the silence. "Pardon me if I startled you."

Mercedee relaxed and exhaled upon seeing Rosalia's face framed in the white coif.

"Oh yes. Yes, Sister Rosalia. Thank you for reminding me." Mercedee dabbed her eyes with her handkerchief. "I hadn't thought to get lunch."

"Shall we, then?" Rosalia asked.

"Certainly." Mercedee pocketed her handkerchief then rose and followed Rosalia across the dormitory and into the hallway.

There, Mercedee walked alongside Rosalia and asked, "Do you stay here by yourself every Christmas break, Tante Rosalia?"

After several steps, walking with her hands behind her back, Rosalia replied, "Normally. But I'm not strictly alone. There are other sisters here, and we have things to do in Halifax."

"Oh? What do you do in Halifax?"

"Well, the Sisters of Charity help with families that are poor, and we serve Christmas dinner at the church in Halifax. We also have the Christmas Eve mass here at the academy. People come from the countryside." She looked at Mercedee as they started down the stairs.

"Goodness." Mercedee sighed. "You have a busy Christmas."

"Would you like to help serve dinner? I'm sure that would be an improvement on staying here on Christmas Day." Rosalia's hand slid down the smooth, dark wood banister, and she glanced at her niece.

Mercedee thought briefly. "I think that I would like that. My friend Bell is here, too, with little to keep her busy. May I ask if she would like to help also?"

"I don't see why not," Rosalia said. "Let me know if she would like to go."

Mercedee and Rosalia walked to the counter in the refectory room, and served themselves roast beef, carrots, and potatoes. There was a scattering of students and nuns at the tables, eating and talking in low voices. Rosalia led Mercedee to a small table away from the others, and they sat facing each other.

After finishing a couple of bites, Mercedee said, "Papa doesn't sound like he's going to be able to afford to pay for the academy after this year."

"Has he said as much in a letter?" Rosalia asked before taking a sip of tea.

Mercedee moved her food around with her fork. "Not

exactly. But he hasn't said anything about his mine in Truro. Or any other deals. I thought maybe Mamma had a portion of some woodland. I just don't know. I have a distinct feeling that nothing is going to sell, and I'm going to have to find a new place to live."

"We don't know that yet," Rosalia countered. "If you focus on your studies and do well in the spring term, you never know what might happen."

"But it's so uncertain. Papa is always hopeful, but I've learned not to be overly optimistic."

Rosalia held her cup of tea in front of her chin with both hands. A wisp of steam rose in front of her eyes, illuminated by an incandescent bulb hanging from the ceiling. "I agree. But if you take care of what you can, you'll have time later to sort out the things that you can't control."

Mercedee took a bite and chewed thoughtfully. "I suppose. But it still makes me uneasy."

"Who knows what you'll decide in the span of several months?" Rosalia continued to sip her tea. "You may decide to join the sisters," she said quietly. She studied Mercedee's face, perhaps hoping Mercedee would choose a path that was more structured.

"I don't know, Tante. I don't think I fit well with the church. I try my best but still get into trouble."

Rosalia said, "As you mature, it may become easier to live according to the order and regimen of a convent."

"Perhaps. But you see, there's so much that I want to do on my own."

Rosalia gave her a quizzical look.

"You know, travel," Mercedee said. "I want to see the West. To row boats and ride bicycles. I want to ride a train all the way across the country. But…"

Rosalia's expression changed to one of concern. "But what?"

"But…" Mercedee thought for a moment. "But I have no resources and little hope for any. I'm just a girl without a home who must ask relatives for help. I want to be my own person and not passed around in the family like an unwanted pet."

Rosalia set her tea down and reached across the table with her thin hands that showed her nearly fifty years of age. Mercedee put her hands on Rosalia's.

"I hope you don't feel that way," Rosalia said. "We're family, and I'm sure my sisters will be willing to help because they care about you. Your half-brother, Ferdinand, lives with Monique, and he doesn't feel like he's imposing, I'm sure. You're almost sixteen and maturing quickly. Something will turn out."

"I suppose." Mercedee sighed. "But Mathilde is going to be traveling this coming summer, and I just wish I knew where I'm going and if there's a chance that I'll be back here next year."

Mercedee looked at the light coming into the refectory from the open door. "Last summer, I felt this way. I had not heard from Papa, and I wondered if I would remain in Concession. I love Tante Mathilde, and Peter is fun to be around, but what would my life be? Would I end up married to a fisherman in Tusket?" She looked at Rosalia. "Then Papa found money for tuition. I despair that next time, he will not."

"I would like to suggest that you concern yourself with what you would most like to do and where you'll have the most chance for security. You may not want to stay with Mathilde, but if you're off on your own, one bad turn could take you to an awfully bad place." Rosalia sipped her tea. "The feeling of uncertainty is because you've not made up your mind where you'll go if you can't come back here. You have some control over that."

"Yes," Mercedee said. "I'll have to see what my options are if I can't return. I wish I didn't have to think of such things after only half a year here."

"I understand," Rosalia whispered. "Life may feel very day-to-day right now. But there's one constant. You. Try to make the best choices and keep your dreams at hand. You may well end up on that train to British Columbia."

"I guess I'll just wait and see and make the best of the options that present themselves," Mercedee said.

"I think that's your best choice." Rosalia smiled then took the last sip of her tea. "Would you like to go now?"

"Yes. I think Bell said she was going to be reading in the recreation room." Mercedee stood and picked up her plate and teacup. "I'll take a look."

They returned their dishes to the kitchen and traversed the large room. Outside, Mercedee bid Rosalia a good day and peeked into the recreation room. Bell saw Mercedee and put down the book she was reading and waved her over.

"How are you doing?" Mercedee asked when she arrived at the table.

"Well, but I wanted to let you know that I was at the main office, and I think I saw that you have a letter. I didn't mean to look, but I couldn't help noticing your name." Bell placed her bookmark in the book and closed it. "Do you want to go check?"

"Certainly. I would love to get a letter today. Let's go, if you're done and want to go."

"I've read enough for one day." Bell pushed her chair back.

Bell and Mercedee hurried up the staircase to the main floor. The sisters kept mail in an office by the main entrance. The girls walked through the office door and along a counter. A nun sitting behind the counter looked up as the girls walked in.

"Hello," she said. "How may I help you?"

"My name is Mercedee Meehan. Do I have any mail waiting to be picked up?"

The nun put her book down and got up and checked the alphabetized boxes along the wall. "I'll certainly look and see. You said Meehan?"

"Yes. Meehan," Mercedee replied as the nun walked along the boxes to the letter *M*.

The sister looked inside and pulled out several

envelopes. "Let's see." She flipped through them. "Yes, there is a letter for you, um, Mercedee," she said as she read the name on the envelope. She walked to the counter and handed over the letter.

"Thank you so much, Sister..."

"Ruth."

"What?" Mercedee asked, confused, and remembered that sisters were to be addressed by their names as well as Sister. "Of course. Thank you, Sister Ruth. Have a nice day."

She and Bell left the office as Sister Ruth wished them the same. On reaching the main hallway, Mercedee looked at the envelope. She expected it was from her father, but when she saw the return address, she squealed in surprise.

"Bell, I can't believe my eyes. It's a letter from my dearest friend, Lottie Kilgore." Mercedee lifted the flap and slid out a letter sheet. She stopped walking and started reading.

Bell stood and watched. Mercedee lowered the paper and looked at her.

"Lottie is my friend from Boston. Actually, Melrose Highlands, which is just north of Boston. When Mamma and I lived in Melrose Highlands, Lottie and I became the best of friends."

"I don't remember you speaking of her," Bell said.

"No, I guess there's been so much going on here I haven't had much of a chance to talk about old friends." Mercedee slid the letter back into the envelope. "Perhaps I'll read it in the recreation room."

The two made their way downstairs to the unoccupied recreation room and sat in comfortable chairs facing windows filled with diffused early-afternoon light. The sun quickly disappeared behind the cloak of a storm blowing off the Atlantic Ocean, which was only a few miles east of the academy. Cold rain mixed with snow was moving over the land toward Mount St. Vincent, and Mercedee sat and watched the sun disappear as large flakes drifted past the windowpanes. Snow was sticking to the grass in the field.

Bell took a book from her small bag, opened it to a bookmark, and started to read.

Mercedee had been waiting to read her letter. She hadn't heard from Lottie in some time and wanted to savor the text. She had met Lottie when they were both only five years old. Lottie lived in the Melrose Highlands, where Mercedee and Mamma lived with Papa when things were good, both financially and regarding Mamma's health. That seemed like a long time ago. She and Lottie played in their adjoining backyards. She remembered the summer sun on the oak and poplar trees, the swing that hung from one of the strong branches, and Lottie's doll collection. They spent afternoons playing when Mamma was weak, and that cemented their bond.

But that summer faded, and the leaves turned to brilliant colors of the New England autumn. And Mamma's health also faded. The cold, dry air of November irritated Mamma's lungs, and she deteriorated under the weight of tuberculosis. So, Papa thought it best if Mamma went south for the winter, where the warmer, moist air might help her fight the dreaded disease.

They sold the house, and Papa moved to an apartment in downtown Boston near his office in the Globe Building on Newspaper Row in the center of the city. After many hugs and tears, Lottie and Mercedee parted, and she and Mamma boarded a train for North Carolina.

Over the years, whenever Mercedee had visited Boston, she made sure to visit Lottie. When she learned to write under Mamma's tutelage, she wrote Lottie short letters from wherever she and Mamma were. She dreamed of settling down somewhere close to Lottie or a place where she could take day trains into the city and visit, but that life was far away from the academy.

Lottie's letter included a small picture of her and told of her family and of the school she was attending in Boston. They had just averted disaster when lightning struck their house. Mercedee so enjoyed Lottie's playful prose, and her letter was, as always, too short. She read it again and resolved to write Lottie back as soon as possible to describe life at the academy. She folded the letter and slid it back into the envelope as Bell put her book down.

"I must write back to Lottie at once," Mercedee said mostly to herself.

"You certainly have time now." Bell smiled. "And I have had perhaps too much time to think."

"I must ask what you're thinking about, but I worry it could get me into more trouble." Mercedee chuckled.

7 THE FORBIDDEN LIBRARY

"All right. I'll ask. What are you thinking about, Bell?" Mercedee spoke across a small table in the recreation room.

"I've been thinking about the sisters' library again." Bell pushed a strand of wavy blond hair from her cheek.

"Oh?" Mercedee tried to shift her mind from Lottie and Boston back to present company.

"Yes. Remember when we were curious about the library and wanted to get one of the books?"

"I think you were the one who wanted to get one of the books, but yes."

"And you got in trouble for that letter to Anne and were allowed into the main building. You saw the library and how to get into it." Bell placed a bookmark in her book and closed it.

Mercedee furrowed her brow and folded her hands on the table. "I guess I was in a bit of trouble, and I was taken back there. I didn't actually go on my own." She paused, thinking about the section of the building she had seen. "There was a small office where Sister Joe Precort guards the entrance, much like our library."

"And Sister Joe likes you, correct?"

"Well, she's nice and is never harsh with me," Mercedee

said tentatively. Then she remembered Sister Joe and the sheet of paper. "Now that I think of it, Sister Joe could be an asset."

"Oh, very well." Bell smiled, picked up her book, put it in her bag, and whispered, "Here's my plan. The break is almost over, and when classes start, the sisters will all be busy. During the morning when only Sister Joe is there, I could go in and ask her about an obscure book that I need for class, just for a reference. Of course, the book isn't in the student library. When she goes to look for it, you can slip in and snatch a book that you're interested in." Bell grinned.

"Perhaps one of those meditation books that they're always using," Mercedee suggested.

"Right."

"All right. So we get the book." Mercedee looked around to make sure no one was eavesdropping. "But how do we get it back without the sisters noticing? This would be awfully bad if we get caught."

"I haven't thought that through yet." Bell sighed. "But it couldn't be that hard. Maybe we could slip it back on Joe's desk when she's out. She won't know how it got there and will probably just put it back on the shelf. The main thing is that no one can know that the book was taken."

"That just might work," Mercedee said thoughtfully. "I'll think about the plan a bit more."

The last days of Christmas break went by quickly, and Mercedee traded letters with her father and Lottie. Anne and the Boston girls returned, and it seemed that the level of tension had receded. At least Anne hadn't made any more snide remarks. Mercedee welcomed that change, as she had other things to deal with.

Clara also returned, and Mercedee and Bell informed Clara of the book plot. She chuckled nervously but agreed it would be fun to pull off. "But after that last caper where Mercedee almost got caught, are you two sure you want to try a prank so brazen?" Clara whispered to Mercedee, who was lying on her bunk with her arm on her pillow.

"This daring plot will have to be at the perfect moment," Mercedee said. "The sisters aren't even thinking we would do such a thing. The book will be out and back in before they know it."

"All right, but you had better be careful."

"We will. And this is Bell's idea. I'm just helping out." Mercedee rolled over onto her back. "And you're correct. We can't get caught."

Classes started again, and as they could, Bell and Mercedee would walk past the sisters' library and get glimpses of the library door. But just as they were about to set a date to carry out their plot, their plans were dashed.

Mercedee woke up with her head pounding, and she sneezed into her handkerchief. She sat up in bed and put her feet on the floor, holding her head. In front of her, Clara was in bed coughing and moaning too. The start of the new term brought all of the students back and along with them, la grippe.

"Oh my," Mercedee gasped. "This is terrible."

"Yes, it is," Clara said. "Let's get dressed and go to the infirmary."

"All right. But let's wait until we have breakfast. We may feel better then." After a hot breakfast, they both felt better, but Sister Fidelis heard them sneezing and coughing and took them to the infirmary.

Sister Fidelis was a cold, unfeeling nun who was convinced that Mercedee—and all students for that matter—had too many privileges. She gave the girls a dose of horribly sweet cough medicine and a jar of mentholated chest rub for bedtime. The cough medicine tasted horrible and didn't seem to afford much relief from the cough. Mercedee dreaded the thought of having to take more. She and Bell suffered through class, and after dinner, they tried to turn in early.

"What did Sister Fidelis say to do with this mentholated rub?" Mercedee looked at the small jar Sister Fidelis had given them. She opened the lid and wrinkled her nose at the strong smell.

"She said something about rubbing it on your chest. And it sure smells."

Mercedee sat on her bed, hunched over the jar. "It's strong, but it's doing wonders for my nose. I can breathe easier."

"That's good. I could use some clearing of my nose." Clara dabbed her nose with a handkerchief.

Sister Rosalia appeared around the end of Mercedee's bunk. Her eyebrows lifted as she saw the menthol jar and cough medicine. "What have you done now?" she asked as the girls shot her quizzical glances.

"Erm, I don't know," Mercedee stammered. "I guess we caught a cold. And we got this mentholated rub from Sister Fidelis, but we're not sure how to—"

"Lie down," Rosalia interrupted, taking the jar from Mercedee. "I'll show you how."

Mercedee slid beneath the blanket and lay back on her pillow.

"Now unbutton your nightgown a couple buttons. You, too, Clara," Rosalia continued impatiently, pulling down the blanket so Mercedee could access her nightgown.

Clara also lay down and unbuttoned her gown.

"You just want to put it on your upper chest from your throat to your sternum. Like this." Rosalia sat on the side of Mercedee's bed, dipped out some of the greasy light-colored ointment with two fingers, and rubbed it across Mercedee's chest and up to her collarbone. The vapors penetrated Mercedee's sinuses, and her skin felt cold under it. Overall, it was nice.

"You're quite lucky girls because this is new and much kinder to your skin than what I had to use when I was young." Rosalia noted that the new mentholated ointment had recently been invented by a Dr. Vick in North Carolina.

It became apparent that Sister Rosalia considered herself the head nurse in the academy. She was strict about students taking their medicine and seemed to believe the students could have somehow prevented their illnesses.

"How does that feel?" Rosalia asked.

"Nice. Um, just fine. I'm sure it will help me slee—"

"I can't believe the troubles that follow students at the beginning of term," Rosalia said. "I have so many duties and obligations. And now I must take care of you. Lord, please provide me with strength."

"You know, Sister, I really don't feel that bad," Mercedee said meekly.

"Every year, I tell the students to stay out of the cold and eat well, but do they? No." Rosalia dipped some more rub from the jar and applied it to Mercedee's chest.

Muffled laughs came from beds in the distance, and Mercedee knew she was going to be so humiliated going to breakfast in the morning while smelling of the concoction.

Rosalia looked at Clara. "You need some of this too?"

"Yes, Sister. But I saw you putting it on Mercedee, and I'm sure I can do the same."

Rosalia paused. She glanced across the room at the laughter and back at Mercedee. She replaced the lid and handed the jar to Clara. "Now you both be careful. Don't get this on your nightgowns or bedding. It's hard to wash out. And one other thing. You need another dose of cough medicine." Rosalia reached into her gown pocket and produced a small bottle and a spoon as the girls tried to hide their displeasure. Rosalia took off the cap and poured some into the spoon. "Here you go." She dosed both girls and admonished them to come by her office after breakfast. "I don't want you coughing through classes. Some of the other girls may come down with this, and I will have to come take care of them." She looked pointedly at the girls behind the curtains.

"Yes, Sister," Clara and Mercedee said together as Rosalia walked toward the door.

When Rosalia left, several girls chuckled and laughed. Mercedee and Clara rolled their eyes.

"That cough medicine tastes horrible. I am glad there is some left for others who may have come in contact with our germs." Clara said.

"I don't think it even does anything for my cough," Mercedee said. "I think I'm going to get a drink of water to wash the taste away."

"Good idea."

They both scurried to the door.

Sister Rosalia doctored them carefully for several nights until Mercedee convinced Rosalia that she was getting better. The girls in their classes teased them—some friendly and some not—about having developed a permanent aroma of mentholated rub.

One day, Bell and Mercedee were walking between classes. Mercedee felt better, although her cough lingered. They came upon the main building's door and paused to peer through the window. Sister Joe Precort was the only one watching the library entrance, and no one else was around at ten thirty in the morning. They looked down the hall toward the conference room and Rosalia's office. An office door opened, and Sister Fidelis walked briskly toward the main door. Before Mercedee and Bell could move, Sister Fidelis quickly pulled the door open and stepped through, nearly walking into them. Mercedee struggled to keep from dropping her cloak. Fidelis turned and, clearly surprised, shot them a stern look. Her narrow face had very French olive skin, and her dark eyebrows and eyes pierced through her white habit. "Don't you have somewhere to be? Maybe class, yes?"

"Yes, yes, of course," Bell replied.

"We were walking to the lavatory," Mercedee fibbed. "Let's go," she told Bell, and they hurried that way.

"Humph. All right, then," Sister Fidelis replied and walked on down the hall.

Sister Rosalia came out of the main door and saw the girls. "Is your cold abating, Mercedee?"

Mercedee started to answer but had a coughing fit. She

finally stopped coughing and tried to talk, but Rosalia cut in, "Come with me. There's a nice warm office right in here." She opened the door, and Mercedee and Bell followed. Rosalia continued past the library to the second door and motioned them inside.

Bell asked, "May I wait here with Sister Joe?" Sister Rosalia nodded as she opened an office door.

"This is Sister de Sale's office," Rosalia said. "Relax in here on the cot or sofa until she gets here. She'll give you some more medicine for your cough, Mercedee."

"Yes, Sister Rosalia." Mercedee sat on the small sofa.

"I must go to the parlor at the main entrance and meet a visitor from Halifax," Rosalia said as she opened the door and walked out and down the hall.

After several minutes, Mercedee grew restless. She pushed the office door open. Bell was standing and chatting with Sister Precort. Mercedee waved for Bell to join her.

"I'm waiting for Sister de Sale," Mercedee said. "Sister Rosalia said she wouldn't be long."

"Oh," Bell said, "I got a good view of the library. There are several interesting books just behind Sister Joe."

"Really?" Mercedee coughed into her fist. "You must be set on doing this."

"I was starting to wonder, but now it looks so easy." Bell bent and looked through the crack in the door, which was slightly ajar. "From that rack of books, one could slip in and take one in the matter of a second or two."

"And by 'one,' you mean me?"

"Well, I could watch at the door," Bell offered. "And you have that shawl. A book would fit nicely underneath it, and no one would know."

"You want to take a book right now? Oh my."

"Why not? We have an opportunity."

"I agree that we do. Be very quiet. If we hear anyone in another office, we call it off." Mercedee looked down the hall through the door crack.

"Sit down. I see someone. I'm not sure who," Mercedee

whispered as voices came from the hallway. They quickly returned to their seats. They listened intently as Sister Michaela talked to Sister Precort about needing help in a classroom. Presently, both sisters left.

Bell and Mercedee looked at each other and then the open door. Stealthily, Mercedee rose and moved to the door and looked each way. "I don't think there's anyone out there."

Bell joined her at the door and walked into the hall. Mercedee went to the library entrance and saw no one. Bell quickly headed down the hall, looking into the offices and conference room. She saw no one either, so she returned to Mercedee and whispered, "I'll go outside as a lookout. You grab a book, and I'll signal through the door if anyone's coming."

Mercedee thought for a second and sighed. "All right."

Bell casually walked to the main door and out into the broad hallway. Mercedee again looked down the hall then took a deep breath and ducked past Sister Precort's desk and into the library. Mercedee saw what she was looking for just behind the desk. The bookcase had glass doors, so those books must be important, and one of the doors was slightly ajar.

Two steps over and Mercedee had the door open. She reached in and grabbed a book. The title was *Sisters of the Charities Morning Meditations*. "Perfect," she whispered to herself. She held the book and covered it with her cloak then walked out of the library and toward the glass door. *A couple more steps and I'm home free.* But walking toward the door, she saw Bell in the hallway, grimacing. She couldn't wave, or she would give the whole plot away.

Everything happened quickly. Mercedee glimpsed a nun on the other side of the glass door's window. She backed up and started toward de Sale's office, but it was too late. Sister Michaela was coming through the door and looking straight at Mercedee, who tried to act casually, but her heart raced.

"What are you doing in this part of the motherhouse,

Miss Meehan?" Sister Michaela seethed. "You know you are forbidden to come here."

Sister Fidelis followed Sister Michaela into the office.

Mercedee started to panic. "Oh, well, I was looking for Sister de Sale, and I don't know where her office is."

Sister Fidelis walked alongside Michaela and asked, "What has this child done now?"

"I haven't done anything," Mercedee pleaded. "I came looking for Sister de Sale to get a dose of medicine. I've been so very ill lately." Mercedee feigned sincerity but also wished she had been honest because it wasn't unusual for students with colds to come to the offices. In any case, she wasn't going to allow Michaela to push her around. Mercedee held the book and shawl close to her body and coughed into her fist.

Sister Michaela told Fidelis, "Sister dear, do you hear the story the child is telling? Go ask Sister de Sale if it's true."

Mercedee's face warmed. "No need. I see Sister Rosalia coming down the hall. She'll get the medicine for me." But Mercedee had to think fast because Rosalia wasn't coming down the hall, and dropping her name wasn't having the desired effect.

With Michaela and Fidelis scowling and Mercedee's nerves raw, Sister de Sale came in through the closed door and saw Mercedee. She walked over and put her arm around Mercedee's shoulders. "I just heard you had the worst cough. You need some cough medicine. Sister Rosalia alerted me to your condition. Come into my office where it's warm and get some rest."

Mercedee tried unsuccessfully not to smirk as she turned away from Sister Michaela and Sister Fidelis. "Oh, thank you, Sister de Sale. You're so kind. This is the worst cold ever," Mercedee said in a gravelly voice, and they walked into de Sale's office. Mercedee still had the contraband under her cloak.

Shortly, Mercedee had swallowed the medicine, and Sister de Sale told her to rest awhile and left for a classroom.

Mercedee was still hiding the purloined book on her lap under the shawl. Hearing no voices in the hall, she casually walked out of the main building and down the hall with the book under her cloak. She immediately went upstairs to the St. Vincent dorm. She found Bell's bunk and saw her lying in it. Bell sat up quickly.

"Mercedee!" Bell whispered. "You made it. I thought you were a goner. I'm so glad to see you. Is everything all right?"

"That was a close one. Sister de Sale happened along, and I think Sister Rosalia told her about my cough. She whisked me into her office, and I was off the hook."

"Oh my!" Bell gasped. "I wouldn't give you up for a hundred like me. You're amazing."

"But the bad news is that I had to take another spoonful of that disgusting cough medicine." Mercedee smirked, and they chuckled. "And here's the book I, um, checked out for you." Mercedee produced the book from under her shawl and laid it on Bell's pillow. Bell stood up as if to make sure no one was watching.

"Meditations," Bell read. "That's the one they use in the mornings."

"Yes. Now let's see what's in this sort of book that only the sisters get to see."

Mercedee and Bell thumbed through the book, reading quickly and searching for something interesting. They spent more than an hour going through the book but found nothing.

"This is the most boring book I've ever seen." Bell sounded exasperated.

"I can't believe I risked my enrollment for this! Nuns must lead the most boring lives."

Bell heard voices and slid the book under her blanket. "Maybe that's why they're so hard on us?"

"Maybe," Mercedee said. "Now how are we going to get the book back?"

"Don't worry. You can leave that to me." Bell concealed

the book in her bag and got up.

"I'll assume you know what you're doing." Mercedee followed Bell into the hall and nervously checked to be sure it was empty. She hurried back across the hall to her dorm and her bunk.

In no time at all, Bell had made her way to Mercedee's bunk, where she was filling Clara in on their escapade. "All taken care of," Bell said.

"How did you manage that?" Mercedee asked.

"Well," Bell started, "Sister Joe wasn't at her desk. There was a stack of books there to be reshelved, and I put our book in the middle. Soon, it'll be back on the shelf, and none of the other sisters will be any the wiser."

"Brilliant, Bell!" Mercedee gasped, then the three of them laughed.

"Yes, and I'm so happy that you came to the Mount this year, Mercedee," Bell said.

"We're indeed having fun now, but I'm finished with pranks and taking chances. If Papa can find the money, I want to be able to come back next year." Mercedee relaxed on her bed, took a deep breath, and coughed as she exhaled.

***

In the third week of February, Mercedee and Clara sat at their desks, waiting for Sister Baptista's mathematics class to start. Mercedee liked math, but she didn't like Sister Baptista. The sister stood at her desk while holding a sheet of paper, looking down her thin nose at it with her small, dark eyes and focusing through her reading glasses. Mercedee glanced at Clara, who sat to her left, and they exchanged looks.

Sister Baptista tapped a ruler on her desk. "Class, this Thursday and Friday, we will not have class because we'll be attending the annual retreat." She walked to the side of her desk, still focused on the paper. "We will be visited by several Jesuit clergy and Father Devlin. There will be several exercises that you'll attend, and Father Devlin will talk about vocation for those interested." She paused and put the paper down on her desk. "Now get out your worksheets from yesterday and turn to page seventy-five of your textbook."

While walking to the line forming for lunch, Clara asked, "Vocation? What do you think, Mercedee? Do you want to become a nun?"

Mercedee smirked. "I don't think that would be particularly good for me. Since I arrived here, I've gotten in so many scrapes with the sisters. Why would I want to become one of them?"

They reached the line at the top of the stairs and waited for the call to silence.

"You haven't been called by God, then?" Clara asked.

"I don't think so. At least—"

Sister de Sale called for quiet, and the line started to move like items on a conveyor belt and disappear into the stairwell.

The girls spent Thursday listening to Jesuit clergymen talk about the mission of the church and the divinity. Mercedee found it interesting, but on Friday, when Father Devlin spoke about vocation, or answering the call of the Lord to join the Catholic Church as a nun, Mercedee didn't hear the call. She didn't feel comfortable devoting her life to a cause that belonged to someone else and living within the restrictive framework of the church, particularly for nuns. Some other girls were much more interested.

On Friday, several of the girls, including Jean, asked to speak with Father Devlin about vocation, but Mercedee went to the recreation room downstairs with Bell and Clara. Later, Jean entered the room and came to their table.

"What do you think, Jean?" Clara asked. "Do you want to join the Sisters of Charity?"

"I feel strongly that it's worth consideration," she replied. "I think my mother would be happy if I did."

"I agree you may be happy as a sister," Mercedee said, "but I hope you'll be more like Sister Joe and less like Sister Michaela."

The girls chuckled. Father Devlin came into the room and spoke with each girl. He was tall with black pants, a coat, and vest over a white shirt with a high white collar. Middle-aged, he had salt-and-pepper hair. He carried himself with authority but also smiled as he spoke in a soft and inviting tone. His charisma pulled on Mercedee and made her nervous, especially when he headed to their table.

"Greetings, young ladies," he said, towering over Mercedee and her friends.

"Hello, Father Devlin," they replied.

He looked at them and asked Mercedee, "Would you like to speak with me about the vocation, my child?"

"Um, no, thank you, Father. But thank you again." She stammered and blushed as she looked at the table.

"I'm always available if you desire to answer God's calling. Your friend Jean here is interested." Father Devlin looked at each of their faces as Jean smiled and humbly looked at the table. "Would any of the rest of you like to speak with me about following your divine calling?"

The other girls also declined or nervously shook their heads. Father Devlin moved on to others in the room, and Mercedee, Jean, and Clara glanced at each other. As he left, Clara said, "Father Devlin was partial to you, Mercedee."

"I suppose," Mercedee replied. "Probably because Tante Rosalia is a nun. She has been for years and is so devoted. I most certainly am not, although I can see the attraction of structure and security."

"Yes," Jean said. "As a sister, you can help people, and you're always taken care of."

"That would be fine," Bell said. "But I can also see why you might not want to have to learn all the ceremonies and rules. Especially if you're not completely invested in spirituality."

"I don't know," Bell said. "Even the morning meditations aren't very exciting."

Bell and Mercedee smiled at each other.

Mercedee thought for a moment. "I don't think that I

really believe strongly enough in a God-dominated life to give up adventures that I may be able to have on my own. Perhaps someday I'll change my mind."

"Why do some sisters seem so hard on you, Mercedee?" Clara asked.

Mercedee looked at the window and then Clara. "I'm not sure. At times, it seems that they think I'm something that I'm not or see more potential in me than I do. They want me to be someone else, someone they see, but I don't know who that person is. At least, that's what I'm sensing."

"I can't see you forcing girls to follow strict rules," Clara said.

"Now that you mention it, I may have trouble with that. There's more to life than wearing a nun's habit, although at least then, I would always have clothes that fit and more than one nice dress." She finished with a laugh.

Clara chuckled. "Oh, so true. And I wouldn't always have to fix my hair!" She stuck out her lower lip and blew a strand of curly hair that had come loose.

Jean and Bell laughed, but Mercedee knew she was right. She didn't feel that she belonged at the Mount on a permanent basis. Although education was important, her adventurous nature was always telling her that she could do it on her own. She always had before, and she would again. But one thing that she couldn't control was that she was growing out of her dresses and blouses, and Papa couldn't afford to buy her new ones. Her clothes seemed tattered, and the embarrassment of walking about with girls from rich families was unbearable. She promised herself that by the end of the school year, she would find a way to acquire or make better clothes. Becoming a sister would be a desperate move that she would always regret because it wouldn't be honest. She resolved to find a better way.

"We need to go to dinner," Clara said, startling Mercedee out of deep thought.

"Right. Yes." Mercedee sighed and slid her chair back.

***

Easter Sunday began with a beacon of sun that warmed the chilly academy. Students of Mount St. Vincent arose, ate breakfast, and filed into the giant cathedral for Easter mass. After mass, Mercedee stood in the recreation room and looked out the window and across the park that was starting to emerge from the long winter. Other girls were going for a walk in the park, and Mercedee decided to join them. Turning toward the door, she nearly ran into Bell Condon.

"Oh, hello, Bell."

"Hello to you. Would you like to stroll around the garden?"

"I'm planning to do just that." Mercedee replied, and she and her partner in crime headed out.

Mercedee and Bell took the stairs to the main level, where Sister de Sale was talking to Sister Loretta. Sister de Sale looked at the two of them and raised one eyebrow as if to ask, "What now?" but then almost smiled as Mercedee grinned at her.

"Sister de Sale," Mercedee said as they approached, "Bell and I would like to go for a walk on the campus grounds. Would that be all right?"

"I suppose," Sister de Sale replied tentatively, probably wondering if Mercedee and Bell were up to something. "Fresh air is always good for the body and spirit. But stay on the path, if you will. Everything is wet, and there's a brisk breeze."

"Oh, of course, Sister," Mercedee chirped.

"We'll be ever so careful not to tread in any mud or wet grass," Bell added.

"Have a nice walk," Sister de Sale said, and the girls walked to the door.

Mercedee reached the building's exit, gripped the brass handle, and pushed open the heavy hardwood door. The cool, humid air of the early Nova Scotia spring greeted her as she stepped onto a landing and descended a short stone-and-concrete stairway to a gravel-and-cobblestone path. Bell followed her, and they meandered along the path across the acres of grassy field. Leafless groves of hardwood trees flanked the field. The leaves wouldn't burst out for at least a month. Several other girls walked along the path, and one held up her ankle-length skirt to keep it dry. She tiptoed across the wet grass and retrieved a ribbon that had drifted away in the breeze.

"I still can't believe you were able to get out of the sisters' library with that book," Bell said.

"I can hardly believe it myself," Mercedee replied. "A bit of luck."

"And you have nerves of steel."

"Oh, please." Mercedee blushed. "I had no other choice."

They walked silently, then Mercedee spoke up. "How are your parents faring in St. John's? Is the city recovering from the fire?"

"In the last letter, my mother said that Father had received some of the settlement from the insurance firm, but the business is still not making money." Bell looked at her feet and kicked a small pebble off the path with her narrow boot. "He can't pay the workers everything that they're owed."

"That's awful," Mercedee said. "I hope things turn around for your father."

"If the business doesn't improve, I'm sure they won't have the money for tuition here next year." Bell stopped and looked out across Bedford Basin. "But things should improve with spring and summer."

"Yes, the fishing season hasn't started yet." Mercedee clasped her hands behind her back and looked at the rounded hilltop beyond the edge of the campus. "I know what you're going through. I've only gotten a few letters from my father in Boston, and he hasn't said anything about his accounts paying off or selling his mine near Truro."

Bell faced Mercedee. "We're the two unknowns. Where will we be in a year?"

"Yes, but I must say that one year ago, I didn't have the

slightest inkling that I would be here. It must be the story of my life, not knowing what'll happen next."

They chuckled.

"Sometimes, the unknown can turn out just fine, I suppose," Bell said.

"That's true."

Mercedee and Bell walked along the path to where it branched into a loop.

"We should go back inside now. I'm a bit chilled." Bell looked at the sun, which was moving near the horizon of the hilltop, and the shadows of large trees grew. The breeze was growing colder as well.

"Yes, let's get back inside. We can wrap up in our blankets so we won't get sick again," Mercedee said.

Early the next morning, Mercedee woke to a pounding in her head and a dry mouth from her congested sinuses, forcing her to breathe through her mouth. She stared in despair at the patterned white ceiling and glowing lamp. Her symptoms could only mean one thing—she'd caught a cold again. She reached for her handkerchief and dabbed her nose. *Not again. Not again!*

Mercedee tried to make do, not wanting to admit that she might be sick. She put on her dress and carried her handkerchief. She tried to hide her runny nose, but Clara turned as she finished buttoning her white blouse.

"Mercedee, your face is pale. Are you feeling well?"

"I'm just fine." Mercedee hoped it was true and wiped her nose. "I just woke up with some sniffles."

"I hope so, because I'm not feeling quite well this morning. I sure hope we're not catching la grippe again."

"I hope you're right. Maybe mine is just a temporary thing." Mercedee looked at Clara. "You don't look too bad."

"Oh, thank you for that endorsement." Clara chuckled.

"You know what I mean." Mercedee smiled back, suppressing an urge to cough, and cleared her throat.

They finished dressing and filed out into the hall to line up for the silent march to the refectory. Bell came up behind them, and Mercedee noticed that Bell also looked tired and pale.

"Are you sick?" Mercedee whispered.

Bell wiped her nose. "I think so. Not too bad, I hope."

"Yes, I've felt worse," Mercedee mouthed as Sister Michaela walked to the head of the line with her hand up.

Sister Michaela headed down the stairs, and the only sounds were the taps of footsteps and the rustle of dresses echoing in the large hall. As Mercedee, Bell, and Clara approached, the worst thing happened. Mercedee felt an itch in the back of her throat, and her sinuses burned. She fought it. She swallowed. She tried to quietly clear her throat. She wiped her nose and held it for a second, fighting an involuntary spasm.

No! Mercedee held a finger under her nose. Then she could no longer hold it back and surrendered. The silence through which the girls promenaded was shocked, jolted, and obliterated by an explosion from her mouth and nose as she tried to cover her face with her handkerchief.

"Ah-choo!" echoed throughout the hall and stairwell.

Girls moved away as Mercedee stood up straight and let out a second booming "Ahhhh-choo!"

The halo around Mercedee grew larger still as she let out her third and last booming sneeze.

Mercedee moved out of line and walked to the lavatory door, leaned on the wall next to it, and blew her nose into her handkerchief as Sister de Sale approached.

"Oh my. You'd better come with me, Miss Meehan." Sister de Sale led Mercedee to the door to the sisters' offices and library. "I'll let you stay in my office where it's warm."

"Thank you, Sister." Mercedee sounded like her nose was completely plugged.

Once inside, de Sale said, "Lie down on that cot, and I'll get you some hot tea."

Rosalia was in her office and preparing to go to breakfast when Mercedee arrived. Walking by de Sale's door, Rosalia glanced in and saw Mercedee sprawled on the cot. "Oh my,"

Rosalia said compassionately. "What do we have here? You look like the influenza has ravaged you again." She caressed Mercedee's forehead, feeling for fever.

"Yes, Tante," Mercedee replied with a hollow voice from her clogged sinuses.

Soon, Sister de Sale returned with a cup of steaming tea. "Here you go, dear." She held out a white ceramic cup decorated with leaves and a painted bust of Jesus looking toward heaven. On the other side was the face of Mary with a halo. She was looking down at something.

Mercedee sat up and put her feet on the floor. "Oh, thank you so much." She sighed and accepted the tea.

"Was that your sneezes I heard out in—"

"Yes, Tante, I'm afraid it was me." Mercedee slurped a mouthful of hot tea. After swallowing, she coughed several times. As her coughing subsided, she wheezed. "I think my friends Clara and Bell are sick too."

"Sister Rosalia has some new cough syrup that'll help that cough. Don't you, Sister?" Sister de Sale said.

"Why, yes. Yes, I do." Rosalia rubbed her hands together. "I'll go put some in a separate bottle and issue it to you." She scurried out of the office and disappeared down the hall.

Mercedee grimaced as she inhaled the wisp of steam rising from her tea.

Finally, Sister de Sale spoke softly. "Don't worry about your coursework until you're better. I'll give you some assignments that you can work on while resting."

"Thank you, Sister." Mercedee sipped the tea. "I've had a cold already once, and I do hope I will have some resistance to this infection and I will get over this one quickly. I can't afford to miss more classes."

"Yes," Sister de Sale said. "Resting will help."

Sister Rosalia returned with a one-pint brown glass medicine bottle with a cork stopper. She reached into a pocket and produced a small spoon. "Here you are."

Mercedee took the spoon and held it out as Rosalia

pulled the cork out of the bottle and filled the spoon. Mercedee reluctantly opened her mouth and swallowed the concoction. She made a sour face and took another sip of tea to cleanse her palate as Rosalia replaced the cork.

"Take this with you." Rosalia handed the bottle and spoon to Mercedee. "Take one teaspoon three times a day, and it'll help you get over that cough." She stepped back and looked at Mercedee, clearly waiting for a response.

"Uh, yes. Yes, Sister Rosalia." Mercedee leaned back and set the bottle and spoon in her lap as she took another sip of tea. "Thank you so much."

"Be sure and take the medicine so you can get well and get back to class. I don't want to come back here and see the bottle full."

"I'll take the medicine," Mercedee said groggily. She drank the last of her tea, enjoying the hot liquid bathing her tender throat. "Thank you for the tea, Sister de Sale. Now I think I should go to my dorm and lie down."

"That's a fine idea."

"I agree," Sister Rosalia said. "As you feel up to it, you should get down to the refectory and get some breakfast. That will also help you recover."

Mercedee nodded and made her way to the door. "I'll try to do that. Goodbye for now."

"Lord's blessing," Sister de Sale said.

"Be well," Rosalia added as Mercedee reached the door.

"Oh, and one other thing." Mercedee stopped. "My friend Bell is also feeling poorly. She may need medicine as well."

"Yes," Sister de Sale replied. "I saw her in the hallway. She will certainly need care, and thank you."

"Indeed," Sister Rosalia said. "I'll take some medicine to her dorm."

"Yes, Sister." Mercedee exited the office into the hallway. She passed the sisters' library entrance that she knew so well. She walked to the stairs, her head pounding with every step. Descending the stairs, she came upon Bell slowly climbing up.

"Are you going to class?" Mercedee asked.

Bell gave Mercedee a pained look. "I'm going back to bed. I feel horrible."

"I'm sorry to hear that. I was just at Sister Rosalia's office, and she gave me a dose of cough syrup. She gave me a bottle of it and expects me to take it three times a day." Mercedee made a "yuck" face while holding out the bottle and spoon.

"Oh no, not the cough medicine," Bell said, a hint of humor cracking through her congested head.

"Oh yes, the cough medicine." Mercedee smiled. "And again, I'm sorry."

"Whatever for?"

"I told them that you're sick too."

"Oh no," Bell gasped.

"Sister Rosalie will be up to your dorm to give you some cough medicine too." Mercedee coughed and wiped her nose. "This would be funny if my head didn't hurt so much."

"Oh no…" Bell trudged up the stairs. "I'm going to lie back down. Jean is sick too."

"I'll get some breakfast and go to bed myself." Mercedee went down and had a light breakfast with hot tea, and by the time she finished, she was nearly the only one in the refectory. The other students had finished their breakfast and gone to class.

Mercedee was anxious about missing class, but she and her mamma had traveled on the eastern seaboard and around Nova Scotia, and both Mamma and Papa had schooled her well in reading and grammar. Geography and math came easily to her. She would make up the work with no problems at all.

She finished her tea, dropped off her dishes at the counter, and headed upstairs. After the first flight, she could feel the virus had weakened her. Her legs ached, and her head pounded. She slowed her pace and kept moving on up.

She made her way down the wide hall, into the dorm, and flopped onto her bed.

"Mercedee. Mercedee?"

The words pulled her back into a hazy consciousness. Sister Rosalia was looking down at her. The ceiling behind Rosalia glowed with the ceiling lights, and the distant window was dark. *What time is it?* Mercedee asked, "How long have I been asleep?"

"I brought you a cup of tea," Rosalia said. "You slept through the day."

"Thank you." Mercedee groggily sat up. "Thank you so much."

Rosalia handed her the cup, and Mercedee sipped the tea and inhaled the steam through sinuses that she could barely breathe through.

"Have you taken any more cough medicine?" Rosalia glanced to her left. "Oh my." She looked at Clara, who was asleep in her bed too. "Miss Clara is ill also. I'll have to get her a bottle of cough medicine as well."

"I'm very sorry, Sister Rosalia. I don't think I took any because I was asleep." Mercedee leaned over and looked past Rosalia at Clara's bunk. "And she appears to be as well," Mercedee said as Clara snored. "I'm sure she'll appreciate some cough medicine." Mercedee's subtle sarcasm was obviously lost on Sister Rosalia. "And is it too late to get a bite to eat from the refectory before I turn in?"

Rosalia paused. "I think there may still be food available."

"Oh, thank goodness." Mercedee swallowed a gulp of tea.

"Are you going to eat?" Clara leaned up on her elbow and rubbed her eyes.

"Yes, I'm going to the refectory. Hopefully, they have some hot soup."

"That sounds very good," Clara said. "I'll go with you."

"We'll be so careful. Thank you," Mercedee said as Sister Rosalia turned to go. "I'll finish my tea and go downstairs."

"Yes," Rosalia said over her shoulder, "and don't forget to take your cough medicine." Rosalia disappeared down the aisle between rows of beds.

For the next week, Mercedee, Clara, Jean, and Bell could not attend classes as their colds persisted. Even regular doses of that awful cough medicine didn't help. But finally, the congestion mercifully dissipated, and on the same morning, they all returned to class.

"I'm so glad the cough has abated. Aren't you, Mercedee?" Clara asked as they walked up the stairs from the refectory after breakfast. "I was starting to wonder if I'd caught the consumption."

"Um, yes."

They climbed the stairs in silence until, reaching a landing, Clara stopped. "I'm sorry. I forgot," she said, remembering that Mercedee's mother had passed away from tuberculosis less than a year ago.

Mercedee looked at the book bag in her hands and then at Clara. "Oh no. It's all right. I'm fine." She met Clara's gaze. "Let's go to class. I'd rather occupy my mind with Sister Michaela's math lesson."

"Sister Michaela? Really?" Clara gave Mercedee a quizzical look, and they both broke into laughter. "I never know what to expect from you."

"Let's go," Mercedee said, and they ascended the stairs.

8 THE SECOND DIVISION

A tall, narrow window opened out of the west side of the motherhouse, and as it peeked over the tall building, the morning sun illuminated just the tops of trees to the west of the academy. In the cold, dense morning air came the crisp sounds of boats in the basin and men banging steel on steel, repairing track.

Sister Michaela ushered Mercedee, Bell, Jean, and Clara into the administrative conference room and directed them to be seated. They reluctantly complied.

"I need to speak with you girls before class," Michaela said sternly as she closed the office door.

Mercedee looked across the table at Bell with raised eyebrows and mouthed, "What's happening?"

Bell shrugged.

"Jean, Bell, Mercedee, and Clara," Michaela said, facing them. She placed her hands on the table. "It is almost Easter, and we are concerned about your recent absences from class."

Mercedee frowned, confused. "But we didn't miss class intentionally."

"I am aware. It was not your doing. The influenza affected a number of students." Michaela clasped her hands in front of her. "But that notwithstanding, it is the policy of the academy that we do our best to bring absent students back up to the rest of the students' progress by letting them focus on missed lessons separately from the other students."

"What are you saying?" Clara asked. "Will we be separated from our classmates?"

"Are we being punished?" Mercedee sighed.

"Now, now, settle down. You're not being punished." Michaela sounded impatient. "This is just a minor change. You will be placed in the second division until you can make up the work and complete the lessons." She paused. "This is for your benefit. It will be very difficult to catch up if you're also being given a full load of new material."

Mercedee opened her mouth and covered it with her hand. Clara and Jean frowned, and Bell's eyes welled with tears.

"We were all doing well in our classes. I can hardly believe that we're that far behind." Mercedee's voice trailed off as she imagined herself becoming a second-class as well as a second-division student.

Michaela gave the girls a stern look. "I'm sorry, but all of you have missed at least one week of classes, and by academy policy, we need to move you to the second division to allow you to catch up more quickly." She headed toward the door. "You will attend the same classes but will meet at alternate times. See Sister Precort at the library desk to get your new schedule. I'm sure that if you buckle down, follow rules, and work extra hard, you can rejoin the first division soon."

Sister Michaela reached for the door handle and pulled the door open. A rush of cool air entered, and Mercedee realized how warm and stuffy the room had become. The air felt good and refreshing but didn't quell the disappointment causing her stomach to flip. She rose and silently walked into the hall. She strode toward the library entrance and Sister Precort's desk.

Mercedee stepped up to the desk and said in a subdued voice, "I need to get my—"

"Of course." Sister Precort offered Mercedee a sheet of paper. "I'm sure you'll all be back in the first division before you know it," she said encouragingly as Mercedee entered the hallway.

Mercedee waited there for the others, looking down at the piece of paper. The top of the sheet read, *Second Division Class Schedule,* and below it was a grid of boxes with course names and room numbers. It was very similar to her original schedule except the order was changed so that she and the other second-division students would meet at a different time and place. Just as that awful Michaela said they would. Reading the heading again made her heart sink. She felt a wave of disappointment, like falling into an abyss of self-doubt and failure.

"Mercedee," Clara said.

"Yes? Yes. I'm all right."

"What are we going to do?" Jean's dark eyes looked quizzical and sad.

"We must do something," Bell added. "This can't be happening. With all that's going on back in St. John's, my father will be so disappointed in me falling to the second division."

"I don't trust Sister Michaela." Mercedee looked at the door they had exited. "She's been waiting for a reason to relegate me. Us for that matter. Policy?"

"I wouldn't put it past her." Bell slapped the schedule on her dress then folded it and slid it into her book bag.

"That meeting caused us to miss our last class of the day," Clara said. "Let's go to the recreation room and talk about this."

Mercedee nodded. "Yes. Let's do that." She started to feel better since her friends shared her predicament. There was only one thing to do, and that was to prove Michaela wrong. To make the best of things.

The four girls walked down stairs to the recreation room

and plodded to an empty table, past a couple of girls talking and another reading a book. Mercedee dropped her book bag on the table and flopped into a wooden chair with a dark-brown leather seat pad trimmed by brass upholstery pins. Bell, Jean, and Clara took the three other chairs.

After a moment of silence, Mercedee spoke. "I don't know if we can make up enough work before the end of the year to get back into the first division."

"You're right," Jean said. "It's almost Easter and then only a month until the end of the year."

"Ahem." Clara sighed. "Perhaps my father can afford for me to stay for the summer and make it up?"

Mercedee looked at the painting of St. Mary on the wall, her head rimmed by a golden halo and her eyes distant. "That will never happen for me," she said softly.

"Oh," Clara whispered. "I'm sorry."

Mercedee glanced at Clara and put her hand on her friend's ruffled white sleeve. "Don't worry. I'm all right." Mercedee put her elbows on the table, rested her chin on the backs of her knuckles, and took a deep breath. "The year isn't over yet. We'll show the sisters that we're just as good as the first division."

Bell's eyes grew wide, and she grinned. "Yes. Even if we are relegated, they'll know that we aren't second-division students."

"*Oui, oui,*" Jean added.

"And if we do well enough, they should still move us to first division for the end of the year, don't you think?" Clara asked. "The academy must have a policy about that too."

"I don't know where I'll be next year. I hope I can stay, but in any case, I want to finish this year showing Michaela that I'm as good as the Boston girls, and she doesn't control me." Mercedee smiled.

Clara smiled back. "I'm in. I feel I also have something to prove."

Jean said, "Whatever happens, we'll at the very least be in the first division next year. Wherever we may be."

Bell looked at the long, ornate hands and brass pendulum of the wall clock as the long hand snapped to the nine and it chimed through the quarter-till progression. "We'd better be going. Our new class is about to start."

"Yes," Clara said. "We must also get our books."

They left the table and marched up the stairs with a new sense of purpose. In the hallway, the girls quickly collected their materials and entered the classroom. Sister Baptista was organizing papers on her desk in front of a large map on the front wall. Mercedee felt strange not seeing her usual classmates. She chose a desk and chair near the front.

Turning abruptly, Sister Baptista said, "Oh my, you are some eager pupils today. You're early."

"Yes, Sister," Mercedee said. "We're ready for geography."

"Agreed," Bell added.

Baptista looked at the girls, at first quizzically, then smiled. "This is wonderful. I was simply hoping that all of you would show up at all, what with the schedule change, but here you are, bright and ready to go." She looked out the door. "Unfortunately, there are two other students who aren't here yet. As soon as they arrive, we can get started."

Sister Baptista walked to her desk and picked up four sheets of paper from a stack. "Here's today's worksheet. You may start looking at it while we wait for the others." She handed a paper to each girl.

Mercedee looked at the sheet and the map on the wall and whispered to Bell, sitting to her right, "This looks easy."

Bell nodded. The map was of North America, and the assignment was to sketch a map of Canada and the United States and locate a list of geographical features. Mercedee and the other girls retrieved pencils from their bags and began sketching.

Soon, two other girls entered the classroom. Mercedee had seen them before but didn't know their names.

"Welcome, girls," Sister Baptista said. "Class, this is Hattie Doyle and Lena Milson."

The girls took seats in the second row as Baptista continued, "Hattie and Lena, this is Clara La Brun, Jean Freal, Bell Condon, and Mercedee Meehan."

The sister handed the newcomers the assignment, and they dug out pencils. Mercedee nodded to Hattie and Lena, but her attention was on the map. Railroad lines crossed the continent in the United States from Chicago through the Wyoming Territory and on to San Francisco, and lines in Canada connected Toronto to Chicago on the south and through Canada to Winnipeg, Calgary, and on to Vancouver. One of the features that students were to place on the map was the Rocky Mountains and ranges along the West Coast. Mercedee drew them in with inverted vees and remembered the days of traveling with Mamma Agnes, living out of her trunk and sleeping in strange places. She yearned to travel and see the world, and the academy felt suddenly confining. But, she reasoned, there was so much to overcome—

"Are you all finishing your worksheet?" Sister Baptista snapped Mercedee back to the present.

"Yes, Sister," the others chorused as Mercedee hunkered over her sheet and rushed to add the Mississippi River, the Great Lakes, and Hudson Bay. She finally whispered to herself, "Someday…" and handed her paper to Sister Baptista.

In the days and weeks that followed, the four girls used their motivation to go above and beyond, even dominating the classroom with quick answers and extended explanations. They were driven to do as much or more for their classes than the first-division students did. The school year was winding down, and there wasn't much time.

"What are you doing, Mercedee and Bell?" A voice came from behind them as they walked down the long hallway toward class.

They turned to see Hattie and Lena following them.

"Why, we're going to class," Bell said with a quizzical look.

As Hattie and Lena moved closer, Hattie asked, "I mean, why do you keep asking for more work?"

"Can't you keep up?" Mercedee retorted smartly.

"Well, yes," Hattie stammered, "but why do you want more assignments?"

"I would like to answer that with a question." Mercedee wrapped her arm around her two books and pinned them to her chest. "Do you belong in the second division? Are you happy here?"

"First off," Hattie said, "that's two questions, but the answer is *not especially* to both."

"But what can we do about it?" Lena added.

Mercedee glanced at Bell. "We don't like being second division. I, for one, feel that I'm better than this. So we decided to do as much as the first division. Probably more because we're behind from being sick, if they were to rank us."

"Michaela will not keep us down," Bell said.

"Oh." Lena looked thoughtfully at Hattie.

"I don't think it'll do any good, but it's worth a try," Hattie said solemnly.

Lena nodded.

For two more weeks, the motivated girls pushed their teachers and dominated classroom discussion, bound and determined to rise to the first division before the end of the term. Sister de Sale for one noticed, and it seemed as if even Sister Michaela might have been impressed, although it wasn't easy to tell. One day, preparing to start Literature with Sister de Sale, Sister Michaela entered the class and spoke briefly with the sister in private then turned to the class.

"I wanted to tell you that your concerted effort over the last several weeks has not gone unnoticed. You have exceeded expectations and made up crucial ground after your absence due to illness."

Mercedee glanced at Bell, who gave a hint of a smile. Mercedee's stomach twitched with anticipation that they might be able to return to the fold of first-division students, and she was excited that their strategy might have worked.

"We even spoke about moving you back to the first division." She paused, and the students looked up at her with wide eyes, their hope and anticipation palpable. "However," Sister Michaela continued as Mercedee felt an intense deflation coming, "the term will be ending in less than four weeks. It just doesn't make sense to rearrange schedules now and put the classes back together for a few weeks."

Michaela looked around the room at the disappointed faces. "Keep in mind that you will no doubt be fully caught up by the end of the term and will rejoin us next year as first-division students. You'll receive assignments the same as your first-division counterparts. You should feel good about the schoolwork you've done, and I hope you continue to perform this well for the rest of the year." With that, Michaela opened the classroom door and walked out.

"Is everyone ready to perform an exercise on the silk route?" Sister de Sale asked.

The class responded with uninspired murmurs of agreement.

As the door closed, Mercedee held her pencil as if poised to hit Sister Michaela in the back. Clara, who had been watching, surreptitiously tapped Mercedee on her elbow and grinned and winked. Mercedee placed her pencil on her paper and returned a wry smile, since Clara clearly knew that Mercedee would have another scheme waiting in the wings.

9 THE BIG DECISION

It was Sunday. Mass had completed, and Mercedee had retired to her bunk in the Immaculate Conception dorm. Clara and Bell had left for the recreation room, where Jean was waiting. Mercedee suddenly appreciated the quiet that was punctuated only by murmurs from a bunk across the dorm.

She felt peaceful until shaken by the realization that she hadn't yet written a letter to Papa. He would be expecting one that week. *Well, this is the perfect time to take care of that.* Mercedee gathered her writing supplies and stationery and headed for the library.

At a table flooded with sunlight coming through a tall window, Mercedee dipped her pen in her ink bottle, dabbed it on the rim, and began to write.

Mount St. Vincent,
Halifax, N.S.
April 28, 1893
My dearest Papa,
Just a line to tell you of our visitors yesterday afternoon. As I passed through the Music Hall on my way to practice, I was much embarrassed on coming upon a formidable group made up of French

religious. However, I continued to take a mental picture of the party, as there is always something of interest attached to such strangers. These nuns were of the order of St. Joseph of Clung and are en route to St. Pierre, where they intend to remain on a mission. Their dress was very peculiar, and they had no outer garments but went out with the same things as they wear in the house.

We had a snowstorm day before yesterday, which surprised us very much, as the weather had been so beautiful before, but I am glad to say that the snow went away before the day was over. Scores of robins have been on the wing for nearly two weeks, and yesterday, while we were out for our walk, we gathered some pussy willows, the first I have seen this Spring.

Do you remember when we used to get pussy willows behind Bennie Dawe's house and bring them home to poor Mamma? Did we not have very good times?

Poor Lottie! I have not written to her for some time. I hope she will not be offended with me, but I fear she will.

As Father MacDonald has not left us yet, we still enjoy his Indian stories. He is going to have an operation performed in Halifax soon, and he has promised us a lovely drive in the latter part of June if he lives through the operation. Indeed, he is so kind, we are all praying for perfect recovery.

My dear Papa, as nothing of any importance occurred this week, I fear you will have to be satisfied with this short letter.

Your loving child,
Mercedee

Mercedee folded the letter, slipped it into an envelope, and addressed it to William Meehan, 53 Globe Building, Boston, Massachusetts. She sealed it, dropped it into her bag, and left for the recreation room.

On her way there, Sister Rosalia summoned Mercedee to her office and quietly closed the door. She circled the desk to her chair, reached behind her and pushed her black dress forward, then sat. Mercedee inhaled and prepared to apologize for her rude remark to Anne, but Sister Rosalia raised a hand and stopped her. "I'm well aware of your

215

difficulties with Anne, but that's not what I wanted to talk to you about."

Mercedee held her breath and gave the sister a quizzical look.

"You know the term is over in a week, and you need to decide where you are to go."

"Perhaps I could go to Boston and stay with my papa," Mercedee said. "I haven't received a letter for some time, but I could write to him again."

"No, I'm afraid that's not possible at this time. I received a letter from your aunt Seraphie saying that your father is having a difficult time financially right now. You know there is a depression from the financial panic last year, and his ventures haven't fared well. Furthermore, Seraphie thinks he is living in his office." She paused and straightened a book on her desk.

"What are you saying? Why didn't he tell me—" Mercedee cried.

"He may not want to burden you with his troubles, my dear," Rosalia said. "I'm certain he will soon have his affairs in order so you can stay with him, but right now, it's not possible. You could go to Concession with Tante Mathilde again and wait. I'm sure that's what William would prefer."

"Oh…" Mercedee sighed in disappointment. "I love Tante Mathilde, but I would rather not do that. I could end up there for some time."

"Mathilde just got back from New York, where she went to see a doctor, but I'm sure you could keep house for her." Rosalia paused. "Or there's the possibility that Tante Seraphie and your cousin Aggie would be glad for you to stay with them in New York."

Mercedee's eyes filled with tears. She turned away to hide her distress and looked at the wall, where a painting showed Jesus praying in the wilderness. *How can life be so cruel?* Her mother was dead, her dear papa was ruined, and she had no one in the world. Besides, all her clothes were too small, and she had no hope of getting new ones. She wouldn't willingly go to Aunt Seraphie and her cousin Aggie. Seraphie was kind and had looked after her, but she couldn't bear Aggie's airs and looks of pity. Seraphie would probably give her Aggie's hand-me-down clothes, which were outdated and too short and would require much alteration. The hemlines would show. *How humiliating!* Mercedee stared into Sister Rosalia's desk, searching for an answer.

But wait! There was another way. *What about Tante Monique?* A plan started to take shape. Monique Gravelle, her late mother's sister, was a seamstress and had a thriving dress business in East Orange, New Jersey. Her business wasn't as big as Seraphie's, but she had just bought a new house. She employed several girls to do the tedious hand stitching needed for finishing ruffles and flounces on the beautiful gowns worn by the wealthy ladies of New York City. Perhaps, if Monique wanted her, she could help with the sewing and make some clothes for herself. For that matter, the previous summer, Monique had written a letter practically inviting Mercedee to go to Orange.

"Sister Rosalia." Mercedee broke the silence, and Rosalia looked up. The silence was becoming tense, and she'd started fidgeting with things on her desk.

"Yes?" Rosalia clasped her hands on her desktop.

"Could I go to stay with Tante Monique? I can stitch, and I'm sure she could use some help."

"I don't know." Rosalia pursed her lips. "We'll have to ask your father. He and Monique haven't been on very favorable terms from what I've heard, although I'm not sure why."

Rosalia looked at her desk then up at Mercedee. "Monique is a very capable, industrious woman. But she rarely gives anything away. Be careful. I would suggest one of the other two." Rosalia gazed into Mercedee's face. "And listen to your father. I think he would be upset if you don't go stay with Mathilde and, if not there, with Seraphie."

"Thank you, Sister—I mean Tante," Mercedee said with the hint of a smile. "I'll be careful. Thank you so much for helping me." Mercedee stood up and walked around the desk toward Sister Rosalia, who rose from her chair. Mercedee hugged her aunt then walked into the hall outside. Sister Rosalia shook her head with concern. She breathed a prayer for Mercedee's protection and guidance but shivered slightly as she felt a premonition of hard times ahead for the strikingly clever and intelligent young lady.

Mercedee briskly headed for the main hallway, intent on getting to her dorm to ponder what to do. Pushing open the door, she saw Sister Michaela coming toward her and assumed an almost sarcastically reverent slow pace with her hands behind her back.

"Greetings, Sister Michaela." Mercedee nodded as they passed.

"Hello, Miss Meehan," Michaela replied with a measuring glance.

Mercedee continued to the stairs and up to her dorm. Her footsteps echoed in the quiet, empty room. She made her way to her bed and lay down. Looking up at the ceiling through the rectangle of the bars holding her curtains, she took a heavy breath. "There's only one thing to do," she whispered to herself.

Mercedee sat up, pushed back the curtains, and rummaged through the top drawer in her small dresser. She retrieved a pack of stationery, extracted two sheets and an envelope, then grabbed her bag and headed for the student library.

There, two other girls were reading at one table, so Mercedee picked a secluded table and sat down, setting the stationery in front of her. She carefully pulled out her pen and ink bottle, unscrewed the cap, and set them on the table. She paused, looking over a dark hardwood bookcase with wood-framed glass cabinet doors. Over the low case and through the window, she could see trees on the hill to the west of the motherhouse.

Mercedee thought for a moment then picked up her pen, dipped the tip in the ink bottle, and tapped it against the rim. Taking a deep breath, she wrote on the envelope, "Monique Gravelle, 37 Orange Street, East Orange, New Jersey." In the return address corner, she wrote, "MMR, Mount St. Vincent Academy, Halifax, NS." She set the envelope aside and adjusted the paper in front of her.

"Dearest Tante Monique," she wrote. "I hope this letter finds you well and in good spirits. I am within two weeks of the end of the academic term at the Mount, and I find myself in a bit of a predicament…"

Mercedee wrote several more lines, pausing to look out the window and compose them just right. Finally, she wrapped up the letter and signed it. She folded the letter, slid it into the envelope, and hurried to her dorm. She found enough money for postage. It was nearly all she had. She walked briskly past other girls coming and going to the hall and saw Clara. "You look like you could use something to do," Mercedee said as Clara got closer.

"I think you're right. Where are you headed?" Clara looked at the letter in Mercedee's hand. "Oh, are you headed downstairs to the mailroom?"

"I am," Mercedee replied.

"Mind if I tag along?"

"Of course not. I was about to ask if you wanted to go."

The girls walked into the mailroom.

"What are you sending?" Clara asked.

"I'm taking control of my life! I'm going to arrange my future!" Mercedee exclaimed with a skip and a jump. "I'm so excited. If my Tante agrees, I will go to Orange and make my own way."

"You're so clever. I hope it works for you!" Clara answered.

"I wouldn't say that I'm clever, and this isn't without risks, but I am finished with waiting for others to tell me what to do."

***

Three days later, after her last class of another demoralizing day in the second division, Mercedee walked downstairs to the mailroom. She wasn't sure whether she hoped her father had written to say he had completed a deal to provide her with the means to return to the Mount or whether he would allow her to choose where to go in less than two weeks when the term ended. She knew what she wanted but was also fairly certain that neither option was likely.

Sister Grace in the mailroom smiled as Mercedee entered. "Hello, Miss Meehan. I just finished sorting today's mail, and I think there was something for you."

"Oh?" Mercedee said nervously.

"Yes, and it is right here." Sister Grace slid a letter across the counter, and Mercedee hesitantly glanced at it as she picked it up.

"Thank you so much, and best of the day to you," Mercedee said as she left.

"And you," Sister Grace said, sorting letters into a neat stack.

Mercedee didn't want to look at the letter. It wasn't from Papa. The return address was East Orange, New Jersey, so it must be from Tante Monique. What would her reply be? Mercedee struggled to walk at a normal pace to avoid the ire of the nuns, but she wanted to run back to her dorm room. In the stairway, however, she decided to check for an open spot in the student library.

Mercedee walked nervously through the small office at the library entrance and into the main room. Seeing no one, she breathed a sigh of relief and made her way to her favorite spot near the back and opposite the windows. She set the letter on the table in front of her and looked at it. It was indeed from Monique. She slid her finger under the flap, tearing loose the adhesive. She took a deep breath and pulled out the letter.

Mercedee's eyes moved back and forth, taking in the words line by line. "Oh," she whispered. "Oh my."

***

Mercedee walked across the recreation room to the

window. Thin white curtains glowed in the afternoon sun and contrasted with the deep-red drapes that flanked the window. Red stripes crisscrossed the valance framing diamonds with roses in the center of each. She pushed back the curtains and looked out at the broad field, woods, and hill on the west side of the motherhouse. "Jean, Bell!" Mercedee called out. "It's a beautiful day. Let's go for a walk." Hearing only silence, she turned around.

"Yes, Mercedee. That sounds like a grand idea." Jean looked up from her book.

Bell closed hers. "I'll join you."

Mercedee closed the curtains, returned to the table where Bell and Jean were organizing their things, and picked up her bag. Soon, they left the recreation room and headed to the stairs.

A few minutes later, Jean and Bell followed Mercedee on the trail that crossed the grass-covered field behind the motherhouse, meandered through the woods, and made a long loop, partially climbing the hill that was something of a backstop for the Mount St. Vincent acreage. Mercedee entered the newly forming canopy of oak and maple trees. A squirrel chattered at them, and their feet sank into the soft, spongy soil.

After hurrying along the trail, Mercedee reached a wide spot where a bench was sitting on a cobblestone pad. She sat down as her friends tried to keep pace. Light filtered through the tree leaves, and she could see the Bedford Basin and the motherhouse through a gap in the branches. Bell and Jean arrived, breathing hard, and dropped down onto the bench next to her.

"My goodness." Bell sighed. "You were leaving us behind."

"Doesn't it feel good to get out and walk?" Mercedee asked.

"At your pace, it's a bit beyond *good*," Bell said with a gasp.

Jean smoothed her dress. "It does feel good. Those stairs

in the motherhouse keep one in shape, but it's so nice to get out into nature. I just wish my legs were as long as yours."

Bell leaned in front of Jean and faced Mercedee. "Doesn't your father have lots of rules about exercise? I hope you didn't sweat." Bell chuckled.

"You're right." Mercedee laughed. "I'd better rest in the shade for a bit."

"Mercedee," Jean said in a much more solemn voice, "I want to ask you what your plans are. Do you think you may be back next year?"

Mercedee looked through the tree branches. "I'm going to miss you two and Clara."

"What do you mean?" Bell asked.

"I mean that I don't hold out much hope that my papa will be able to raise the money for me to come back." Mercedee paused. "He might. I think he would need a good amount of luck, but he could get it."

"Well, I certainly hope you'll keep in touch," Bell said.

"I will." Mercedee looked down the trail. "Who's that?"

A girl was walking toward them. The shade and light from behind made it hard to distinguish her face. As she got closer, Mercedee said, "Hello, Clara. I'm sorry we didn't find you before we left."

"That's all right, I guess." Clara sighed. "Sister de Sale saw you leave and told me you were probably up the hill. I see she was correct."

"We were just discussing plans for next year," Jean said.

"Oh? I hope I can come back. Everything is a question mark after the financial panic in the United States."

"That's what I was just telling Bell and Jean in so many words," Mercedee said. "I doubt that my father will be able to find the money to send me back here."

"What will you do?" Bell asked.

"I've been entertaining three options. Papa only wants there to be one, but I think I can convince him otherwise."

"Three choices?" Clara shifted on her feet.

"Yes. You see," Mercedee said as the others looked on,

"my papa wants me to go back to Tante Mathilde in Concession, north of Yarmouth, until I can find something better or he can come up with the money for the Mount."

"Concession is in the middle of nowhere," Clara said. "I'm sorry. I know your Tante lives there, but what would you do? Isn't that a small farm?"

"It is, and I'm not going to go regardless of what my papa says. Do you remember Tante Seraphie? I'm sure you do, Clara."

"Oh yes, I do," Clara said.

"I think I saw her when you came to the academy, because I was here early," Bell said.

"Oh, right," Mercedee said. "Well she has a dressmaking shop in New York City, and she's starting a second shop from what I understand. There's the possibility that I could go live with her and make money sewing for her." Mercedee held her bag on her lap.

"That sounds nice for a while," Clara said, "but I know you. You would go out of your mind after a time if all you were able to do was sew dresses."

"Perhaps," Mercedee said, "but there's a third option." She pulled an envelope out of her bag and slipped a letter from it as the three friends looked more engrossed.

"Tante Monique also has a dress shop in New Jersey," Mercedee continued. "And I wrote her a letter last week telling her of my predicament and my lack of presentable clothes. I've outgrown most of my dresses."

"I wasn't going to say anything." Clara ribbed Mercedee with a smile.

Mercedee rolled her eyes. "You see, I also told her of Tante Mathilde being ill—she knows this because Mathilde was in New York recently for medical treatment—and I asked if I could stay with her just for a while."

Bell leaned away from Mercedee, looking at her. "Really? What did she say?"

"I'll bet Monique has a lot of sympathy after hearing all that," Jean said.

"I think you're right, Jean. I just got a reply from Monique in the mail today." Mercedee unfolded the letter and read aloud. "My dear Mercedee, your little letter came today. It made me shed many tears."

Clara put her hand over her mouth. "She sounds so compassionate."

"My dear child," Mercedee read on, "always rely on my sincerity and feel that there is one who will guide your steps. And since you so sincerely appreciate what is done for you, it will make it doubly sweet. Now, it is my duty and pleasure, combined."

"She sounds like the best tante ever." Bell sighed.

Mercedee glanced up from the letter, nodded, and continued, "I wrote to Sister Rosalia last Friday about the small balance you have with the academy, and I have not changed my mind, because I know it to be best. It will not offend Tante Mathilde if you do not go to Concession. She is too intelligent and sensible a woman to take umbrage when she is aware of how hard it is to earn money."

Mercedee held the letter to her chest. "I can't believe that Papa would be upset with me not going to Concession. This is the good part." She raised the letter in front of her eyes again. "It is best if you come right here. Now, my dear Mercedee, the season will soon be over, and my seamstresses all want their vacation, but before I can let them go, I want your sewing all done, so I think you had better take the Boston boat, which is a lovely one, and come right on."

"Oh, Mercedee!" Clara gasped.

"That sounds wonderful." Bell put her arm around Mercedee's shoulders and hugged her.

"I think so too." Mercedee sighed. "She says I should stop briefly in Boston and see Papa and then take the Fall River line down to New York, and her niece, Aggie, will pick me up at the pier. And when I'm finished with my new clothes, I can go spend a whole week with Papa." Mercedee dabbed a tear from her eye. "She goes on to say that I can see Papa again on my way back here." Mercedee read on then commented, "I'm not sure about the last part."

"Does she know something that you don't?" Clara asked skeptically. "Has your papa told you he has the money for next year?"

"I haven't been told that he has the funds, and I have to doubt it. Although maybe Monique is going to help? I don't know." Mercedee scanned the letter some more. "What do you think?"

Jean crossed her feet in front of her. "It indeed does sound like the best option."

"Of course it does," Bell said.

"Oh yes, it does," Mercedee agreed. "I just wonder about Papa and if Tante Seraphie will be upset. I don't know what Papa has told them. And maybe I should help Tante Mathilde."

Clara looked Mercedee in the eyes. "You have to take the best option for you right now. Especially if it'll help you get back here and further your education."

Mercedee read on, "Monique goes on about Mathilde. She writes, 'she came here on June 1st and stayed one week. Consequently she was here on the anniversary of your dear mother's death. Oh, how we wept that day. Poor Aunt Mathilde was really sick, and we spoke of your coming here this summer to have you fitted out, and she said she much wanted to see you (for she loves you dearly).'"

"Yes," Bell said. "If you tell your father what Monique has said and that Mathilde is under the weather, he has to see it's the best thing."

"You're right. And did I mention that my half-brother, Ferdinand, is also living with her?" Mercedee looked back at the letter.

"Maybe you'll be able to catch up with Ferdinand," Jean said. "Are the two of you close?"

"I wouldn't say that Ferdinand and I are close. I haven't seen him since I was very young. He lived with us when Mamma and Papa and I lived in a house in Melrose

Highlands in north Boston. Maybe that would be a blessing."

Mercedee looked at the letter again and read, "Now, my dear Mercedee, the season will soon be over, and my seamstresses all want their vacation, but before I let them go, I want your sewing all done, so I think you had better take the Boston boat, which is a lovely one. And come right on. Your father will put you on the Fall River line, and Phillip will meet you in New York at the Fall River Pier. Remain on the boat until he comes."

"Who is Phillip?" Bell seemed enthralled.

Mercedee thought for a second then said, "He's Phillip Gravel, Monique's husband. Her son is also named Phillip, but he's a student. There's more," Mercedee said, reading from the letter again. "In the fall when you return, you can remain with your father and spend some time with Tante Mathilde. Let no one know when you are coming, and after you are here, you will write to Aunt Seraphie and Agnes letting them know."

"Oh my," Jean said. "She assumes you'll be returning here to the Mount."

"Yes, she does say as much," Clara agreed. "But it also sounds a bit clandestine, don't you think?"

Mercedee gave Clara a quizzical look.

"I mean, Monique is very positive. She says it is fine and the best option, but then she says not to tell anyone until you're there," Clara said. "I don't know your family, but that gave me pause."

"Hmm…" Mercedee thought.

"Perhaps Monique just doesn't want to cause any misunderstandings before you get there," Bell theorized.

"Indeed," Mercedee said, "everyone can get the wrong idea when it comes to family. And I'll be back here in the fall. It'll only be for the summer."

"Where does Monique live? Would there be enough room?" Clara asked.

"She and Phillip just bought a big house in East Orange,

New Jersey. Tante Seraphie said there was lots of room, even with Phillip and Ferdinand living there too." Mercedee sounded more hopeful. "That settles it. Monique sounds so loving. I'm going to write Papa a letter. Maybe I'll make myself a copy of Monique's letter and send the original with my letter."

"Perhaps he'll be proud of you showing some independence," Clara suggested.

"I don't think I would go that far," Mercedee said, "but he can't be upset. It sounds like Monique will be very good for me, and I should get a chance to see Papa at times if he or Monique will purchase a ticket on the steamer from New York to Boston." Mercedee paused thoughtfully then added, "I could see Seraphie at times as well."

Clara looked at Mercedee. "Have you considered that you could work for Monique and make enough money to return on your own?"

"I don't know. This school is expensive, isn't it? At least I could help my father pay." Mercedee peered into the tree branches. "There are many possibilities."

"Let's walk on around the trail and stretch our legs again," Clara said.

The others agreed, and they went farther up the hill, meandering through the maple trees, then traversed the slope and dropped back down on the north end of the motherhouse. Along the way, they passed through small meadows with spring flowers and more trees until they reached the cleared field near the motherhouse. Instead of going into the back door, Mercedee led them to the north end, where the trail looped around to the roundabout in front.

"Why are you taking this route?" Clara asked.

"I don't know. It just seems like the direction that I should go." Mercedee continued on, following the roundabout that would take them to the vestibule and the main entrance.

At the road, the four girls walked together, with

Mercedee and Clara side by side followed by Jean and Bell. Just down the hill, the clanging and rhythmic huffing of trains carrying passengers and freight to and from the harbor piers in Halifax invaded the peaceful day and the coastal wind rustling the large maple trees.

Mercedee, Clara, Bell, and Jean walked through the half-circle vestibule and large open doors and into the hallway. Mercedee glanced back into a window of the parlor they had just walked past. Beatrice McDowell and her sister Dottie were standing at the window and waving excitedly at her. Mercedee was on good terms with the always lively McDowell sisters, so she stopped and smiled back.

Mercedee started to raise her hand to wave but saw two teenage boys in the room, also peering at her and grinning. "What?" she gasped in great alarm. She halted before she could wave. Then she froze, fixed in time, realizing that her sin would no doubt be witnessed by one of the sisters.

"Who's that?" Clara asked.

"They must be Beatrice and Dottie's cousins that they're always talking about," Mercedee answered softly. "They must be visiting from Northwood."

"They sure seem happy to see us," Bell said. "Or at least you—"

And then, in an instant, Mercedee's greatest fear, her worst-case scenario, came true. The one thing that she feared most happened.

"Ahem!" came a voice from behind them, farther down the hall.

The girls turned and saw Sister Michaela walking toward them, scowling and motioning them over to her.

"But, Sister, Beatrice waved, and I was just looking back," Mercedee said.

"You will come with me and either go for a walk in the back or go to the recreation room until those boys have left," Michaela snapped as she stepped back and motioned for the girls to pass. "Especially you, Miss Meehan. You were the one waving at the young men. Don't talk to anyone at the parlor, especially the young men."

The girls murmured in agreement as they passed. Mercedee stifled an urge to defend herself but decided against it, although her anger festered as, with clenched teeth, she followed Bell down the stairs. *I didn't even wave!* Mercedee wanted to yell it at Sister Michaela.

Mercedee, Bell, Jean, and Clara went straight to the recreation room and sat in chairs in the corner. Two of them were wicker chairs with cushions on the seats, and the others were rocking chairs.

Clara was first to speak. "I think Sister Michaela will always have it in for you, Mercedee."

"Don't I know this?" Mercedee replied, overflowing with frustration. "She had to have seen the whole thing."

"Yes," Jean agreed. "She had to know that none of us had any part in that."

"We were just walking past," Bell said.

"I'll say one thing," Mercedee said. "I will not miss Sister Michaela when I leave here, and it doesn't matter where I go. At least she won't be there."

"Are you still not sure where you're going?" Bell asked.

Mercedee put her elbows on the armrests. "I know where I want to go, and I know what I need, but I don't know where I'm going." She took a breath and looked across the room. Painted on the far wall was the scene of a river with hills in the background.

"You see," Mercedee continued, "I don't have any money. I can only go if Papa, Seraphie, Monique, or someone sends me enough money to get there."

"Oh my, you are truly adrift," Jean said solemnly.

"I don't know what I would do." Clara sighed.

The recreation room door opened, and Anne and Gertie, whom Mercedee and Clara had hardly seen in some time, came into the room. Seeing Mercedee's group, they sauntered over.

"Hello, Anne," Clara said.

"Yes, hello," Mercedee added.

"And hello to the girls who were gawking at the boys, and the lead gawker, Mercedee," Anne mocked as Gertie howled.

"Well, I see that good news also travels fast at the Mount." Mercedee looked directly at Anne.

"Good news?" Anne rolled her eyes. "I wouldn't call being disciplined by Sister Michaela for fraternizing with a boy *good* news. But that speaks to your character, not mine."

Mercedee curled her lip. "I was being sarcastic."

"I don't think you want to start a conversation on character, Queen Anne," Clara teased.

"And you shouldn't bring that up, Clara. I know you wrote the insulting letter, and I'm going to prove it to Michaela someday," Anne fumed, putting her hands on her hips as Mercedee's table erupted in laughter.

"Anne," Mercedee said, stifling a chuckle, "I know you came here to poke fun at me since Michaela got cross with me for no real reason, but I'm not worried about it. I actually feel sorry for you that you must be so disappointed that the boys were waving at us and not you."

Anne pursed her lips and extended her fists straight down at her sides and harrumphed. "Let's go, Gertie. Lunch will be starting soon, and I don't want to miss it because of these country girls."

"Country girls?" Clara scowled as Anne and Gertie disappeared.

Mercedee rolled her eyes. "Let's eat quickly. I just thought of something, and I need to see if I can find Sister Rosalia."

"Sure," Jean said, and the others nodded.

10 NEW BEGINNINGS, NEW CHALLENGES

Mercedee walked purposefully to the stairs and ascended to the main office. She pulled open the heavy door and walked down the hallway to Rosalia's office. *Oh, thank goodness.* She saw Sister Rosalia through the slightly open door, sitting at her desk. Mercedee gently tapped on the door, pushing it open farther, and Rosalia motioned her in.

"How can I help you, my dear Mercedee?" Rosalia looked tired.

Mercedee sat down in the simple wooden chair facing Rosalia's desk. "You see, I have a question for you. Did, um, my father send any money for me to travel or ship my things?"

Rosalia appeared to think for a moment. "Yes, you're in luck. He did. I'm surprised it slipped my mind."

Mercedee's face lit up.

"You see, he sent thirty-five dollars in a letter. He told me to keep it so that you would have traveling money. Your account isn't balanced—you owe a dollar and something—but he was planning on sending more to cover that."

"Oh, that's the best news I've heard in months,"

Mercedee gushed. "That might just be enough for what I'm planning to do."

"And what are you planning, pray tell?"

Mercedee reached into her bag and pulled out the letter from Monique. She handed it to Rosalia. "Please read this. It's from Monique, and she's made a very generous offer."

Rosalia studied the letter as Mercedee watched her face for any sign of how she felt. After what seemed like an hour, Rosalia folded the letter up and handed it to Mercedee.

"Monique is my little sister, and I have watched her grow up and do many things. I must say I have certain reservations," she said as Mercedee's face grew concerned. "But knowing what I know about your choices, I think this may be your best option."

Color flushed Mercedee's face, and she put the letter away. "I'll be all right. I promise, Tante Rosalia."

"Yes. But first things first. Sister Michaela has been up in arms about your account not being balanced. She will be wanting to find you before you leave and get the account balanced. Or at the least contact your father and have assurance that he'll sort out the books." Rosalia gave Mercedee a serious look.

"But I don't have any money. Papa hasn't sent any in some time," Mercedee said. "And if I pay the account with my travel money, I'll not be able to leave."

"I assumed as much. Don't worry. I'll write to your father and get the money one way or another after you've left." Rosalia waved her hand.

"All right," Mercedee said, relieved. "Thank you so much."

"Now, here's what we need to do," Rosalia said as Mercedee leaned forward. "The Distribution is in one week. Yes, next Monday. We must attend that. Have all your things packed and ready to go."

"Yes."

"The Distribution will continue until the afternoon, but if we leave after lunch, we should be able to catch the one thirty train to Halifax. We can get to the pier and purchase a ticket to Boston and another on to New York as detailed by Monique in the letter."

Mercedee's stomach flipped and flopped as she realized that was really going to happen. Her excitement mixed with trepidation. "I understand. Should I send a telegram to Monique or Seraphie so someone could meet me?"

"I'll do that. I'll have plenty of time after you've gotten on the steamer. I think the best chance would be to see if Seraphie or Aggie could meet you. Probably Aggie. They live much closer to the piers where you'll be arriving."

"That's what I was thinking too. I've never been to East Orange," Mercedee said.

Rosalia looked at her young niece. "Are you ready?"

"Quite. And one other thing."

"Yes?"

"Would it be all right if Clara or Bell joined us going to the pier?"

"I suppose, but they need to be ready to go on time. And they should have twenty-five cents for the train."

"Oh, of course," Mercedee said. "And thank you so much. I can't even say how—"

"Think nothing of it, dear child," Rosalia said, "but do one thing for me, and don't run afoul of Sister Michaela again between now and the Distribution. Please?"

"I'll do my best, dear tante."

"Hmm…" Rosalia pursed her lips. Mercedee's best had not been enough thus far.

"Honestly, Tante. I will do nothing to get in trouble."

"All right. Well, go take care of what you need to do." Rosalia smiled as Mercedee opened the door and walked out.

In the main hallway, Mercedee thought of something else she had to do. She needed to write a letter to her papa and explain things. He wouldn't be happy, but he needed to know. She walked across the hall to an empty table—her recently adopted refuge—in the student library. It wasn't

Sunday, so no one would be checking out books, and she should have the library to herself.

She took the letter from Monique out of her bag and quickly copied it. Mercedee then addressed an envelope to her father in Boston and took out a sheet of stationery paper. She dipped her pen in ink, tapped it on the rim of the bottle, and started to write.

Mount St. Vincent
Halifax, Nova Scotia
June 26, 1893
My own sweet Papa,

I received your two welcome letters this morning and also one from Aunt Monique by the same mail, which I shall include in this letter.

Of course, dear Papa, after having read Tante Monique's letter, you may easily imagine what caused me to write so soon. Well, it is this, dearest Papa, that Sister Rosalia and myself have decided that it is better not to wait but to take the boat in Halifax and go straight to Boston, and from thence to New York, so that Tante Monique will be able to fix my clothes. I am sure that you will think, with me, that this is the best and wisest thing to do, and after I get my clothes finished, I can return to Boston if you are able to have me. I will always be treated very nicely there in East Orange, so do not worry on my account. And I will be able to see you in Boston on my way to New York. It will only be for a few moments, but it will be soon, dearest Papa. I am going to write to Tante Monique tonight and tell her that I am willing to go as soon as she is willing, and I hope, dearest Papa, that you will not be offended with me for going. I suppose that I will write to you once more before I start.

I am sure, Papa, that if I go to New York, they will do everything possible to make me happy, and as she is so kind as to make my clothes, I must show a little gratitude to her. I am doing it for the best, Papa, because you might not be able to put me up in Boston now... but maybe after my clothes are fixed and fit, I can go to stay with you in Boston and see my good friend Lottie.

And now, dearest Papa, I will close with much love and hoping that you will not be at all offended with me for deciding the matter

myself.
Your devoted child, Mercedee Meehan

Mercedee read the letter again to catch any errors in grammar or spelling. She took a deep breath, folded the two letters, and slipped them into the envelope. She packed up her pen and ink, placed the letter in her bag, and left the library. With butterflies in her stomach, she walked straight to the mailroom and mailed the letter.

Things were moving quickly. She had spent the school year growing, learning, making friends, and dealing with antagonists and, even worse, Sister Michaela. However, she was leaving a relatively safe and known world. Michaela made the move one that Mercedee looked forward to, and there was so much out beyond the motherhouse that she wanted to see and do, yet the sting of losing friends—or at least not seeing them very much anymore—was there. In her heart, Mercedee understood that that was how it had to be.

Mercedee decided that on Sunday, she would tell Clara and Bell of her plans. She needed to pack her things, secure her trunk, and move it downstairs to a storage area so it could be shipped to East Orange and catch up with her.

For the time being, however, Mercedee just wanted to sit down with her friends and tell them that she had made up her mind. But where were Clara and Bell? Mercedee climbed the stairs and looked in the dorm. Not there. She headed to the recreation room.

Mercedee pushed open the recreation room door and peeked in. She was happy to see Bell and Clara sitting at two chairs in the corner. A girl at the piano played a soft piece of music. Mercedee walked quickly over to her friends and sat down.

"What are you up to?" Clara asked.

"We were just talking about summer plans," Bell said.

"Oh, I was just making plans of my own." Mercedee sat in a rocking chair.

"Tell me about your plans," Clara said. "I'm relieved that you might know what you're going to do."

"I'll tell you in a moment," Mercedee said. "First, tell me, what are your plans?"

Bell shrugged. "I'm just finishing things up and waiting to hear from my father about when I can go home."

"Same for me," Clara said.

Mercedee looked them in the face and said softly, "I'm leaving for New York." She lowered her voice. "I'm leaving tomorrow right after lunch at the Distribution."

"What? Really?" Clara said.

"You must be going to stay with—" Bell said.

"I'm going to stay with my tante Monique in New Jersey," Mercedee said confidently.

"So, you're going to do it?" Clara asked.

"Yes. I've made up my mind. There's more. Earlier, my papa sent some money for me to travel on, and Rosalia has it."

"Oh, that's a fine discovery," Clara said.

"But there's one problem."

"What's that?" Bell asked.

Mercedee looked around to see if anyone was eavesdropping and continued in a low voice, "My account isn't balanced, and I owe the Mount some money. Sister Rosalia says she'll try to get the money from my papa." Mercedee paused. "Once again, the problem is Michaela. She's known about my account for some time and has been stewing about it too."

"But what can Sister Michaela do?" Bell asked.

"Sister Rosalia says that Sister Michaela won't let me leave until the account is squared or she has assurance from my father that he'll sort it out." Mercedee took a deep breath. "I'm concerned she might take my travel money to square the account."

"Do you need help?" Bell asked.

"I don't think I need help except for not getting cornered by Sister Michaela. Sister Rosalia and I will take

the train into Halifax to the pier where the steamers depart."
Mercedee paused. "And I was wondering if you would like
to go with us. We can say goodbye there."

"I would love that," Bell said.

"Me too," Clara said. "Perhaps if we accompany you, it'll
appear as if we're on an outing and not raise any attention
from Sister Michaela."

"Oh, that's a good point, Clara," Bell said.

Mercedee nodded. "It is set, then," she whispered. "I
was worried that with all of the commotion of Distribution
and my rushing around, that I wouldn't be able to say
goodbye. Just don't forget to bring twenty-five cents for the
train fare. And of course, don't speak of this plan."

"Of course," Clara said.

"All right," Bell agreed. "But there's one other thing."

"What's that?" Mercedee asked with panic in her eyes.

"It's just that, well, it's almost dinnertime," Bell replied.
"Would you like to take a break and eat?"

She and Clara chuckled.

"Oh, my goodness, yes. Thank you, Bell." Mercedee
sighed and sat back in her chair.

Mercedee looked across the recreation room at the
translucent white curtains that glowed in the afternoon sun
like the beacon in the Yarmouth lighthouse. As the girls
milled about and sang a song at the piano, she could see a
mural on the far wall. It was a faraway place, and during her
year at the Mount, she had spent long moments looking at
it and daydreaming about visiting such a place. The mural
had enough detail to identify the type of landscape, but
enough was left to the imagination so that the mind could
paint its own picture and invent its own adventures. It had
dark-green trees and light-green grass on the banks of a river
that flowed around brown rocks. The scene didn't look like
Nova Scotia or the Appalachian Mountains that Mercedee
had seen in North Carolina as a child. It looked like pictures
and paintings she had seen of western Canada. The river
flowed along the wall and around the room, connecting

walls between doors and windows.

"Mercedee. Mercedee! We're going to eat," Clara called through the white noise of girls chattering.

"Yes. Yes, of course." Mercedee blinked and followed Bell and Clara to the stream of girls funneling out of the room. As the line slowly moved into the refectory, Mercedee motioned for Bell and Clara to stand closely and whispered, "Don't let on to anyone that I'm leaving tomorrow or that you're going with me to Halifax. All right?"

Bell and Clara nodded.

"I just don't want any fuss."

"Of course," they said.

After picking up their plates of food, silverware, glasses of water, and serviettes, they walked into the room of tables and looked for familiar faces. Waving from a table in the corner, Jean captured Mercedee's attention, so she walked in Jean's direction. Arriving at the table, Mercedee saw the smiling faces of Dottie and Beatrice McDowell sitting with her. *Oh no!* Mercedee faked a smile. She liked the silly McDowell sisters. They were funny and generally harmless, but right then? On that day? If Sister Michaela were to walk into the refectory and see them laughing together—and one could rest assured that Beatrice and Dottie would be laughing at some point—it would be bad. Very bad. It was far too easy to get in trouble.

"Sit down, Mercedee." Freckles dotted Beatrice's cheeks, and her big grin was framed by strawberry-blond hair that was braided and wrapped in a bun. "And you, too, Bell and Clara."

"Um, sure." Mercedee scanned the room and the door to the common area. "Sure."

She and Bell and Clara took seats and put down their dinners, completely filling the six chairs at the table. Mercedee was glad the room was packed with students and their noisy talking. If Michaela entered the room, Mercedee would be alerted by the quelling of the din.

"First of all, Mercedee, I want to apologize for getting you in trouble earlier. I had no idea that Sister Michaela would be so intolerant. She always feels the need to be particularly strict toward the end of the year."

"It's all right, Beatrice. You didn't know." Mercedee spread her serviette on her lap and hoped for a way to change the subject.

"Oh, and our cousins are so gregarious," said Dottie, who was every bit Beatrice's sister.

"Does that run in your family?" Mercedee asked, and after a moment of silence and quizzical looks, she broke into a laugh, and the table erupted.

"Good one." Beatrice chuckled.

"Well, no hard feelings," Clara added. "I think we were just in the wrong place at the wrong time. We have a knack for that."

Bell swallowed a bite and said, "You know, Sister Michaela doesn't really need a reason."

"That's quite true," Jean said.

Mercedee hurriedly ate several bites and dabbed her mouth with her serviette. "So, Dottie and Beatrice, you're singing in the choir at the Distribution tomorrow?"

"Yes, we are," Beatrice said with an enthusiastic smile, "and I can hardly wait."

"This is some excellent shepherd's pie, eh?" Jean commented. "Considering that it's coming from the cafeteria?"

"Indeed," Bell said and took a drink of water.

"It was tasty and filled me up." Mercedee patted her tummy under her white blouse.

The room quieted, reflecting the mass consumption. Mercedee again scanned the room and dabbed her lips with her serviette. She finished her glass of water and said, "Thank you for a most enjoyable dinner. Now I'm going to return to my dorm and read and relax." She got up and collected her dishes. "Perhaps we could meet back here later for tea?"

"Yes, that would be wonderful," the McDowell sisters said in unison and then laughed.

"I'm going to head upstairs too." Clara pushed her chair back.

Bell looked up and said, "See you soon."

"See you then." Mercedee winked.

"I need to go upstairs too." Jean followed Mercedee and Clara from the table.

Approaching the counter to dispose of their dishes and serviettes, Clara spoke softly. "We got up just in time."

Mercedee glanced around, and Sister Michaela was walking into the refectory, her permanent scowl prominent.

"Indeed." Mercedee set her dishes on the counter and waited for Clara. They walked casually toward Sister Michaela and the door with Jean in tow.

"Hello, Sister Michaela," Mercedee and Clara said in unison.

"Miss Meehan and Miss La Brun." Sister Michaela's arms were crossed, and she gave them a measured look as if she were trying to guess what the two would do next.

In the hallway to the dorms, Jean spoke up. "Oh, Mercedee, before I go to the St. Vincent dorm, I have something for you."

"Oh?" Mercedee asked, surprised.

"Me too. I mean, I have something for you too," Clara stammered.

Mercedee gave them a quizzical frown.

"Don't worry. It's nothing big." Clara looked at Jean.

"Here you go." Jean pulled an envelope from her bag as Clara did the same.

"Postals? You don't need to send me a letter. I'm right here." Mercedee chuckled.

"You see, they aren't letters. You can't read them until you've left," Jean said.

"Yes, you're forbidden to open mine until July 9," Clara added.

Mercedee accepted the envelopes and looked at Clara's.

"And one other thing," Clara said.

"Yes?"

"You have to sign the envelope as a promise you won't open the letter" Clara said.

Mercedee rolled her eyes.

"Here's a pencil," Clara said, offering her one. "Bell and I have already signed ours."

"All right." Mercedee smiled. "You're watching?" She wrote on the envelope next to the other printed names and signatures.

"Thank you, you two." Mercedee sighed. "You're very good friends."

"You're welcome," Jean said before she turned and entered the dorm.

Moments later, Clara and Mercedee sat on their beds in silence. Mercedee was thinking about the end of the school year and perhaps the end of their relationships with other students. Clara was probably thinking about her family and readjusting to life at home. Mercedee was imagining a better situation with Monique. Perhaps she would prosper as Ferdinand had.

After a few minutes, Clara looked over at Mercedee, who was staring at the ceiling. "Are you all right?"

Mercedee broke her stare and glanced at Clara. "Yes. Yes, I was just thinking." Mercedee sat up and sprang to action. She pulled her travel suitcase from under her bed and sorted her clothes. She retrieved her clean clothes and those in the best condition, which weren't anything special. She also pulled out her overnight bag and all essential items. It felt like second nature.

When she finished, she slid the bag under the bed and got up. "Clara, would you help me go down to storage and get my trunk? It would be best to put my things in it and take it back down to storage so that it can be shipped to me."

"Sure," Clara said. "This could be good timing since most students are still out and about, and we won't have to explain what we're doing."

They walked downstairs to the bottom floor and surreptitiously slipped into the storage room.

"I hope no one saw us," breathed Clara.

"Let's see." Mercedee turned on the lights. "My trunk was three rows this way…" She walked along the ends of the shelves, looking for her trunk.

"Here it is." Mercedee looked at a trunk on the first shelf. She grabbed its handle.

Clara reached for the handle at the other end, and they slid the trunk to the edge of the shelf.

"It's much lighter than when we hauled it into the building from the wagon," Mercedee said.

"I'll say. But it's easier for you since you're so tall."

The two shared a smile. They carried the empty trunk to the door and, after passing through, set the trunk down so Mercedee could turn off the lights and close the doors. As they neared the stairs, Clara stopped. "Wait, I hear voices on the stairs."

"Go this way," Mercedee instructed, and they carried the trunk past the door to the refectory and the recreation room to a hallway that led to the north end of the building. "The other stairway is down here."

"Of course. Good idea," Clara said.

"Did it sound like Michaela?" Mercedee asked.

"I don't think so, but it was hard to tell."

They turned in at the stairwell. Mercedee was the last one through and looked down the long hallway to see two nuns emerging from the opposite stairwell. They were talking to each other and clearly didn't notice Mercedee disappearing from view.

She and Clara lugged the trunk upstairs. It was heavy even when empty. In the dorm, only a couple of girls commented on their task, and Mercedee felt relieved to see some other girls also packing bags.

"I need to visit the lavatory. I'll be back right away," Clara said.

"All right," Mercedee replied, looking into her trunk.

She sat on her bunk, folding clothes, organizing odds and ends, and sorting what she would need in her travel bag and which items she could do without until the trunk caught up with her. Folding a pair of socks and placing them in her travel bag, she heard a sound over her right shoulder and glanced up. It was Anne.

"Um, Mercedee?" Anne broke the silence.

"Yes?" Mercedee sounded exasperated.

"Well, I just wanted to say…" Anne paused. "I was in the main building the other day, and I overheard Sister Rosalia and Sister de Sale talking."

"Oh?" Mercedee grew concerned and looked at her trunk. She sincerely hoped whatever Anne had to say didn't take long.

"I wanted to say that I'm sorry about your mother. And perhaps I shouldn't have gotten you into trouble."

Mercedee sat up straight on her bunk and looked at Anne. Her eyes appeared to be honest enough. "Well," Mercedee started, not sure what to say.

"I just wanted to say that I'm sorry," Anne said kindly.

"Thank you." Mercedee looked at Anne and wondered whether something else was going on. "Apology accepted."

After an awkward pause, Mercedee continued, "And just so you know, your apology will not get me to admit to participating in the posted letter." She smirked.

"I must say, *whoever* did that was taking a very bold risk but pulled it off rather brilliantly. I must admit that it was quite clever." Anne showed a hint of a smile.

"I'll agree with you there. Whoever did it had quite a plan." Mercedee winked. "Are you going back to Boston soon?"

"Perhaps," Anne replied. "My father may want me to stay a few days longer. He's having some problems with the financial panic. He invested in a mine out west, and now it's basically worthless."

"Really? My father invested in land with coal mines here

in Nova Scotia." Mercedee started to feel a connection with Anne. "Those properties are now failing as well."

"Oh my. Father said in a letter that we may have to sell our house in Melrose Highlands and move to the city. I'll dread that if it comes to pass."

Mercedee raised her eyebrows. "You live in Melrose Highlands?"

"Yes."

"I used to live there. Papa has an office downtown, on Newspaper Row, and Mamma and I lived in Melrose Highlands when I was young. Unfortunately, she had tuberculosis, and when she couldn't keep a house any longer, Papa had to sell the house."

"I can't imagine." Anne sighed. "We have more in common than I thought."

"I must agree with you," Mercedee said as Clara made her way across the room.

Anne saw Clara and quickly said, "I should let you get back to packing. Best of luck to you in whatever your plans are."

As Anne turned away, Mercedee said, "Thank you, and best of luck to you too." Mercedee watched Anne walk away as Clara came up from the other direction.

"What was that about?" Clara asked. "One more insult before you leave?"

"No. She was actually quite nice. I almost trust her sincerity."

Mercedee packed the rest of her belongings into the trunk and called out to Clara. "Are you ready for our last caper?"

Clara giggled. "Yes. Yes indeed. Do you want me to help you carry this trunk back to the storeroom?"

"I think it's ready to go," Mercedee said.

With that, they both grabbed an end of the trunk. Heading to the north stairwell with the loaded trunk, Clara started to wonder if her burning arms could carry the load all the way to storage.

At the top of the stairs, Clara spoke up. "I need to rest. Could we put the trunk down?"

"Yes," Mercedee said, and they set down the trunk and worked their hands and fingers.

"Who's that?" Clara asked as a figure moved behind Mercedee.

"Could you two use a hand?" Bell asked.

"Oh, hello, Bell, and yes!" Mercedee said with a smile.

They traded off lugging the trunk down the stairs and to the shelf in the storage room. As far as they knew, Michaela and the other nuns were none the wiser.

"I'm going to go lie down," Clara said. "And hope I can even pick up my bag tomorrow."

"Me too," Mercedee and Bell agreed.

Walking back to the south stairwell, Mercedee said, "I can't thank you both enough for your help. I'm almost there."

"You're most welcome," Bell said.

"I hope things work out for you in New York," Clara added.

"Thank you, Clara. I think things will go well with my tante Monique."

Back at the dorm, the room buzzed with girls talking. They were planning their summer and reminiscing about the year that was. Mercedee was thinking about the trip that would begin in less than twenty-four hours. Clara was reading but put down her book.

"How long is the trip to Boston, Mercedee?" Clara asked. "I just take the train across to New Brunswick. It only takes a day."

Mercedee thought for a moment. "If I remember correctly, it'll take at least two days on the steamer. Weather and seas should be fine right now, but it's still a long trip. And about a day and a half to get to New York Harbor from there." Mercedee hadn't been on a steamer for four years, since she and Mamma had traveled to Digby from Boston, but she remembered spending two days on that big ship.

"That's a long time to be on a boat. I don't think I could take the rocking and such." Clara turned back to her book.

"It's not that bad, especially on calm seas. Without a storm, the big steamers don't rock that much." Mercedee continued, "I'm going to go to the lavatory and then turn in. Tomorrow's going to be a big day."

The next morning, the dorm and most of the motherhouse were full of activity. Mercedee got up and went to the lavatory. She fixed her hair and tried to clean her worn dress as well as she could. Looking in the mirror, she lamented the state of her clothes. Her white blouse was starting to look too small, and it had spots that she wasn't able to completely wash out. Her dress was frayed around the bottom and at least an inch too short. She adjusted her waist to compensate, but she had already tried that, and there was nothing left to gain.

Mercedee shook her head and despaired that she would just have to look like the daughter of a pauper on the ship to Boston. She was alarmed and saddened to think that perhaps that was what she was. Would Papa ever become financially solvent? She hoped against hope that Monique would help her at least look the part of a girl of means. She turned away from the mirror and walked past other girls getting ready for Distribution. Every one of them had superior dresses and blouses. She swallowed and walked toward the Immaculate Conception dorm. *Someday, my life will be different. I shall make it different.*

The Distribution went well, with much pomp and circumstance in the main auditorium. They enjoyed musical performances and choirs. Older girls graduated, and others received awards. Watching other girls get academic and Child of Mary awards stung Mercedee, Bell, and Clara because they'd had no control over their relegation to second division.

On the way to lunch, Sister Rosalia stopped her in the hallway.

"Mercedee dear," Rosalia started, "as soon as you finish

your lunch, get your bag and other items and meet me out front. I have a wagon coming around to take us to the train station."

"All right. I'll be down there as soon as I can make it."

"With Bell and Clara?" Rosalia asked.

"Yes. They're coming also, and they know what to do."

"Godspeed."

Mercedee relayed the message to Bell and Clara at lunch, and they ate quickly and headed upstairs. Mercedee took a few extra rolls in a serviette for the trip.

The dorm was quiet as Mercedee grabbed her bag and jacket and placed all other small items in her purse. "Do you have your train fare?" Mercedee asked Clara and Bell.

"Yes, we do," they replied, rolling their eyes.

"Well, then," Mercedee said, taking the hint. "Let's go."

They walked along the hallway and down the stairs. Mercedee didn't even think of taking one last look around. She was preoccupied with getting to the wagon so she could get to the train. All the way through the main hallway and out the double doors, she was especially relieved that there was no sign of Sister Michaela.

The small buggy that Sister Rosalia had used to pick up Mercedee, Seraphie, and Clara more than nine months ago sat inconspicuously off to the side of the main entrance of the motherhouse. Sister Rosalia sat in the seat, holding the reins.

"Get in, girls," she called.

Mercedee set her bag in the back and climbed in beside Rosalia. Bell and Clara climbed in and sat on the second seat. Rosalia snapped the reins, and the horse pulled on the harness. The wagon rolled past the main entrance to the roundabout. Rosalia steered the horse to the right and headed for the train station.

"Where are you going?" came a voice from the motherhouse. All heads in the wagon turned to see Sister Michaela in front of the rotunda.

Rosalia pulled on the reins, and the horse came to a stop.

"Don't take exception, Sister Michaela. I'm just taking these girls to, um—"

"We begged Sister Rosalia to take us on one last tour along the Bedford Basin during the lunch break," Mercedee interjected, sparing Rosalia from having to perhaps mislead Sister Michaela.

"Yes," Sister Rosalia said. "We'll return before the ceremony commences unless something comes up or we have wagon trouble."

"Of course, Sister Rosalia," Sister Michaela said skeptically. "Just one more thing before you go. I need to speak to Miss Meehan."

Mercedee's palms started to sweat. She felt time slipping away. If they missed the train, they would be in real trouble.

Incredulously, Anne was coming out of the rotunda and asked for Sister Michaela. *What's she doing? Was that conversation a ruse, and she's going to ruin this day?*

"Sister Michaela," Anne said as she approached. "I'm terribly sorry if I'm interrupting, but I have a very important question about one of my grades. I was just wondering if you would look at it before it's recorded. I would greatly appreciate your attention to this immediately."

Sister Michaela walked toward the rotunda with her gaze still on the wagon. "Yes, Anne. What is the issue?" Sister Michaela finally turned away.

Sister Rosalia snapped the reins, and the horse again took off at a brisk pace around the roundabout.

"That was fortuitous that Anne needed Sister Michaela right then," Clara said.

"Yes, very much so," Mercedee said. *Just how much does Anne know?* Mercedee wondered, but it was obvious that Anne knew what she was doing, although it was a mystery how she'd been aware of the situation enough to distract Sister Michaela.

Out of earshot, Mercedee asked, "Did Michaela not see my bag in the back?"

Clara chuckled. "We moved it under our seat before we

started off."

The three girls laughed.

Mercedee wasn't sure, but it looked like there was a hint of a smile on stoic Sister Rosalia's lips.

As they headed into the trees and the motherhouse disappeared from view, Mercedee felt suddenly very independent. She was going to have a real adventure.

At the train station, Rosalia tethered the horse out of sight, and they waited on the platform. The one thirty train was on time, and they boarded. When the conductor came through the car, they each gave him twenty-five cents, and he gave them a ticket with a single hole punched. Clara and Bell could use it for the return trip. The train chugged east then turned north and rolled into Halifax. It was only a few more miles to the Deep Water Terminus at the west end of the city.

"Mercedee," Rosalia said, "a number of people have traveled to the Mount for the Distribution, and some came from Boston. The ship for that line is still at the pier, so you'll be able to get on the return passage."

"Oh, wonderful, Tante!" Mercedee cried. "I was thinking that I would have to wait here for some time."

"You're having good luck thus far," Clara said.

"Hush, or you'll certainly jinx me." Mercedee chuckled.

After ten minutes, the conductor walked through the car. "Deep Water Terminus! Pier Two and Three!" Minutes later, the train came to a stop.

Mercedee picked up her bag and coat, and they filed off the train. They headed down north Richmond Street toward the pier. A large grain elevator was there along with other buildings, including a big building where the government processed immigrants to Canada. The walk took at least ten minutes, and Mercedee was starting to wonder where the pier was when they rounded the grain elevator and she saw the large steamship taking on supplies, freight, coal, and passengers. An office along the way had a window and a sign that read Tickets. They stopped and inquired about the trip to Boston and New York City.

A man in a dark uniform and hat looked up at them and said, "One fare to Boston on the Yarmouth Line will be twelve dollars. This line only goes to Boston. You'll have to purchase a ticket to New York City in Boston."

"Very good," the cashier said. "The *SS Boston* is at Pier 2 over past the immigration shed. The dock workers can stow your trunk. Be sure it's marked so you can retrieve it."

"Yes, sir," Mercedee said softly.

The cashier paused then continued, "Now, this is the Yarmouth Line. Our steamers go as far as Boston. When you get to Lewis Wharf in Boston, you'll need to use this ticket to get credit for a ticket to New York on the New England Steamship Company ships. They're leaving Boston for New York City all the time. Your best bet is to get a train ticket to Fall River and take the Fall River Line to New York."

"Yes. Yes, I will take one ticket to Boston." Mercedee handed him two bills.

While the cashier made change, Mercedee looked over her shoulder at the long ship with a low profile and two black stacks emitting wisps of black smoke above a long, low, two-level galley. She looked at the cashier, frozen, as if grabbing for straws in a fast-moving river.

The cashier raised his eyebrows beneath the short bill of his black hat and slid the ticket and change across the counter. "Is there anything else?"

"Oh, um, of course not." Mercedee noticed the line behind her, and some were becoming impatient. She turned, and the foursome left the ticket window. After a few steps on the cracked concrete leading to Pier 2, Mercedee stopped again. "But how am I going to get a ticket in Boston? Will I have enough money?"

"You have twenty-three dollars left," Rosalia said. "That should be plenty for the fare to New York. And here are two dollars for food so you don't starve to death on the trip." She looked into Mercedee's astonished face and took one of Mercedee's hands in both of hers. She placed the two folded dollar bills inside and wrapped Mercedee's fingers around them.

"I don't know what to say." Mercedee had tears in her eyes.

"Just take care of yourself and do as well as you can. This next chapter won't be easy, I'm sure." Rosalia gave Mercedee a hug and continued, "Your papa cares a great deal, but I suspected he wouldn't send enough, so I was prepared."

"Thank you again, Tante," Mercedee said. "I'll write to tell you that I made it."

"I'll appreciate that," Rosalia said.

"And one other thing, Tante Rosalia." Mercedee pulled out a sheet of paper that listed the ship port itinerary that she had gotten with her ticket and looked at it. "Will you send a telegram to Papa William and tell him that I'll be changing ships in Boston Harbor on July 5 and will stop for two hours in Providence later that day? I hope to see him either of those places."

"Yes, I'll see if we can send that out later today," Rosalia replied.

"Perhaps on our way through Halifax?" Bell asked.

"Yes, we can make a stop for that. Certainly, William will greatly appreciate that."

They separated and walked down the pier alongside the huge ship as people passed them on both sides. A long line led into a building opposite the ship, where immigrants waited after coming across the Atlantic from the United Kingdom on the massive steamships. A sign showed the direction to processing and the quarantine building. Mercedee and the others walked on past to where a gangplank led up to the main deck of the ship.

"Well, we're here," Mercedee said. "Thank you all. Thank you so much."

"I'll miss you," Bell said. "The Mount won't be the same without you. I hope you can make it back next year."

"Me, too, Bell," Mercedee said, and they tearfully embraced.

Mercedee turned to Clara. "I feel like I've known you for such a long time. I'll miss you so much."

"I'll miss you too," Clara said. "I hope we can meet again." She and Mercedee hugged for a long moment then separated and wiped away tears.

"I'll try my best to find a way to see you all again. And thank you for seeing me off, Clara and Bell. You're very special friends."

Rosalia stepped toward Mercedee and took her niece's hand in both of hers. "Remember, the Lord is always by your side, and he is the only one who deserves blind trust. All people can have ulterior motives and other ideas."

Mercedee looked into the wise and kind wrinkled eyes that had seen so much over the years. "Yes, Tante. I understand."

"I hope so." Rosalia let go of Mercedee's hand.

Mercedee wiped her eyes again and picked up her bag and coat. She walked up the gangplank. On reaching the deck, she headed along the railing toward the bow and waved one last time. She turned and walked away as her friends and Rosalia waved back.

Late the following afternoon, Rosalia was walking down the main hall outside the sisters' offices when Sister Precort approached and handed her a piece of paper. "This came in from the Western Union office. Actually, the telegram came in yesterday afternoon, but no one could find Mercedee. I thought I'd pass it on to you."

"Thank you, Sister Precort." Rosalia read the apparently hastily written telegram as Sister Precort started down the hall.

Western Union Telegraph, July 3, from: Boston
To: Miss Mercedee Meehan
Obey Your Papa. Do not go to Orange. Go to Mathilde in Concession.

William Meehan

"Wait, Sister Precort." Sister Rosalia walked after her and said, "I need to get to the Western Union telegraph office. Could you help me?"

"Sure," Sister Precort said. "I was there not so long ago. It's getting late, but we can send a night message, and he'll get it tomorrow morning."

Sister Rosalia thought for a moment before looking again at the telegram. "I suppose that I had better do that."

The two nuns walked quickly down the stairs, past Sister Michaela, and out the main entrance.

Later that evening, the Western Union office on the ground floor of the Globe Building in downtown Boston received a telegraph.

Western Union Telegraph night message, July 4, from: Halifax NS

To: Wm Meehan, 53 Globe Bldg., Boston

Mercedee left this morning. Meet her. Your telegram too late.

Sister Rosalia

EPILOGUE

After Mercedee left Mount St. Vincent, Marie Ann Potier (Sister Mary Rosalia) conversed with Mercedee through letters but never saw Mercedee in person again. Marie Ann stayed at Mount St. Vincent until her death in 1925 at the age of 81, a revered figure at Mount St. Vincent Academy. The Sisters of Charity - Halifax provided this quote from *The Acadian Recorder* newspaper in Halifax:

"The death took place this morning, at Mount Saint Vincent, of Sister Mary Rosalia Potier, aged 81 years. Sister Rosalia, who was 61 years in religious life, spent thirty-five years at Mount Saint Vincent, where she was beloved not only by pupils, but by the sisters and all her acquaintances.